Romancing The Bone
ISBN 978-1-909934-26-9
Copyright©2013 Barry Lowe
Cover art and design by Dawné Dominique

First published by loveyoudivine Alterotica

Published by
Lydian Press 2013
Find us on the World Wide Web at
www.lydianpress.com

ROMANCING THE BONE

GAY ROMANCE EROTICA

Barry Lowe

Lydian Press

$\mathscr{C}$ONTENTS

† All previously published as individual eBooks by loveyoudivine Alterotica.

* Previously published in Best Date Ever: True Stories That Celebrate Gay Relationships, Edited by Lawrence Schimel (Alyson, 2007)

$\mathcal{D}$EDICATION:

*For Wally, thanks for four decades of
unforgettable love and romance,
and Tofu, who hates to be left out*

Love is a Many-Gendered Thing

Carbon Dating

$\mathcal{I}$'m as embarrassed as hell. Normally, I wouldn't even consider appearing in public like this. Naked, except for handkerchief-sized red Speedos strung up between my ass cheeks like those Aussie lifesavers. I hope none of the neighbors is watching as I knock on the door to my best mate Robbie's house, hoping he won't answer the door. I'm praying it's his dad.

You see, I have a problem. I'm 19, pretty good looking, not an ounce of body fat on my slim, okay skinny, frame. Long, black hair, which hangs seductively across my face. My dick is average size, between 6¾"-7", depending on which porn movie is in the DVD player when you measure. My body is twink hairless except for a clump of pubic seaweed, and my ass is smooth as butter and as bubbly as a balloon.

Okay, what's the problem, you're asking? The problem is I just can't get laid. Let me rephrase that. I can't get laid by the guys I fancy. I suppose two telling points I should mention here: I'm a bit on the, shall we say, less than macho side, nothing flaming, but you'd never mistake me for Russell Crowe. Plus, I'm a top. Sure, I'd love to reciprocate, but just the idea of a cock entering my butt hole sends my body into shutdown and sphincter central locks all entrances to the building.

Oh, did I mention my homme (yes, I'm studying French at college) of choice is a delicious, mature daddy with just a fleck of grey through his temples highlighting his desirability. Alas, most men of that age either find it too arduous to douche or simply only have time to stick their dick in any available twinkhole and squirt before racing home to the wife, husband or spouse of unspecified gender.

I usually satisfy myself with a quick fumble in a borrowed bedroom, a suburban shithouse, or a noirish alleyway, only occasionally going upmarket for a quick blowjob in someone's Ute or family sedan with baby seat attached. Once I encountered a truckie, who was everything I ever dreamed of, until he took off his trousers to reveal he was wearing pantyhose.

No wonder then that last night I was running off at the mouth on meeting a gentleman of such proportion and charm that I was practically drooling. It was the occasion of a charmless party that I'd attended with mates Robbie and Viz. Unusually, none of us scored that night.

"There was no one there over 35," I had moaned dramatically. Robbie and Viz in the back seat were indulging me, though not without a certain amount of eyes heavenward.

"And this was a problem why?" asked Robbie, the perfect straight man, in the theatrical sense and not in the sexual.

I put on my grandest voice. "It's the same problem you will face one day when you realize you are no longer a Robbie and have become plain Rob, Bob or more pretentiously, Robert."

He smiled. "Did that really answer my question?"

"There was a guy in the kitchen said he was 29, but he looked 40," Viz said hopefully.

There was no stopping me. I was playing to the gallery. Actually to Robbie's dad, known to me and Viz as Mr. Wardrop.

"Forty to me is like 12 in twink talk," I said. "You should know that by now."

Viz smirked. "So what is the age of consent for daddy lovers?"

I looked over at Mr. Wardrop and tried hard to ascertain his age. "I guess I'll go as low as 45, if ..." Damn! If only I had known Robbie's dad was so hot I may have taken more interest and got strategic info, like his age.

"Cradle snatcher," Robbie yelled.

I had been flirting outrageously with Mr. Wardrop since he turned up in response to our mayday message when we came out of the world's most boring party to find our transport missing. Not stolen, but gone. Our driver, Gene, was notorious for dumping whoever he was with if a stray fuck presented itself. Obviously, it had and regardless of his protestations that he would not, he had stranded us. Problem: Too far out of town for a taxi, too early to get a lift with anyone else, and too close to curfew to take a chance. Solution: Call Robbie's dad.

What a miserable party bunch we must have looked when he turned up. I was so pissed off I yanked the back door open and was clambering inside when his voice made me look up. "Let me guess. You must be Vincent." He half-turned in the driver's seat holding out a strong, masculine hand. His face was tanned and fit, and fucking gorgeous. I wanted to see more of him. So I elbowed Robbie out of the front seat and grabbed it myself.

And that's why I was knocking at his front door. Alas, a very tired and disheveled Robbie answered.

"What are you doing here?" he asked.

"I thought it was a great day for a swim. Got to keep healthy. And your dad has a pool."

"It's ten after seven in the morning and it's 52 degrees outside. The sun's barely up."

"Depends on whose son you're talking about," I said as I adjusted my package in expectation.

It went right over Robbie's head, "And why are you wearing your togs stuck up your ass like that? You better come in, otherwise you'll get arrested."

He led me to the kitchen and put on the coffee.

"What drugs are you on?" he said, appraising my provocative swimwear.

I couldn't help myself. "He's fuckin' gorgeous." I was jumping up and down in my enthusiasm.

"Who is?"

"Your dad!" I screamed.

"Ewww!" Robbie grimaced. "I wouldn't go there. Anyway he's not even gay."

Robbie and his elder sister, Kylie, had grown up dad-less after their parents had divorced when Robbie was five. There had been no contact until a few weeks before, when Robbie's mother had announced she was running off with a young shoe salesman and that his dad would be back to help out with his college education in an effort to make up for all those years of invisibility. Robbie wasn't sure he needed a dad cramping his lifestyle, especially now that he was stretching his sexual muscles.

"How do you know?" I was pouting.

"There are no Judy Garland, Barbra Streisand or Bette Midler albums or movies in his collection," Robbie admitted.

"Shit!" Disappointment number one because I am and always will be a show queen. Are you beginning to grasp my problem here?

"What about ...."

"No, it's all classical and jazz shit."

"Porn?"

"None that I've found yet."

"That's unnatural for a man his age not to have porn," I said. "Girlfriends?"

"Nup," Robbie replied.

"Boyfriends?"

"Definitely not!"

"Underwear?"

"Boxers. Generic brand."

"Cologne?"

"Stuff I gave him last birthday, practically untouched. You're barking up the wrong geriatric here," Robbie said.

"He'll never be able to resist my charms once I get going," I boasted.

"May I point out," Robbie interrupted, "that you are speaking about my dad here, and there is no way you are sticking your dick up his ass. It doesn't bear thinking about."

Robbie pulled a face as I smirked and got instantly hard.

"You're disgusting," he said.

"Who's disgusting?" Mr. Wardrop asked as he came into the kitchen in his terry-toweling dressing gown that came down to just below his waist. He saw me. "Oh, hello, Vincent. You're up bright and early," he said as he looked directly at my barely concealed erection.

"Just a close friend of ours," Robbie said while his glare warned me to be quiet.

"Is there enough there for three," Mr. Wardrop asked as he nodded at the percolating coffee pot but kept his eyes fixed on the flimsy material covering my cock and balls. "I just can't get started without my morning caffeine fix."

Note to self. Buy coffee beans on the way home.

He poured three cups and went to the fridge.

"Shit! We're out of milk."

I love a man with a dirty mouth.

"Rob, be a good boy and duck down to the mall and get some milk and maybe some croissants for breakfast." He took some banknotes from a jar on the breakfast counter.

"Okay, dad. Coming Vince?"

"No. I think I'll stay here and keep your dad company. I'm not really dressed for the mall."

Mr. Wardrop looked me over and nodded. Then he tossed Robbie the car keys and said, "Drive carefully, son."

That assuaged Robbie's temper a little, and he raced upstairs to grab his jeans. Once dressed, he was quickly out the door shouting a departing, "I won't be long."

"Any orange juice while we're waiting," I said as I wrenched the fridge door open. Mr. Wardrop had jumped up to stop me, but was too late. Yes, there was orange juice. On the top shelf. Just behind the milk.

I closed the fridge door slowly and turned toward him. As I pushed him back in his chair, I buried my tongue in his smile. Then I had his robe open and was running my hands through the fur on his chest. His nipples were already hard as I sat on his knee facing him, feeling something else hard, as well.

He held me at bay for a moment. "Vincent, we really shouldn't," he said, but his cock said otherwise.

My response was to grip his throbbing meat in one hand while I fastened my lips to his nipple and sucked. He gasped as I slowly jerked him, and he brushed the hair from my face. He grabbed my wrist to stop me pleasuring him and then engulfed me in his arms. He was strong and masculine. And warm. He just held me and his heartbeat thumped against my chest.

He looked me squarely in the face and asked, "Why are you doing this?"

"Because you're hot!"

He laughed. "I haven't been hot for the past decade or more. I'm not even sure what constitutes hot in this day and age. I'm out of touch."

I held his face in my hands and to reassure him, I leaned in and kissed him while rubbing my hard-on against his belly. His tongue explored my mouth as I sucked, gently teasing him, and then we swapped. I entered him. There was no attempt at supremacy like there is most times with younger guys. No eager rush for release. Here was a man who knew how to take his time. His hard cock poked at my ass crack and I rubbed myself against him. I couldn't help but sigh. Sex with Mr. Wardrop was going to be a gourmet meal not a rushed takeaway.

"Um ..." I said as I came up for air.

He sighed. "Yes, Vincent."

"Now that you have your cock wedged in my butt cheeks, I don't think it's proper to call you Mr. Wardrop anymore."

He laughed so loud, I fell off his lap. I got to my knees and engulfed his cock before he realized my intent. I ran my fingers lightly across his hairy balls as my mouth and tongue worked him.

"Ned." He shuddered with pleasure.

I licked his piss slit and was rewarded with his sweet precum. I wanted to taste him bad. I impaled my face on his thick, hard cock until it tickled the back of my throat. He let out the longest sigh I had ever heard. He stood to pump in time to my oral rhythm. It was now or never. As he hurtled toward climax, I gamely moved my hands to his ass and ran my fingers down his crack. I went on and pulled his fleshy cheeks apart and dared to finger his humid butt hole.

I could tell from the short gasps of his breathing that he was close. I prized his sphincter open with one finger. It met no resistance, but as I was about to gently penetrate, I felt his sphincter grip my finger as he shot a load of cum into my mouth. A few more contractions followed a few more squirts until he backed against the kitchen table a little unsteady on his feet.

"Hoo boy. With a mouth and a tongue like that you must make a fortune." He grabbed for his robe. "Hold on, I'll get my wallet."

I was struck dumb. I was shattered. Then I was incensed.

"I don't want your fuckin' money," I yelled as I stormed toward the front door almost knocking down Robbie as he entered with milk. He stared at me as I swept indignantly down the front path. Then I heard him call out, "Dad, what's been going on here?"

It took me a few days to calm down, and in the meantime, I refused to answer Robbie's calls or his emails. He was my best friend and I was sure his dad would have painted some crap picture of my perfidy and how I had seduced him. Robbie would never forgive me. Hell, I'd never forgive myself.

It was a different matter when Robbie turned up at my apartment banging loudly on the door screaming, "You blew my dad, you sick fuck!" I had to open the door because my lease specified no loud noise or profanities allowed. Robbie marched in, and I waited for the deserved abuse.

"I knew it was the only way to get you to open up," he said. "Why the fuck aren't you taking my calls?"

"You know why," I muttered miserably.

"So, you blew my dad. Okay, Ewww! Tacky. Bad taste. But you are both adults, so I guess it's really none of my business although you as my stepmother, I can't go there. But you're my best friend."

"He told you then?"

"Of course he did. He was as baffled as I was. Until he told me what he said. So I don't blame you being upset. He thought I'd set it up as some sort of gift to him."

"Gift?"

"Yea, he thought I knew his life story and I was helping him out."

"How?"

"I'll let him explain it to you. He wants you to come over for a pool party and barbecue so he can apologize for the misunderstanding and make it up to you. You up for that?"

I smiled for the first time in days. "I'm up for him any time."

"Don't. I do not want to hear this." Robbie put his hands over his ears and stared me up and down. "You look like shit. I suggest a hot shower, a ginseng scrub and some of that spray cologne you're so fond of."

"How many people are going to be at this barbecue?" I was hoping to get Ned to myself.

"Not sure. Dad was ringing around when I left."

I didn't feel in the mood for a party, swinging or otherwise, but I couldn't miss the opportunity of seeing Ned, especially when he was going to grovel. I skipped the ginseng scrub and was at Ned's place in under half an hour. Robbie told me his dad was out by the pool, although I could hear no gaggle of voices.

I went out through the glass doors and almost creamed my jeans. Ned was lying on his stomach on the pool lounge totally naked. His tanned body rippled with muscle and his short-cropped hair complimented his stubbly chin and cheek growth. His bubble ass pouted like an unappreciated cheerleader at a drunken gay party.

He smiled when he saw me. "Hey, Vince. I'm getting a little burnt. You want to rub lotion on my back?"

"Sure, Mr. Wardrop," I said.

"I thought we were on first name basis."

"I wasn't sure."

"You better take off those good clothes of yours. Wouldn't want to get oil over them."

I didn't want to look eager, so I stripped slowly down to my jockeys and left them on. I glanced back into the house to see Robbie pulling the curtains and making vomiting motions with his fingers.

I mouthed 'Fuck you!' and he disappeared. I turned my attention to Ned. He handed me the bottle of sun tan lotion and I squeezed it directly on to his back. He flinched at the splash of cold oil. Normally, I would have warmed it in my hands first, but I was still miffed.

"I don't blame you for being angry," he said as I began to rub the lotion into his body, hesitating to admire his love handles. "I was stupid. Insensitive. I've been out of the loop for so long I naturally thought …" He hesitated. "It never occurred to me that you would be interested in someone as old as me without an ulterior motive."

I massaged his back firmly but gently. "There was an ulterior motive. I wanted to fuck you."

"Yea, Robbie told me. I guess I was having such a good time I didn't notice your finger in my ass until it was gone."

I kneaded his shoulders and neck and felt the muscles tense. He raised his head and half turned to me. "I guess I just couldn't understand that such a young, good looking guy could be interested in an old man like me."

"You think I'm good looking?" I teased.

"You're fucking gorgeous!" he said and turned over on his back almost knocking me over with his steel hard prick as proof. "Come here." He opened his arms. "And take those things off."

I stripped and my cock was the equal of his in hardness. I lay against his chest and looked into his eyes. "I thought Robbie knew all about me, my life and why I came back into his. I find out you guys didn't even know I was gay," he said. "Robbie's mom and I split amicably when I realized. I fell in love with a wonderful man named Todd. I wanted him so badly that I broke down one night and told Robbie's mom. She carried on a bit but eventually we worked out that Todd and I would move to another state although I would pay support. I was not to come near Robbie as he grew up, but I was always supplied with letters about his progress and photos from special occasions. Truthfully, I didn't miss Robbie all that much because I had Todd. We had fifteen wonderful years together."

"Did you guys split up?" I asked.

"In that inevitable way that comes to all of us," Ned said with a slight ache to his voice. "He died. Killed rather. Hit-and-run. I was devastated. I withdrew. Months passed. Then two years. Friends were always at me to get out. Find a reason to keep going. But in the years with Todd I'd lost all my dating skills. Just about every one of the gay survival skills. Oh, I tried a few times, but always got burned. The rejections sent me into a spiral of despair."

I scrutinized his face intently as he told his story, so intently he looked away in embarrassment.

"Then I got a call from Robbie's mom to say she'd discovered that it ran in the family and she thought I would be a better role model. She bowed out to allow me to get to know the son whose life I'd never shared. It was a lifeline and I grabbed for it. That's why I'm here."

"Some story," I said as I stood up.

"I thought you were a sort of gift from Robbie to help ease me back into the marketplace. Forgive me?"

"Turn over, old man," I commanded. Ned lay back on his stomach, exposing his beautiful ass. I slapped it hard, admiring the red stinging slash across his buttocks. I slapped him again and was delighted as he sucked in air as an expression of his pain. Then I bent down and kissed the warm flesh. I parted his cheeks and kneeled to put my lips to his asshole, my tongue lapping to moisten his hole. I sucked and probed as he wriggled beneath the onslaught.

My face awash with my own spit and the sweat from Ned's ass, I came up for air. I was aching for release. I drizzled sun tan lotion between his cheeks and massaged it into his inviting hole. I took my time even though every muscle in my body ached to get to the action. I teased his ass entrance with first one finger then a second. The rhythm was smooth and met little resistance. His asshole was hot and inviting. As I kept up the finger fucking, I greased my cock with the other hand. Then kneeling behind him, I extracted my fingers and lowered my cock.

As I sank into his ass, I groaned. I pulled him up so that we were fucking doggy style. He pushed back gently, his ass sucking me back in as I withdrew. And with each thrust he grabbed my cock with his ass muscles and milked me. The pace was leisurely; we were in no hurry here. I leaned over and nibbled the back of his proud neck. He attempted to turn his head so we could kiss, but all I could do was lick the corner of his mouth. I picked up speed, felt for his cock and wanked it gently in time to my thrusts, but he took my hand away and said quietly, "Not yet. I want to concentrate on giving you pleasure."

And it was the pleasure he was giving me that was tipping me over the edge. I had never been able to hold off for so long on a first penetration before in my life and all my pent up excitement was eager to explode.

"I've got to come soon," I grunted, and Ned began to back up on my cock to meet my increased rhythm. That was it. My cock spewed cum inside Ned's ass, squirting so many times I shuddered with pleasure. The orgasm was so intense it seemed to go on and on so that I thought perhaps I'd hemorrhage cum until I died.

I collapsed in a puddle of our combined perspiration on his back. Ned was the first to move. He disengaged my cock from his ass and lay me down on the sun lounge. He covered me with his body and kissed me gently. "Thanks, I needed that," he said.

"Not as much as I did." I tried to stifle a yawn.

I felt my legs being elevated and my asshole exposed. "Don't," I said softly. "I don't like that." He brushed aside my arms that were feebly attempting to block his passage as easily as he brushed aside my objections.

He lubricated my asshole with the oil, but took so much time massaging and making brief forays internally that I thought he'd accepted my protestations. Yes, a finger would slip in gently without fuss and wiggle about a bit so that it felt good, but I was so warm and relaxed that it scarcely registered the finger was penetrating deeper each time and that eventually it was joined by a companion.

My "mmmm" of contentment gave him the permission he was seeking. He pushed his cock between my cheeks to the door to my bowels. It wasn't until the pain from his initial assault registered with my brain that I realized how far we'd come. I gasped, but it was more a reflex than a reflection of the actual circumstances.

"Relax, Vince," he cooed, lulling me into a comfortable lethargy. He knew what he was doing and slowly penetrated me so painlessly that it came as a shock when I felt his balls slapping against my ass.

I had never been fucked like this before. Normally my sex partners rammed at my asshole like invading hordes against a castle wall. Ned had breached my defenses with stealth and perseverance. He was in for the long haul and not the quick spurt of satisfaction.

He rode me slowly at first, so that his thrusts eased me into trusting him totally. Every now and then, he would fuck with increased vigor. I would cry out not in pain but that having a cock in my ass could feel this good. He didn't mistake my vocabulary of sounds. I didn't need to tell him anything; he played my body expertly like a tightened musical instrument. He knew the right movements.

I surrendered to him. He picked up the pace, filling me with the most extraordinary feelings. I opened my eyes to see that he was watching me carefully, reading his success in my face. I surrendered as his cock began to pick up speed and strength, and although I was not the expert he was, I attempted to imitate the sphincter control he had used. He smiled the first time I did it. He leaned over and stroked the sweat-matted hair from my face.

I was so full of love for this man I had to look away. He didn't misinterpret my action, but caressed my face and began to fuck me with added strength and aggression. I attempted to match him, but he motioned for me to relax. As I did, he continued to dominate me and made my ass feel so good I thought I would blow my load without touching my dick. His breath came in short bursts. I put my hands to his back, attempting to pull him further inside me.

Then he grunted and gave one last thrust. I felt his cum flooding inside me. His mouth flew open and his gasps were my reward for allowing him my ass. He spasmed a few more times, and then with a look of disbelief pulled out and lowered my aching legs. He lay beside me to catch his breath. I held him until his heart stopped beating so violently it threatened to split through his chest.

The late afternoon sun cast its watery heat over us. We were both afraid to speak.

"Can I see you again?" I asked more timidly than I had wanted to sound.

"You mean a date?" he smiled.

"Yeah, I guess."

"Something more permanent?" he ventured.

We spent the next half hour discussing our options, and we agreed we knew so little about each other apart from being great at sex that we wouldn't rush it. 'It' being a more permanent relationship. We'd explore the possibility and meanwhile we'd explore each other's bodies with renewed vigor.

And just before we fell asleep together, we agreed that the only problem we could see was how to tell the kids.

ℒᴇᴛ 𝒯ʜᴇ 𝒢ᴀᴍᴇꜱ ℬᴇɢɪɴ

𝒴ou may have seen me on television advertising a certain brand of lawn mower. I've got a great body; stripped down to shorts I look fucking amazing! I've appeared on a few sporting calendars and in the buff in a couple of women's magazines, where I listed my favorite food as lettuce, my favorite movie star as Jeff Stryker, favorite car as a Black Stretch Limo with a king-size bed, and my favorite woman as...the one I haven't met yet.

The funny thing is, though, I don't go out with women. But these mags never seem to get around to asking who my favorite man is. Mine? Well, the answer would have to be the one who's fucking me right now. That's just about anyone I pick up at the bars.

Cruising bars is something I'm very good at; fame is a powerful aphrodisiac. Even though I'm getting long in the tooth in gay years, I am, at least, an Olympic Athlete. With a tight, sexy swimmer's body. Beijing was my last Olympics. Guess it's unlikely I'll make it to Rio. Anyway, it's not the competition I ache for any longer, though I have set a few world records and have a shelf full of cups and medals to show for my trouble. What attracts me is the cock.

Any sports meet there's bound to be a whole range of new, hot studs and hangers on eager to soak up the advice and friendship of a veteran winner. Some guys go for the babes. I go for the boys. And I get 'em, too.

But the Olympics are something special. The camaraderie: win or lose it's an experience you'll never want to forget. And Athens for me was certainly that. The gold medals were great and there's all that great Aussie backslapping from the media and the politicians and the people back home—that just makes it better for the day I stand up and tell the fuckers I'm a nelly queen who loves cock. That'll make a few sporting officials shit 'emselves. And it'll probably make a few more of the guys hammer themselves more securely in the closet.

I know I should have done it sooner but, well, I guess I'm a weak bastard. I knew if I told 'em too soon, I'd never be picked for the national team. I had a good reason to want to be selected: Matiss.

I saw him at the games in Athens. Great little piece of chicken meat. Far too young for me. But four years later—that's a different matter altogether. There he was in the Olympic Village. God, he was a beauty. About five foot nine, hair as black as obsidian, gorgeous round face with slightly plump cheeks and thighs that could hug a bear to death.

His English language skills back then had been perfunctory, but we'd had a few mumbled and mimed conversations in the canteen. He'd been chaperoned by the swim team manager and had clocked up decent times without snatching medals. But he was going to be a champion. In more ways than one. When I saw him in Beijing, my heart went straight to my cock. And Denise noticed.

She smirked. "My, hasn't little Matiss blossomed. Put your tongue back in your mouth, you're drooling."

I love Denise dearly as a fellow athlete, and as a cocksucker, she's one of the best, but Matiss was going to be mine. First. She could have him afterwards. Once I'd broken him in.

"You can have him at the Glory Hole Games." Denise flicked her sweaty practice gear at me. "That's if I don't drain his balls beforehand."

The last night of the Olympics was what many of us, male and female, looked forward to. A sort of sexual competition for anyone who wanted to be involved. And they gave out medals. Not officially, of course. This was all behind the backs of the officials. But my gold for the 2004 Glory Hole Games takes pride of place on my mantle at home.

"Nicky, you look good," Matiss shouted across the canteen.

He had been chatting with a group of team managers who looked like thugs. One of them ambled over and whispered conspiratorially. "Meester Neecholas, Matiss 'ee would like for you to join him for a welcome wodka in our room." It was as if Maria Ouspenskaya had suddenly morphed into a bulky Lithuanian weightlifter.

"Our room?" I said, imagining this big bear of a man, obviously a competitor, using me as meat in his sandwich.

"I will be at training. You will be alone." He winked and strode off like a muscle-bound gorilla with an oversize butt plug up his ass.

Denise leaned over and vamped in her best Greta Garbo. "Zo, chew vont to bee halone?"

I laughed. "Fuck off. This is true lust."

"Remember," she warned. "Don't fall in love."

"I never do."

Later, in Matiss's room, he was nervous.

"You look good," he repeated.

"So do you."

"You think my English, she has got better?"

"And your muscle tone, too, by the looks of it."

"You think so?"

"Take your shirt off and let me take a look. Then I'll be able to give you a considered opinion."

If you play pro sports, it's amazing how far you can go with other men when you tell them you want to admire their physique. Matiss quickly shucked his baggy ill-fitting shirt. My jaw hit the floor. This man was god! He almost turned me into a true believer.

"Wow!" I whistled in appreciation. Yeah, queers can whistle despite what you may have heard.

"You like?" Matiss smiled.

If he'd been working on his body to produce these results I don't know how he'd had any time left to work on his English. Or his swimming.

He produced a bottle of contraband Vodka and paper cups, telling me about his sporting scholarship to the university in Vilnius as we chatted like two old friends. I suspected he needed the courage of the grog to ask me if I wanted to actually feel how solid his muscles were. It began with a few puppy punches to his stomach and moved on to my caressing his biceps, running my hand over his stomach to his chest and then playfully tweaking his nipples. I could have died in this man's chest.

His trousers were so baggy I couldn't tell what effect, if any, I was having on him, but my jeans were tight enough to reveal that my reproductive organ was pumping blood like a vampire at a blood bank.

"You have big muscle, too," he said, squeezing the outline of my hard prick playfully. In jest or in earnest? When he didn't take his hand away even someone as slow as me could take a hint.

I tickled my fingers back down his chest and stomach. This time there was no macho pretense about admiring physiques. Wiggling my finger in his belly button—it's an innie—made him giggle, and when my hand finally found his solid cock in the folds of his trousers, I gasped. This boy was big all over.

"I make my body like this for you," he said before he gently pulled me to him and lathered my mouth with his tongue. This guy's kiss was dynamite. Needing to breathe I pulled away. But Matiss was back on the job almost immediately.

"Whoa boy," I managed, when I came up for air again.

"You not like Matiss?" he asked, with a pout.

"Yes, I like Matiss, but my body needs oxygen every now and then or it goes into coma."

He smiled. "Let me see body of Nicholas. I dream about four years."

Now that's flattering in anyone's language. To think this young guy had stored away four years of fantasies about me. "I have photograph of Nicholas," he added as he rifled through a drawer and produced a battered newspaper photo of me in Aussie colors at an international meet flashing that shit-eating grin of the winner. "I carry it everywhere. It help me to win." Then he added shyly. "And to learn English."

Oh, oh, I thought. *This guy's a clinger. Gorgeous. But a clinger.* He obviously had plans for the two of us raising pigs in a little cottage on the Baltic coast. All my future held for him was a bed romp of uncertain duration and "Thanks a lot!" So, the sooner I got on with it the better.

I ripped off my clothes. His stare sizzled me to such an extent I thought I'd get sunburn. He smiled. I stood naked in front of him, before he dropped his clothes to the floor. Matiss went for the old Lithuanian chest press, but I suddenly dropped to my knees rather than face certain death from the suffocation that was involved in yet another passionate kiss.

His cock was swarthy and generous and had a slight bend in it like a mature banana, but the taste was more salty and aromatic than sweet. I felt him flinch and drop a few Lithuanian expletives in appreciation.

Sucking Matiss's prick brought on thoughts of all those other endowments I'd be gobbling to my heart and throat's delight at the sexual Olympics in about three weeks' time.

Matiss was good practice. No, Matiss was great practice. I relaxed my throat muscles and took his cock to the base. He was a gentle lover and made no attempt to force himself on me so that I could control the pace. That's always the sign of a good top in cocksucking. But if I was eager, Matiss was determined to show he could reciprocate. Lifting me off the cock I was so reluctant to vacate, he kissed me briefly and led me over to the bed.

He engulfed my prick with his mouth. The sensation was total, as if my soul were being sucked out and channeled into his incredible mouth. My entire body felt like oozing honey. This man was little short of a miracle. I'd heard the occasional story of this sort of incredible passion, although I'd never experienced it before. I'd never wanted to.

Attempting to break free because I wouldn't willingly allow him to smother my individuality, he merely responded by holding me tighter. A feeling of delirium overcame me as I was rolled on to my stomach and fingers doused my asshole with lubrication.

"I wait four years for this," Matiss muttered.

I couldn't resist, even as I felt my asshole being breached. There was no pain, though this was a position in which I rarely indulged. His playful initial thrusts gave way to enthusiasm, and finally, to a toughness I began to enjoy.

Pushing back against all he could fuck into me, I grunted in appreciation. Matiss gave a sort of bellow each time his stomach slapped against my ass cheeks. There was no stopping the momentum, and my head was bucking from the ramrod shaft that was teaching me the meaning of being fucked. I slammed my ass backwards to try to take more of him inside me. We were both reaching a peak ...

FLASH!

My cum spewed out all over the bed. I yelped with pleasure from the intensity of the orgasm and from the fright of the flash of bright light. When the spasms had subsided and Matiss had pulled out, I dared glance at the doorway.

Matiss's gorilla roommate was holding a digital camera, which had just recorded our intimacy.

He smiled. "Gold performance, Matiss. And seelver for you, Meester Neecholas."

"What's the meaning of this, Matiss?" I demanded.

He merely shrugged and it was then I noticed the condom on his prick. He hadn't cum.

I was in deep shit!

"The Lithuanians are on our side now, Nick." Denise was commiserating with the fucking stupid situation I'd managed to get myself into.

"When it comes to sport there are no friends, only competitors," I whined.

We were marching around the stadium during the opening ceremony, waving to a local crowd that was going totally berserk and a global television audience in the millions. I knew I had a good chance of another gold medal and no half-assed Lithuanian git with a digital camera was going to get me to throw it away. It just meant my cover would be blown earlier than expected, losing me a shitload of sponsorship deals. What the hell, I'd be the gay world's pin-up boy for a few weeks. I'd get even more cock.

The following week I concentrated on the team effort although I was continually thinking of Matiss; not so much about what he planned to do with the photo, but about the tingle I'd felt in my ass as he fucked me.

Matiss continued to smile across the canteen, waving to me on a number of occasions, but I gave him the finger. Everyone who knew us thought it was merely a routine form of psychological intimidation. Fortunately, we were drawn in different heats, but we both coasted to wins in easy times. I secretly watched from the stand as he surged to the lead early in his swim and stayed there. As he got out of the pool, I'd made the mistake of standing up to leave. He'd seen me. That cute face of his lit up with one of the shit-eatingest grins I've ever fuckin' seen. And his gorilla saw it, too.

"You like a copy of photograph?" he said in his slimiest English.

"I'd like all the copies and the camera card, if it's all the same to you, Lurch."

"Perhaps you would like for your Australian papers to have copy?" He smirked.

"Not just at the moment, thanks. I'd still like to bask in a bit of geriatric glory before I come out."

It was no use using subtlety on this man. He didn't understand it. Or sarcasm, for that matter.

"It would be good idea you come second to our champion."

"Do what you like with the fucking photo," I said with as much Dutch courage as I could muster. I was counting on most media not wanting to smear the record of an Olympic hero—at least until the whole bloody thing was over.

Denise had captured a bronze and a gold in her events before I found myself on the starting block for my main race. And wouldn't you know it; there was Matiss in the fuckin' lane next to mine. We'd made the two best times. I was pissed off that his was two one-hundredths of a second better than mine, although I knew I'd coasted in the preliminaries. But then, maybe he had as well.

He smiled and said, "Good luck, Nick" as if he meant it and held out his hand. We were on international television and this wasn't the way things were done.

I shook his hand to uproar from the stands and between gritted teeth mumbled, "You'll eat my farts, fucker," hoping the world's microphones didn't pick it up.

Here we were, the two fastest men over 1000 meters. One with his career ahead of him and me, well, mine was all behind me now. In more ways than one. I glanced over at Matiss and noticed the outline of his cock snuggled in his national swimming togs. And my ass ached to feel it again.

But there wasn't time for more of that maudlin shit as we both flew through the air in our starting dive. The first lap separated the chiefs from the soldiers. I realized Matiss and I had it sewn up even if we didn't break any records. We had a Canadian and a Netherlander close on our tails, but I knew the Netherlander would run out of puff around the third lap. Our only real danger was the Canadian. Cute he was, too.

Matiss and I were toying with each other. He'd burst ahead, and I'd let him go. Then I would do the same. We were rounding the ends within a butterfly's breath of each other, the spectators screaming hysterical partisan encouragement. We were both up to giving them a show.

We put distance between ourselves and the Canadian, so the outcome would never be in doubt. We were like two porpoises frolicking, and, at times, I almost forgot where we were. It was dream-like when we hit the final lap. The Canadian was a good three to four body lengths behind and the rest of the pool out of serious contention. I lapped Matiss and thought I saw that smile again. Fuck him.

Matiss dropped farther and farther behind until it looked as if there would be no competition. He was deliberately throwing the race. What the fuck was going on?

I slowed imperceptibly to allow him to catch me. We were level now, the Canadian closing fast when, with a slight nod of my head, which he acknowledged, we sprinted the last ten meters, Matiss touching the pad just ahead of me.

The crowd went berserk! Matiss punched the air just as I had four years earlier in the same event. He hugged me excitedly. I half expected a triumphant kiss. The times showed we'd both broken the world record for one thousand meters. Big deal! The record had been mine anyway.

Gold: Lithuania. Silver: Australia. Bronze: Canada.

We stood like slabs of meat and listened to what passed for a patriotic ditty in Lithuania. Don't get me wrong, I think all anthems are crap and bring out the worst in people. It was what happened next that would be read about in newspapers or seen in countless loops on YouTube. We three winners were full of fake bonhomie and backslapping when Matiss leaned over from the winner's podium and planted the biggest, wettest fucking tongue kiss on me that I'd ever known. Cameras shrieked, microphones spluttered, and a few thousand pacemakers packed it in.

What did I do? What d'ya reckon? I fuckin' kissed him back. Everyone blamed Lithuania, but Matiss kept a regal silence. He'd obviously voided his sporting scholarship to university and would return home in disgrace. There was serious talk of stripping him of his medal.

That was his concern. Mine was the Cocksucker Games, although I was finding Matiss in my mind more than I cared to admit.

"Snap out if it!" Denise yelled. "You won't even get the bronze if you carry on like this."

There are no starters' blocks for the Cocksucker Games, though you are allowed to bring a cushion, provided it is of official dimensions and contains sponge rubber, not feathers. The contestants line up in front of a paneled wall, the females at one end and the males at the other. The wall is riddled with a row of glory holes at various cock heights all along. At the starter's gun, we drop to our knees and swallow the cock that protrudes from the hole. This goes on until the last cock has been drained or there is only one contestant still kneeling. The winners are determined by the number of sperm-filled scumbags in each person's possession. Hands are allowed only to remove the overflowing rubber.

The cocks are supplied courtesy of male competitors in the village, as well as friendly journos, sportscasters and various auxiliary staff. There is never any scarcity of volunteers. I just hoped the lesbian competition was as well organized.

The gun cracked while my mind wandered. Denise was already on her knees at work on her first big purple headed number before I realized we were away. Mine was a cute uncut number of medium size. I was wrapping my lips around it as Denise yanked off the condom on her first triumph. God, she was good. And fast! Though they did tend to put the premature ejaculators at the beginning to add spice. Of course, the depositors could always come back for seconds.

They were all shapes, sizes, colors and ages, and the only thing they had in common was that they were cocks! Glorious cocks! The smell of fresh cum was already rampant, but every cock that invaded my throat would become the flavor, the texture, the length and breadth of Matiss's.

Fuck off, I told myself. *Get back to the job at hand, well, at mouth.* This was crazy. Surely, I hadn't fallen for that Lithuanian Mata Fairy.

I had four condoms oozing against my knee to Denise's five. I put on a spurt, so to speak, and drained my next two sets of balls in record time. Now I was getting into it! My mouth and throat were machines, hoovering sack loads of sperm from overflowing balls. I was in cock hog heaven. Drool poured from my lips as I sucked and swallowed rubber and the hard gristle of cockdom. There was a feeding frenzy as the ocean of sperm was being dumped at our failing knees.

In time we'd all come down with arthritis and repetitive lip injury. Another cock poked its way into my inviting sludge of a mouth. I'd lost count of the tally, and I didn't fucking care. I'd drown in oozing condoms before I'd let a fucker like Matiss and his gorilla make a monkey of me.

I sucked and dribbled like I've never fuckin' sucked and dribbled before. I gulped and belched until my breath stank of burning rubber; still more horny manhood poked through the aptly named glory holes and turned me cock-eyed. There were six of us left in the competition, many having retired satiated or having bettered their previous personal best. I was awash with perspiration and drool and the smell of cock cheese and stale piss. I finished off my latest, who had taken an eternity to cum, which under different circumstances I would have approved. Great cock, great technique, but in bed; not at the Glory Hole Games.

Bending forward for my next prize it seemed reluctant to appear, but appear it did, eventually, while I cursed the lost seconds. I made a mental note to complain to the organizers.

I knew that cock before it had even poked through its entire length. It was Matiss's. I shook my head to clear it, but it wasn't my imagination. My heart sank and my throat seized up. I couldn't. I attempted to push the cock back through the glory hole, which would lead to instant disqualification. It made a tentative effort to return, but I had my mouth to the hole whispering "Matiss? Is that you?"

I saw the look of horror on Denise's face, not because she knew I was now out of competition, but because she knew with certainty I was in love. Something I was forced to admit to myself.

Matiss squatted. I could see his face through the intimacy of the glory hole, hating myself as I said it. "I love you, Matiss. Fuck it!" He smiled that beautiful, young smile he has. "I love you too, Nick. Fuck it!" Kneeling in the detritus of over a dozen orgasms, the watery cum crushed beneath my aching knees, I kissed Matiss through the glory hole that had finally brought us together.

A few of the more romantic judges applauded, and I was on my feet racing around the barrier to find my man. He grabbed me and flung me in the air almost knocking over the guy whose cock was firmly embedded in Denise's vampire-like mouth.

We found a quieter spot to talk, and all the questions tumbled out of me. The photograph had been taken not only to intimidate me, but to keep Matiss on a leash. They'd threatened to show it to his family, because he'd already told the Lithuanian swimming coach of his intention of migrating to Australia. The coach had believed the incriminating photo had forced me to throw the race, as well as keeping Matiss in line, right up until the fateful kiss on the winners' podium.

"I will need a very personal trainer if I am to get in shape for the London Olympics," Matiss explained.

I didn't listen after that. My stomach felt funny, my head filled with marshmallows, and my mind with plans that included a queen-sized bed and a harbor-side apartment with a swimming pool. Then the young man stopped his babbling and stuck his tongue down my throat. Who am I to fight true love?

Oh, yeah. Fuckin' Denise won Cocksucker gold. And she bought the apartment next door. She's threatening to install a glory hole between our living rooms. But that's taking friendship a step too far.

Taking The Bait

He stood under the shower at the Seaspray Surf and Lifesaving Club, just north of Sydney. And he really was beautiful. The refracted sunlight through the beer glass tiles added to the luster of his tan. His impossibly perfect torso was caressed by the cascading water, his hair limp and dark over his softly chiseled face. He had a nipple ring that looked comfortably at home on his luscious chest, and a dragon tattoo that hugged his back like a proprietorial lover. But my attention was attracted by his muscular hand pumping his slim, tanned cock with such force the veins stood out on his forearms.

Without glancing my way, he knew I was watching. He was performing for me, so I felt like holding up a placard with a bold 10 on it like they do at diving competitions. Instead, I just said, "Put it away, son. I know who you are." He glanced over through his mop of straggly hair matted with sun and saltwater, uncertain whether to continue.

"You're one of Eric Layton's sons, aren't you? Not sure which one but..."

"Todd," he muttered sheepishly as his cock began deflating. "You don't like?" he asked, meaning himself.

"Oh, I like a lot," I said and meant it. "But I'm not a complete fool."

I was hoping to read disappointment in his features, but if it was there I missed it. "Why don't you dry off and I'll see you outside," I said. He nodded and began to spray the salt from his body. I took one last appreciative glance and he caught me. He smiled at the compliment.

I walked down the concrete steps to the beach, seating myself among the spinifex grass fighting an interminable battle against surf and wind erosion. Truth be told it wasn't much of a beach; a small strip of sand in a bay sheltered just a little too well by prominent headlands that enclosed it like almond crescents, my favorite kind of shortbread when I was a kid.

It was from this vantage point, physical and emotional, that I had first seen him: a lone surfer out in the distance waiting for unenthusiastic waves. It was mid-week, so he was bound to be a local.

Seaspray was named after an old wooden sailing boat that plied the east coast until it ran aground. The town had sprung up near where it sank. Seaspray came alive, and then only marginally, on weekends when knowing city folk made the trek north from Sydney to the sylvan unspoiled village of clustered weatherboard cottages that had lain dormant and largely undiscovered for most of its existence. It would be size-queen talk to call it a town. Created in the nineteenth century as a fishing village, it supported a few dozen families until the fish, and consequently the accompanying industry, departed almost two decades since. Those few denizens who remained drove the thirty kilometers to the nearest major town, sometimes farther, each day for employment.

The reason for Seaspray's somnambulant existence was that it lay off the freeway between Sydney and Newcastle, a few meandering miles from the turn-off signposted on rotting wood and rusting tin. The roadway was uninvitingly asphalt-free, its verges overgrown with the prickly blackberries that thrived in the area, and which the secretive locals did nothing to cut back. Itinerant surfers normally bypassed it for beaches farther north with waves less lazy, leaving Seaspray's beach to families and hobby surfers whose daring amounted to little more than actually standing upright on their boards.

This influx was the town's lifeblood. The small Seaspray Inn opened Friday night through Monday morning. If locals wanted anything mid week, they knocked. And the village would have remained this way had it not been for the invasion of the rowdy, the patronizing and the nouveau riche looking for a trendy real estate investment and somewhere cozy. It was a convenient drive from the city. The villagers were suddenly alive to possibilities; those at least who still needed to earn a living. The retirees and the old-timers sided with the environmentalists to petition the government to list Seaspray as a natural treasure to save its heritage from the development bogey.

It was my job to recommend to that government whether development should be permitted or refused.

The surf indolently churned itself on to the sandy beach as if it couldn't care less about the politicking. Todd came out of the surf club and walked casually over to where I was sitting, his board under his arm. He sat much too close. I sidled away. He made no attempt to breach the distance. "Beautiful, mmmm?" I said.

Todd grinned. "You mean me or the beach?"

"Both," I said. "But then everyone tells you that, don't they?" I looked him over. "Is that why you were chosen?"

He almost got the tone and pitch of genuine surprise: "For what?" He realized he hadn't carried it off and had the good grace to look down at the sand he was sifting through his fingers.

"You could have had me in there, you know," he said. "But I'm glad you didn't."

"Yes, I know I could have," I told him truthfully. "But it would not have been of your own free will. And there would have been consequences."

"I'm of legal age."

I turned to look at him. "They weren't the consequences I was thinking of," I said before turning back to the waves.

"I haven't had a lot of experience but..."

I glanced at him again. "Does your dad know?"

He flushed slightly, which merely made him more attractive. "No. He only chose me because I'm family and he could control the outcome."

The townspeople of Seaspray knew me; after all, I'd grown up here. And they knew why I had returned. At least one of them had his own idea about how to get me to make the decision that he wanted.

Todd was silent for a moment then he turned and nodded toward my car. "That your board?"

"Yep."

"How about it?"

In response I stood, peeled off my stifling city casual wear down to my board shorts, which I'd taken the precaution of wearing, tossed my clothes on the front seat of the car and unstrapped my board from the roof rack. "I guess there's no point in locking it?" I asked.

"Nah, they'll just damage the car if they have to force it open."

"I thought so. But they won't find anything." It was a paramount rule of my department that you never carried any papers that gave the slightest hint of your thinking. Rule number two was to never underestimate the skills of nosy townsfolk or prying journalists. Plus it was unprofessional to make up your mind about a decision before the facts were all correlated.

I ran down the beach and into the sea with Todd in pursuit. We paddled out slowly, playfully, like two porpoises until we were far enough out. Then I noticed that a number of townsfolk had made an appearance on the beach around my car.

"They're not very subtle, are they?" I said.

He looked at the savage scar across my chest. "It's not a subtle town. You of all people should know that."

"I suppose there was a security camera in the surf club?" Graphic footage of me and one of Seaspray's finest would have done little for my reputation and my career advancement.

"You're no dummy, are you, Mr. Holden ?"

"Greg."

Looking back to the shore, I saw a glint of sun reflecting off glass.

"Telephoto lens?" I asked with a rueful shake of my head.

"Uh huh."

"Someone thinks I'm going to fuck you in the surf?"

"I could always fuck you, if you'd rather."

I roared with laughter, splashing a handful of seawater at him. He retaliated, and we began a juvenile water fight that ended when he fell off his board. When I leaned over to give him a hand, he pulled me under.

In the quiet stillness beneath the surface, he clung to me. I gazed into eyes so appealing that, bait or no bait, I took the hook. I pried his mouth open with my tongue. He allowed me entrance, reciprocating by running his hands down my body, hesitating momentarily before he pushed his hand eagerly beneath my board shorts, grasping my hardening cock.

He pulled my board shorts loose as he slipped farther into the depths, wrapping his lips around my cock. I gasped, taking in water. His underwater oral skills would have been the envy of a mermaid. I surfaced briefly, gulping in fresh air. With Todd still grappling with my cock, I twisted like a synchronized swimmer in competition until my head was at Todd's crotch level. I maneuvered his white Speedos down, slipping them onto my arm as he had with my board shorts, and was at last able to kiss the magnificent cock I'd seen being pumped so expertly in the shower. He made for the surface and fleetingly broke contact with my prick to suck in air before diving again. From the beach, it must have looked like two men attempting to drown each other.

Todd truly was a man of the sea. He could hold his breath while sucking and swallowing my erection longer than I could his. I was gasping each time I surfaced briefly, but I was determined to bring him to climax. He was too magnificent a specimen to let get away. I wouldn't be able to hold out much longer. Todd's mouth was a suction pump. To surface now for breath would kill the momentum.

Fingering his balls lightly, I licked his cock head as I drove my mouth down to his silky pubic hair. I was going to pass out soon, but I was not willing to let go of my prize. As I shot between his beautiful wet lips, I suctioned his prick until he, too, could no longer control himself. His sperm shot down my throat.

Then like two aqua park porpoises, we shot to the surface gulping in oxygen before our lungs burst. But only after we'd covered our modesty below the surface.

"Not bad for an old guy," Todd yelled as we competed on our boards back to shore.

"Were you a bribe or blackmail?"

"Either. He didn't care," he said as he walked off the beach.

The Seaspray Inn had opened for the duration of my stay—an indication of my importance. Shelley ran the quaint establishment, and I'd known her growing up. "Not much call for wine up here, Greg," she said as she scoured through her paltry wine cellar and scrounged up a serviceable cabernet sauvignon of not too recent vintage. At least the grapes had had a chance to ferment. "This is a beer town."

"That may change," I said slyly, winking.

She slapped me playfully. "Now don't you go getting my hopes up."

We talked over old times as we devoured the bottle. "You happy in the city?" she asked.

"I like the excitement. The beaches are good. I miss the quiet sometimes."

"That's not what I meant."

"Still looking."

"What about young Todd?"

"Oh, come on, Shelley. It was all a bit obvious."

"I'm not talking about that. I told him you wouldn't fall for it." Shelley looked in my eyes. "What do you think of Todd himself?"

I was noncommittal. "A very personable, young man."

"Take him back with you, Greg. For his sake, take him with you. This town is poison. Look what it did to you."

"That was a long time ago," I murmured.

"And if you weren't so important to the future of this town they'd bloody well do it again, and you know it. And what do you think young Todd's future will be if you make the wrong decision in their eyes?"

I was known for my impartiality, but my task was to examine communities and extrapolate communal consequences, not the affect on individuals.

That thought was not a pleasant one to take to bed. I lay listening to the waves on the sand, watching the gauze curtains flap listlessly in the breeze, hoping they would lull my conscience to sleep.

The dream was the most arousing I had ever experienced. Todd crept into my bedroom, his near silent stirrings awakening me. I gazed up at his body in the eerie orange glow of a street lamp outside the window as he shucked his clothes. He leaned forward and pinned me to the mattress. I wanted to put my arms around him, but allowed him to take control, surrendering to his tongue tracing the slash of an old wound across my chest.

It released the trapped memories of the night it happened; the night that I had plucked up the courage to admit to Eric, Todd's father, that I fancied him. We were both untutored youths back then, and his response had been to punch me on the shoulder and tell me not to be silly. But he'd confided my secret to our mates at the Saturday dance at the surf club. They'd dragged me into the change rooms, and while one stood guard, they had taken turns raping my mouth and spitting their contempt. When it was all over, they panicked.

They concocted a story that I had been involved in a brawl with an out-of-towner who had questioned my masculinity and I'd come off the worse for the ordeal. Needing my corroboration to the lie, Eric broke an empty bottle from the beers they'd consumed and slashed it across my chest.

"That's just a taste of what will happen if you ever tell," he threatened.

After I left the hospital, I never went back. To the village, my parents were a constant reminder of the cancerous secret that ate away at Seaspray's innards and there was relief all round when they died in a car accident a few years later. I buried them hundreds of kilometers away. None of their neighbors attended.

My body jerked as I re-experienced the slashing.

"Are you all right?" Todd sounded concerned.

"You're not a dream?" I mumbled groggily.

He moved my hand to his cock. "Do I feel like a dream?"

I was disoriented and sweating from the unpleasant memory. I got out of bed and went to the window. "What are you doing here?"

"I thought you might want company."

"Oh? You thought that or you were told to think that?"

"Okay, I guess I deserve that, but I'm here this time because I want to be." He raised himself on his elbow, watching me in silhouette.

"I'm old enough to be your father," I said.

He grinned. "You're a very attractive man, that's all I know. You didn't take advantage of me when you could have."

I turned on him angrily. "What sort of man sends his son out to have sex with a stranger for the sake of the future of a town nobody really cares about?"

"That's not true," he said. "If nobody cared about us you wouldn't be here."

I had to admit the truth of that.

"Come back to bed. Please," he said.

I lay next to him while he stroked my hair.

"Nobody gives a fuck about this place really," I said. "You're just the frontline in a wider debate. A convenience. Environmentalists are using you as a test case. They want the town left as it is, a museum piece for residents and weekend picnickers. Developers see dollar signs and want to turn you into a summer holiday Mecca with high-rise hotels and condominiums."

"I don't care about any of that," he said and kissed me, almost melting my resistance.

"You'll resent me if the decision goes against you."

"I don't care what you do. Really, I don't."

My anger flared again. "It disgusts me that you would allow yourself to be turned into a whore by your father and whoever else is involved, just to get their own way. Have you no pride?"

He didn't allow my name calling to get the better of him. "Listen, okay. I was doing what my dad wanted at first. I'm not proud of that. But when it didn't work..." he shrugged, "...well, I respected you. I told my dad and he got angry. He told me to try harder."

"So, here you are."

"No, fuck you! I told him I'd have no more to do with it. It would have been easier if you'd been old, gross and lecherous. But you're not. I'm here because I couldn't stop thinking about you and...and the way you held me under the water in the bay. I've never been held like that before. It's more than sex—"

"But to force you into the situation in the first place—"

"You don't understand," he said. "He didn't force me. My dad will be destroyed if the decision goes against him. I had to help. It was my duty."

"Destroyed? How?"

He paused, and I made no attempt to help him. "He's been secretly buying up old properties in the town as they become vacant. All the best land. The area that's most likely to be the site of tourist hotels or blocks of apartments."

I smirked. "I see. And no one knows that the man who struts about parading his anti-development credentials is in reality hoping to make a killing from these very same developers."

"That's about it."

"And this sob story is not another attempt to get me on your side?"

Without a word, he jumped out of bed and began searching for his clothes. "Think what you like," he said at last. "I made a mistake about you."

I rushed him, throwing him on the bed. He resisted, and I felt him wriggle beneath my superior weight, my strength inflaming his passion so that soon his hard cock was pressing into my stomach.

"Resistance is futile," I said. I bit his nipple to prove it.

He pouted. "Ouch, that hurt."

I was lighter on the second nipple. Then I followed the curve of his smooth belly into the dark bush that housed his cock. I lapped his balls, sucking them into my mouth as he thrashed about on the bed. I nibbled my teeth lightly along the length of his shaft and tongue lapped the sensitive knob. He tried to hold my head away in case he blew his load, but I would not give up. My tongue snaked around the stem of his cock as I took him in my mouth and down my throat. He groaned, so I teased him by stopping. He pushed my head down almost gagging me, but I resumed control of the rhythm, the suction. He shuddered.

"I can't hold…" was all he had a chance to say before he grunted. His cock twitched three or four times before his sweet cum flooded my mouth. I held it in as he sank into the bed spent, and then I grabbed his legs, forcing them back over his body. The button of his asshole was directly beneath me. I dribbled his cum from my mouth into his ass crack, lubricating it into his hole with my fingers. When it was slimy enough, I spat the remainder of his cum into the palm of my hand and lubricated my own cock.

I pushed against his muscular ass, but the pain was too intense as the head of my cock met his determined sphincter. I leaned between his legs and took his face in my hands. "You are one of the most beautiful men I have ever seen." He couldn't help it, he smiled. I felt him relax, and I pushed my way in. His sharp intake of breath meant I was hurting him, but I stayed my ground. I kissed him. He was hungry for it, searching my mouth with his tongue. As he did, I picked up the pace, fucking his warm, inviting asshole. It crossed my mind at that moment what poetic justice it was that here was the man who was scarred for life fucking the son of the man who had done it.

Allowing me to enter him fully, Todd closed his eyes, his breath flat lining soft and accepting. I brushed the hair out of his eyes. I wondered that such a man could give himself to me. Picking up rhythm, I began to fuck him harder, forcing his body deeper into the bed. He began to match me stroke for stroke, squeezing his ass around my invading cock. I thought of everything I could to avoid shooting too quickly, but I banished the image of his father. I would not visit the sins of the father on this son.

I gasped as I began to shoot inside him. He clasped me tighter with his sun-tanned legs, attempting to make me part of him. With my cock satisfied, I collapsed on top of him. He rolled over and my cock popped out. He brought his face close to mine. "I could get to like you," he said. I caressed his biceps until he fell asleep.

It was the sharp rap at the door that woke me. I looked over at Todd's sleeping body, covering his nakedness with a sheet.

"Come in," I croaked.

Shelley entered with a breakfast tray. I noticed immediately it had tea and toast for two.

"How…?"

Shelley smiled. "I let him in the back door. Even if I hadn't I would have known because you two made enough noise to wake the entire town."

"Morning, Shell," Todd said as he sat up sleepily. He grabbed a piece of toast and spread it with thick country jam.

"There's a one-man reception committee wanting to speak to you downstairs. Urgent, I think he said. What should I tell him?"

"Tell him I'm—"

"Tell dad we're having breakfast and that we'll be down in an hour, after we've showered, shit and shaved."

Shelley looked at me. I shrugged. She quietly closed the door, leaving us alone.

"No, it's not what you think," Todd mumbled through his munching. "It was not a set up. So have your breakfast and stop anticipating."

We ate in silence, neither daring to discuss our coupling, too frightened to ask if it would be repeated. We showered separately, suddenly coy in each other's presence. An hour later, we were downstairs in the dining area of the Seaspray Inn confronted by what looked suspiciously like a one-man lynch mob: Todd's father.

"Fuckin' pervert," he yelled. "You should be run out of town!"

"Now hold on," I said. "For a start, Todd is of age and can make his own decisions. Furthermore, nothing that we did last night is considered illegal activity in this state."

"It may not be illegal," he growled, "but it's fuckin' immoral."

"Dad..." Todd tried to speak to his father, but Eric wouldn't even catch his eye.

"Anyway, you're hopelessly compromised," Eric shouted at me.

"I would have thought that as you sent your son on a mission, you'd be happy for me to be compromised."

Eric's eyes widened. "I don't know what you're talking about."

"Exactly which side is it you're batting for, Eric?" I asked quietly.

"Why, that's obvious…" he spluttered.

"Course it is, mate. You want the town to stay the way it is. No development. No hotels. No apartment blocks."

"And no faggots like you!" he added with a spiteful sneer.

"If that's the case, then, I wonder why the facts don't gel with your public stand. After all, you've been buying up any piece of available land. Is it to save the town or could it be you hope to monopolize negotiations with developers?"

Eric looked at his son and turned pale.

"You malicious bastard!" he spat at me. "I knew you'd hold it against me just because of that little cut to your chest…"

Todd rounded on his father. "You did that to him?"

"Yeah, and the fucking faggot deserved everything he got!"

Todd looked at me, shocked, shaking his head. "I didn't know."

"Well, he's got his fuckin' revenge. He'll send me to the fuckin' wall. I need the money from the developers or I'm skint. Stony broke. And son, if you think he fucked me, he really fucked you!"

Todd turned on me. He was about to speak, but thought better of it. The look of betrayal said it all. He shook his head and rushed out.

Eric quivered with rage.

"Tell me," I said calmly. "What sort of man sends his son to do what he's too afraid to do himself?"

I could tell at that moment he wished he had the broken bottle in his hand again. But he didn't. He had to be satisfied with a door slam that shattered the rusty hinges.

When we were alone Shelley whistled. "Well that sure pulled a few scabs off!"

The entire scene depressed the hell out of me.

"Was it spite? Revenge?" Shelley asked later as she poured me a coffee. I'd spent the day gathering photographic material. We were on the Seaspray Inn's front veranda as the sun sent the last of its warmth scudding across the still surf.

"Hell, no," I said. "Honestly, it crossed my mind once and that was all. But I really like him, Shelley."

"Take him with you then."

"I can't. I'd always wonder. And so would he."

I wandered off to my room. It was strange how much I missed Todd's warmth next to me. I got up and went to the window. The moon was at its brightest. It cast a blue glaze across the bay. I knew I would never come back. This visit had been a mistake. I walked downstairs to let myself out the back door. The sand crunched under my feet as I walked toward the surf's edge with my board. The water was warm. Against my better judgment about surfing alone at night, I soon put distance between myself and the shore. It was calm and peaceful, and it gave me the space to think.

But eventually solitude turns cold. I wrapped my arms around my body and thought of Todd. I looked toward the shore and thought I saw myself sitting there staring out to sea at a lone surfer as I had on that first day. I was hallucinating. I paddled in. After landing on the beach, I felt heavy, weary. On impulse, I headed to the surf club. Inside it was all dark angles and shadowy doorways except where the moonlight's beam shone lustrously. I had been hoping my dark surf angel would once again be displaying himself under the spray of water. Disappointed, I turned to go.

"Hey, old man," a voice called from the shadows.

Todd walked into the stream of moonlight. He was naked.

He held out his hand. "Now it's my turn."

Revenge begets revenge; the cycle goes on forever. I didn't care. All I wanted was to feel Todd again. He was rough. There was no kissing, no cuddling. He bent me forward, plunging in hard enough to wind me. I made no complaint as he fucked silently, afraid to give sound to his desire. He knew he was hurting me even though I made no complaint. "Now we're even," he spat. But even as he continued to fuck me savagely, I felt the warmth of his tears on my back. He pushed me away from him as disgusted with himself as he was with me. "I can't do it," he sobbed.

I wrapped my arms around him. "I'm glad you couldn't."

The next morning as I loaded my car, strapping my board to the bonnet, Shelley came to see me off.

"So what decision have you come to?" she said.

I smiled. "It was never my decision to make. I knew that I couldn't be dispassionate about Seaspray. I all but disqualified myself long ago on the grounds of conflict of interest. I was just doing the groundwork. They'll appoint someone else to decide your future. I came up to see what was left of the old place."

Shelley was still laughing as I drove toward the beach. In the distance, I saw a lone surfer waiting for errant waves. As I watched, one rose from the mouth of the bay. The surfer waited patiently, anticipating its every move. He caught it, cutting through the water majestically, riding it close to the shore. As he emerged triumphant, excited, from the surf, he walked up the beach carrying his board. I opened the car door and waited.

Party Whip

The young, dark-haired, tattooed Goth boy was faking a confidence he certainly did not feel, sprawled over the coffee table, totally naked, vulnerable, with a cigarette protruding from his asshole.

Brad unfurled his stock whip. The Red Sea could not have parted for Moses as swiftly as the other partygoers parted to move out of harm's way. The whip looked lethal, not like the riding crops prissy queens used to smack each other across the buttocks playing at being masterful. This was a man's whip. It could flay the skin. Brad had seen just that when two stockmen with a decades-old grudge finally settled it with a stock whip fight. They had cut each other to ribbons, but, after a quick patch up by a local doctor, both retired to the pub to celebrate their new-formed mateship.

The whip looked like a deadly coiled black snake. It went everywhere with Brad—a man never knew when he might have use of it. He was a fixture on the rodeo circuit; the Thunder from Downunder was his *nom de whip*, given him for making the hide crack like thunder around the arena. For those exhibitions, he used his 12 foot by 12 plait bull whip. It was built for show.

But Black Beauty was his favorite. Hand crafted from kangaroo hide, as all his best were, by the finest whip masters to suit the secret rituals to which he subjected it with his big broad hands. He had chosen the skins himself to ensure they were free from blemishes and tick marks. It was 12 plait because the more strands to the whip, the more fluidity he got in the movement. This was not a whip for thunder; this was for special performances. It had a spring reinforced cane handle covered with kangaroo leather as smooth as the skin on a virgin's ass and as fiery red as the stripes he would brand there. It was a short whip, a six-footer, because he used it in confined spaces.

At the party, he stood out, not least for his flamboyant, bondage-tinged rodeo regalia, which he toned down as far as he felt comfortable when in the Big Smoke so he didn't look like a total rube, but more to do with his 6'2" frame and solid build. He wouldn't win any bodybuilding championships, he knew that for a fact, but he was brawny, wiry, with muscle. It drove the rodeo chicks wild.

But there were no chicks at this party. It was all men.

Some of them had attempted to start conversations by bringing up *Brokeback Mountain,* as if that had anything to do with his life. He guessed what they were hinting at and just answered their inane chatter with a smile. Hell, why did everyone think that damn movie stood for every gay cowboy in the world? They were as individual as, well, the guys at the party. Sure he sometimes found the drag queens annoying, but that was because some of them wouldn't take his polite 'no' for an answer, retaliating with their smart mouths in an attempt to humiliate him. Most of the time a slow unfurling of his whip was enough to quiet them down. If not, he would haul them party central for his whip show, and if that didn't make them shit scared, then the cigarette-in-the-mouth routine usually did.

Arthur, the party host, smiled when the burly cowboy first arrived.

Brad smirked back. "What's your pleasure?"

"You know what my pleasure is," Arthur said as he gripped Brad by the arm. He didn't mind, for Arthur was his protector. It was Arthur who, while cruising the farmers and cowboys at Sydney's Royal Easter Show a few years before, had picked him up as a raw 19-year-old and inducted him into the pleasures of whip sex, although back then, he felt he was abusing his whip each time he'd used it on Arthur's scarred body.

At the end of ten days, their friendship had been cemented and Brad's unease with the sex whip had disappeared. Arthur taught him the signs to look for in other men, particularly married men, men on the land who had to keep their secret as locked up as their real feelings. During the following year, he had made contact with the Outback underground that carried news of the new boy along the bush telegraph. He found a different claque of admirers turning up at rodeos, male admirers who wanted his company for a quick fumble. Most times he was eager to oblige.

Arthur loved to read Brad's emails of a life that was as alien to him as if he came from Mars. Every year Brad would come to the city for the duration of the Show, his visit culminating in an extravagant party at Arthur's classy inner city apartment. Invariably, Brad supplied the centerpiece entertainment and, just as inevitably, Arthur would try to pair him off with someone so totally unsuitable that he headed back to the country sexually sated, but more lonely than ever. Their own relationship had lost its sexual frisson some time before. Arthur liked variety.

"Come and meet Dex," Arthur said, dragging the cowboy across the room.

"Aw, you're not going to try and pair me up with another twink?"

"I think you and Dex will have an awful lot in common."

Brad laughed. "Now where have I heard that before? What is it we'll have in common?"

"He's an arrogant bastard. Oh, and you'll loathe each other on sight."

Before he could resist they had reached the youth in question. It took just one look before he realized Arthur's assessment was spot on. This guy gave off surly like most men give off pheromones. He was around twenty, to Brad's twenty-eight, a character cobbled together from scraps of pop culture: a Goth slogan tattooed along his arm in Old English script, a half glove on his hand complimented by a leather wrist band, and long, lank dark hair that hung down to his shoulders, green eyes, and a scrappy personality to match. Beneath his battered leather jacket, he wore a tattered T-shirt with some equally tattered slogan that had been sun-bleached to near invisibility, jeans that had seen better days, and boots that came to a point sharp enough to poke out the eyes of leprechauns. He even had spurs attached.

Arthur smiled. "Don't rub your spurs against the furniture, Dex; there's a good lad."

In response to the request, Dex merely rubbed his boots against the drinks cabinet with increased vigor.

Dex nodded at the whip. "You posing with that or is it for real?"

"You mean Black Beauty here?"

Dex sneered. "Your whip's got a name?"

"Yeah." Arthur had been correct. Brad loathed this cocksure character. "I originally called him Ipilya—"

"—the Aboriginal lizard god of storms"

Brad was gob smacked.

"I'm not just a pretty face," Dex said with a fabricated ennui.

Brad looked, really looked, at his antagonist. Yes, he was a pretty face. Not soft pretty, but rugged pretty.

Pretty with the effeminate edges chipped away. But chipped away by whom? Dex attempted to obscure his good looks with a blend of arrogance and a demeanor that seemed to threaten dire consequences if you approached too close.

He took a chance and flicked at Dex's dark locks that had tumbled over one eye. "Why the camouflage?" Before he could do it a second time, Dex's hand shot out and held Brad's at bay. Real firm grip. He realized Dex's appearance belied his strength. This kid had reserves of power.

Dex was savage in his response. "No one touches."

"You hiding behind it or you really like it like that?" Brad asked.

"That's the best you can come back with, man?" he said with a note of boredom in his voice.

"There," said Arthur, who had been watching the exchange with interest. "Didn't I say you'd both loathe each other?" He wandered away happy.

Brad grinned. "Looks like we're meant to be the floor show."

"Doubt you'll survive round one with me," Dex said. "Most don't."

"Fellow queens, whores and twinks," Arthur yelled at the top of his voice. "I've got some great news. Cowboy Brad has consented to a little display of his...um...prowess, something so mysterious that even I don't know half of what he's going to do. You won't see this in the center ring at the Easter Show; it's exclusive to Chez Arthur."

All eyes turned to Brad, some scarcely concealing their utter contempt for something as banal as a whip show. He noted the pursed looks as he uncurled Black Beauty, feeling it slide across his palm as he flicked it and the sound exploded from the tip. There was an immediate hush. Until Dex began a slow handclap.

"What do you do for an encore?" Dex asked with a sneer. "That tired, old trick of snapping a cigarette out of someone's mouth?"

The partygoers laughed.

Brad's voice rose above the tittering. "I need a volunteer."

There was a momentary calculation on the part of certain members of the assembly who weighed up their chances of bedding Brad versus permanent whip burn. Not one volunteered. Dex began to walk across the room to the door.

Brad's movements were so agile no one noticed until the whip curled around Dex's chest. "You'll do." He didn't want to cut the lad, but he did it with enough flick that it would sting. He began to haul the angry Dex back toward him.

"No thanks," Dex spat, barely keeping his cool. "Circus skills are so last century."

"You chicken?" he asked as Dex attempted to make his escape.

It was a cheap trick, but he knew it would work on a guy whose whole life revolved around attitude.

The room watched and waited. Now, this *was* going to be interesting.

Dex turned and only Brad saw the flash of loathing in the boy's eyes. No one had ever cornered him like this before. Dex did not like being the prey.

"I'm a vegetarian." Dex smiled. "I don't believe in using skinned animals for entertainment."

Brad aced him. "Just clothing!"

The crowd's loyalty began to turn from Dex. Most in the room had suffered humiliation at his hands one time or another. They spurred him on to accept the challenge. Brad saw the line of perspiration under the dark fringe. He had to be careful because animals were at their most dangerous when trapped.

"What do I have to do?"

That was how Dex came to find himself bent over the coffee table, naked, with a cigarette wedged in his ass.

Brad stepped back. He removed his shirt with the large silver buttons as if he were a cheap stripper —he knew how to give a show—and ran the whip handle across his chest, paying particular attention to each nipple. There were whispers of appreciation at his tanned, trim torso as he caressed his biceps with the lethal inflictor of pain. It made him hard. While everyone's attention was on his body, Brad flicked his wrist, and the whip snaked out like a bolt of leather lightning. It missed the cigarette just as Dex flinched. Brad was admiring that cute ass and thinking what a shame it was that it was only a cigarette inserted there. He had done the honors himself, managing to run his finger along the perineum as he positioned the boy over the bench. Dex merely grunted his displeasure.

"That was a practice to judge distance."

"Get on with it," growled Dex. "I've never had a cigarette in my life, and I don't aim to start now."

The last of his words were drowned out, deliberately, by the savage whistle of the whip, and the uniform gasp of admiration of the audience as the cigarette was ripped from Dex's rear. He stood up and felt his buttocks gingerly, smiling only when he realized he'd come through it intact.

"Now for my next trick…" Brad grabbed Dex before he could put on his clothes. He bent close to his ear and whispered, "You didn't think you'd get off so lightly, did you?" At the same time, he ran the handle of the whip between Dex's cheeks and up to his asshole.

Dex brushed him aside and turned to face him. For the first time his audience could see Dex was semi-aroused. There were murmurs of appreciation, particularly as the engorged cock was of an impressive size and a string of precum gossamer adhered to his leg like the fine strands of a spider's web.

"Good, I see you're already anticipating my next move." Brad smiled to the confusion of the young man. "Stand over against the door. No, with your back to the wall. Anyone got a match?"

Arthur handed Brad a box.

"Now, could I have a volunteer please…" Brad hesitated, smiling broadly at Dex, "…to insert a match into this young man's penis."

There was uproar. Multiple hands grabbed for the matches. Dex went pale.

"Unless, of course, you're not up to the performance." Brad stared straight at his squirming victim.

He gave the matches to the least attractive volunteer and watched as the man kneeled in front of Dex and fumbled to insert a match into his piss head.

"Oh, did I not say that the volunteer must be erect for this trick to work. Of course, if he's too shit scared to maintain an erection…"

"Put my cock in your mouth," Dex whispered to the volunteer on his knees. The young man, only too eager to oblige, engulfed the semi-hard prick in one gulp. What he lacked in looks he made up for in technique and more than one onlooker added his name to their dance card.

Dex was hard in no time, and the volunteer was eased reluctantly off his prick. The match stood out proudly from his slit.

"Now, I need everyone to be completely still. This is a dangerous trick. It could lead to permanent damage if it goes wrong."

Dex laughed his contempt at the feeble effort to scare him.

"Most of all, um, Dex is it?" he said. "You must remain perfectly still even after I have completed the trick. Hold your breath when I instruct you and count to twenty. Then, and only then, can you relax." And because Brad had used his name, Dex realized he was deadly serious. *Not long now,* Brad thought, *and it will all be over.* He had to admire Dex's spunk. The guy had balls. Unless, of course, he missed.

Dex stood stock-still. The onlookers drew in their breath.

Brad shouted "Now!" The whip spat through the air and caressed the match head, which burst into flame. He had seconds to watch Dex's reaction before deciding whether to continue or not. Dex was still counting, so Brad chanced it. The whip thundered again and the lighted match was ripped from its moorings. Dex remained rock hard, so Brad went for the big finish.

He flicked the whip with the most subtle of wrist movements and the leather hummed through the air and...and wrapped itself tightly around Dex's cock. There was a scream of panic in the room. Dex's eyes widened and his mouth flew open as a grunt came from deep in his gut. He snorted again at the stinging pleasure. With a final guttural sound like the death of a giant animal, his summer storm of spunk spattered against the parched imaginations of the front-row partygoers.

Brad was at his side to catch him when he collapsed, picking up the limp boy like a groom with his bride to the thunderous approval of the crowd. He noticed Arthur smiling wisely at the back of the room.

He carried Dex into one of the bedrooms. The poor guy was exhausted from the tension...and from the best orgasm he'd ever had in his life. In the Outback, the two men would have buried their differences by going to the pub and getting pissed together. In the city, the niceties were different. Dex was just as likely to charge him with assault.

Brad brushed the long, black hair out of Dex's eyes after he laid him on the bed. Slowly, he stripped his clothes off.

Dex was disappointed. This was not the way he wanted it to end. He had revised his distaste for the cowboy. Brad was a man of infinite possibilities. A man who knew the finer alleyways of erotic fulfillment.

Dex knew his humiliation would be complete at the hands of this man he'd underestimated. He would allow it, but he would not enjoy it. Brad lay down next to him and caressed his body, but Dex was disgusted with himself that he was aroused by the strong fingers that brushed his chest and abdomen. He wanted nothing more than to get it over with and leave the scene of his humiliation.

Dex sneered. "To the victor go the spoils, I suppose. Well, if you're gonna fuck me then do it and get it over with."

Brad pressed his lips against his unresponsive mouth. He felt the cowboy's breath against his skin. Knowing he would not move until he got what he wanted, Dex reluctantly opened his mouth.

"I hate you," he whispered even while his body revealed the lie.

Brad moved down the bed and between Dex's legs. *Here it comes,* Dex thought, but to his surprise, Brad bypassed his ass and greedily swallowed his cock right down to his balls. He bucked in an agony of desire as saliva slicked his cock, the cowboy working his throat like a glove around his prick, gagging just enough that the mucous slime made the pole greasy. The rodeo star raised his body over him, then, parting his cheeks, he squatted, impaling himself on Dex's leaking cock.

Dex gasped. The cowboy was not claiming him like some triumphant bull; he was surrendering. He pushed his cock to meet the moist cavern, realizing he wanted Brad more than he'd ever wanted a man before. Fuck those outside the door who would be waiting to see him slink out of the party totally humiliated and hope to pick up the shattered pieces of his ego for themselves. Brad had bested him. If the situation had been reversed, why he would have…

He didn't want to think about the cruelty he would have inflicted. He didn't have to. Oh sure, he would now have to surrender his ass to Brad later, but then he would do it gladly.

Brad flexed his sphincter as he pistoned up and down his cock, milking it with a firmness the youth had never experienced before. Dex spat in his hand, wrapping it around the throbbing head of Brad's cock, still not prepared totally to relax his guard. Before he shot his spunk into his eager ass, he read the thousands of lonely nights and the loveless fumbles in the dark in the cowboy's face.

With that knowledge, Dex let go of his own posturing. It took too much energy to maintain. He gripped Brad's oozing cock and brought him off. He allowed himself a smile as his cum shot over his neck and chest. The moment did not go without notice. Brad had tamed wild horses. They were persuaded, though never mastered, through love not brute force alone. They shared a lot with a creature like Dex.

He watched as Brad ran his fingers through the squirts of ropey cum on his chest and presented it to him. There was a moment's hesitation before he leaned forward and engulfed the sacrifice on his tongue, then swallowed it. Still impaled on his shaft, Brad leaned over to kiss his conquest. This time Dex offered no resistance.

$\mathcal{T}$EAM $\mathcal{P}$LAYER

"$\mathcal{F}$uck, it's hot!" Kevin said for the hundredth time that day.

I agreed and was beginning to wonder why we'd chosen to come to Mexico instead of jetting off to Bangkok with the rest of the team as their prize for winning the Aussie Rules Football Grand Final for three consecutive years.

They'd all be snoring through a beer haze or else chock-a-block up the female dancers at Pattaya. We could have gone with them, but no, Kevin had wanted to go to Mexico to scramble up the pre-Hispanic pyramids at Chichen Itza and Uxmal. Not even Acapulco or Puerto Vallarta where at least there were women who panted over a bit of Aussie sausage.

Our team mates thought we were mad when we'd announced that this year we were going to try something a little different. They mocked us with their usual ribaldry about a "poofters' honeymoon", but they were joking, of course. If you were a poofter, you didn't play football, particularly Aussie Rules.

We just smiled and said we were going for the Hispanic pussy. And we'd found precisely zilch of that. Not that I cared. I had a crush on Kev and that's why I was there. Sure, the pyramids were breathtaking and we'd startled a few tourists by recklessly running up the Soothsayer's Pyramid and then running down the equally steep other side.

But what I wanted to see most was Kev in another sort of action.

No chance that was going to be with me; he was a real ladies man. Everybody said so, particularly Kev himself. But when I saw him on the field in his extra brief maroon shorts and his team singlet, well, let's just say I had to be extra careful the television cameras weren't trained in my direction and could pick up my hard on.

So why was I here when there was not much chance to hook him for myself? I suppose I thought close enough was good enough, and I was trying to maneuver Kev into a three-way. Him and me and a piece of pussy. That way I could watch him in action and store up a lifetime of images to beat off over later.

So far, we'd had no luck finding that elusive threesome. The Mexican women looked down their noses at us uncouth antipodeans. And the Indian women were too chaperoned.

Here we were in Merida on Mexico's Yucatan Peninsula, at 11 o'clock at night, tramping down 60th Street toward our hotel half an hour walk from the Zocalo. About 30 minutes too far in this heat.

There was a disco nearby, but they wouldn't let us in wearing our shorts. Not respectable enough. I suspect they thought we were going to make trouble. We were much bigger than their bouncer.

All we managed to do was catch a glimpse of local school kids dancing in the street near the Zocalo for the benefit of tourists—traditional Mayan dances with young kids balancing trays of drinks on their heads while tap dancing.

At 11 o'clock it was finished, the streets clearing in near record time. A few forlorn, exhausted vacationers clip-clopped along the near deserted streets in tourist-hire horse and buggies.

As we passed Santa Lucia Park, it was crammed with locals attempting to escape the oppressive heat.

"Hey, look over there," Kev said suddenly, his face brightening.

A woman, flirting with a group of men, was waving.

Kev waved back. "She's cute."

"And she's with a group of guys who are just as likely to slit our throats for our wallets."

"Don't be such a racist. See, she waved again."

"You go over. I'm hot, I'm tired, and I'm smelly. And besides, she's the only woman over there."

"I thought we might...um...share her."

"That's a joke right?" My heart hammered in my chest at the prospect.

"Hey, we're grown men," he said with a smirk. "We can do what we like. I'm game. You too scared, eh?"

Scared? Hell, here was the opportunity I'd been waiting for, and he'd suggested it himself. There was only one flaw to his scheme that I could see. "Ah, Kev, do you realize...um..."

"She'll want money? Look mate, I don't care. I've got something here that I need to get taken care of real bad. And I don't mind paying for it. You in or out?"

Oh, what the fuck, I thought. *I'm not Kev's keeper.* "Count me in."

Both of us waved, and she waved back. Now, I discovered very early on that I'm a cock man, but I've done it with women in the past, so I wouldn't totally disgrace myself at tonight's little three-for-all.

We waited as she crossed the road and introduced herself as Conchita. There was a little sexual banter as we had to persuade her to come back to the hotel, fairly safe ground, I thought, and then a little further encouragement to take on the two of us. It was just a ploy to get extra money out of us because her eyes lit up when she got a good look at us under the street lamp.

Kev's a six-foot, blond wet dream on legs that stretch all the way to his ass. I'm not too bad either at five foot eight, although I tend toward the Mediterranean look.

Conchita's modesty was overcome when I hailed a horse and buggy and bid her enter. Because I'd done the gentlemanly thing, she chose to sit with me much to Kevin's chagrin, but I could see from the bulge in his jeans he'd wreak his revenge in other ways.

After smuggling Conchita past the desk clerk back at our hotel, we discovered she was very modest about disrobing. She insisted we turn out all the lights, which rather thwarted my idea of watching Kev in action.

Kev refused as he shucked his clothes and revealed his already hard cock.

Football kept his body in good nick. He had just enough blond wispy hair on his chest to be attractive and thin fuzz that snaked across his rock hard belly to the curly blond patch of pubes that were dwarfed by his monster cock.

I'd never seen it hard before and my mouth watered at the fantasy of wrapping my lips around it. Conchita, still fully clothed, gulped it down with an expert technique that confirmed my earlier suspicions.

"Come on, mate, this is paradise. Get your gear off and let her get a taste of your prick. This is fucking great."

I stripped as I stared at his giant rod sliding in and out of Conchita's mouth. Although she was doing an admirable job of controlling the action, I knew from previous braggadocio of his sexual prowess that Kev would go for the old chokehold.

There he goes, I thought, as he grabbed the back of Conchita's head and rammed his cock down her throat. I heard her gag and watched as she began to struggle to get air back into her lungs. As Kev was close to dumping a load, he had no intention of letting her go, and her struggles became more and more desperate. She clawed at his chest and must have drawn blood because Kev let out a yelp of pain and withdrew his squirting cock, a few globs falling on her face. He was mad and struck out as Conchita ducked for cover, but not quite fast enough. Kev connected with her hair. It came off in his fist.

I don't like to say I told you so but, yeah, I'd been right all along.

"She's a fuckin' bloke!" he roared.

Conchita, or whatever his name was, cowered in the corner, preparing for the worst. So I did the only thing possible. I laughed.

"You knew all the time, you fucking asshole?" Kev screamed, turning his attention to me.

"Of course I knew."

"And you let him suck my dick?"

"You liked it, didn't you?"

"And you were gonna let him suck yours?"

"Sure. Why not?"

The young man made a dash for the door, but was quickly grabbed by Kev and catapulted back into the room.

"What's your real name?" I asked Conchita.

"Juan."

"Well, Juan, we're going to get you out of that dress and out of your make-up and then you and I are going to have a good time."

"What about him?" Juan said nervously pointing at Kev.

I shrugged.

"He can go to sleep if he wants to, or he can watch, or he can go down to the bar until we finish. There's the bathroom, go and get washed up."

Juan disappeared gratefully.

"No more rough stuff, okay." It wasn't a question, it was an instruction.

Kev sulked about for a while until Juan emerged from the bathroom to reveal what a great looking stud pup he was. He was already hot and bothered as his hard cock revealed, and I got a boner just looking at him. Kev moved away from the bed. I intended to have a good time whether he liked it or not.

I smiled. "You like my cock, Juan?"

"I like plenty." He bounded to the bed, engulfing me in his warm wet mouth. Now I knew why Kev had liked it so much. Out of the corner of my eye, I watched Kev's dick hardening as he half-heartedly played with it while relaxing in one of the hotel armchairs.

Juan gulped me down to the balls and swirled his tongue around my shaft and my ticklish knob. I dived for Juan's beautiful pecker and took the whole uncircumcised beauty in one greedy gulp. I heard Kev spit. Without looking, I knew he was lubing up that monster throbber of his with his own saliva.

I lapped my way down to Juan's puckered brown asshole. He groaned in appreciation. I teased his fuck hole with my mouth and my fingers. It was doing the trick because his attentive slurping on my prick had given way to gasps of delight as I drove my fingers deeper inside him.

Reaching into the top drawer of the bedside table, I grabbed a condom and ripped the packet apart with my teeth. The lubricant was nearby, and I squeezed it straight from the nozzle into Juan's wiggling, receptive ass. He giggled as he felt the gluey liquid penetrate him.

He arched up on his knees and hands, and after adjusting the condom, I sank into him. It was tight at first, and Juan gasped, attempting to push me back a little to ease the pain. I took my time and encouraged him verbally, stroking his hard prick in time to my thrusts.

"Fuck you're hot up there," I whispered into Juan's ear. "Hot and tight. Great fuckin' ass." Juan only groaned deep in his throat and tightened his ass muscles around the base of my cock. I held him tight as I withdrew almost entirely out of his body and then sank the entire length back into him: slowly, deliberately, teasingly.

We both heard Kev's groan and turned nervously toward him, but he was too far gone to cause trouble. Pre-cum was already oozing from the slit of his massive cock as he jacked it and stared at the two of us fucking and grunting like animals.

"His mouth's free," I encouraged.

"Nah, mate," he gasped back.

I saw Juan was as disappointed as I was, but we weren't about to let that ruin our fun. However, I had an idea. We tried every position we could think of as I ploughed my prick into his pretty hole: on his back, over the edge of the bed, over the bedside tables, in the bathroom, and finally, we ended with me fucking him doggie fashion on the floor. Kev was just out of reach of Juan's lips which made him feel safe enough until with a few hard thrusts I'd moved Juan far enough along the floor that he was within spitting distance of the prize. One final thrust and I knew Kev felt Juan's hot breath on his balls.

The Hispanic's tongue flicked out gently and lapped at Kev's hairy sac. He tensed, but Juan continued his licking gently, almost tenderly. He relaxed the grip on his prick and allowed Juan to lap up and down the straining shaft. Finally, he took Juan's face in his hands and gently lifted him on to his swollen prick and pushed him down. He was all gentleness this time. There was no hurry, no brutality. Just pleasure.

"I guess I owe you an apology, mate," Kev wheezed. "Sorry for that rough stuff earlier."

Juan was past caring as he slobbered over Kev's magnificent Aussie cock. I felt a twinge of jealousy. As if to punish Juan for his good luck, I pounded his ass ruthlessly. He took me stroke for stroke, his ass flexing as if it could take a much harder battering. Blindly, uncaring of the consequences, I reached out and stroked Kev's balls while Juan swallowed his cock.

The touch was electric. Kev flinched and his cock plopped out of Juan's mouth, swamping his face and hair with another load of thick, slimy juice as I dumped a load. With his free hand Juan had been manipulating his own prick and I felt his sphincter muscles contracting as he splattered his spunk on the carpet. Kev lapsed back in the chair; Juan and I collapsed on the floor. It was quite some time before any of us stirred.

Neither Kev nor I spoke as Juan got himself respectable. We gave him a pair of my jeans and a T-shirt and wrapped his drag in a plastic shopping bag. As well as the dollars, we handed him a pocketful of condoms. He tried to return the money, but we insisted.

After he'd gone I could do nothing but face the music. I saw my entire pro football career going down the proverbial gurgler.

"Look, Kev, I..."

"You a poof, mate?" was all he asked.

Deciding honesty was the best course at this point, I said a little too aggressively, "Yeah, as a matter of fact. What about it?"

"I suppose you wanted to fuck me all these years, too, eh?"

"Want the truth?"

"Uh huh."

"Every time I look at your fucking body I get a hard on. I've wanted to fuck you for years. I've wanted that cock of yours down my throat, and I've wanted to shove my tongue up your ass crack and suck and lick 'til your brain caved in."

With that, he gave an almighty roar. Of laughter. I was a little slow on the uptake.

"You bastard," I shouted at him. "You knew Conchita was a guy all the time, too, didn't you?"

"Yeah, mate." He doubled up with hysterics so that tears ran down his cheeks. I charged, knocking him on to the bed. Although he's bigger than I am, he was winded, and I managed to clamber on top of him pinning him to the bed. He was helpless, but not for long.

His face, still creased with amusement, was just inches away when I crushed my mouth against his. I kissed him like I was a drowning man gulping for air and, rather than resist, I felt him reciprocate. I released his arms and he grabbed me pulling me back to him until I thought he would squeeze all the air out of me.

He rolled over and lay on top of me, grinding his slimy cock against my belly and shoving his tongue so far down my throat I thought he'd be able to tell what I had for breakfast.

Pulling his head off me, I gasped, "For God's sake, Kev, let me breathe."

"You sly fucking dog." He laughed again and punched me playfully on the shoulder.

"Me? You had this planned all along, didn't you?"

He grinned and a faint blush crept up into his face. "Well, yeah. I was hoping. That's why I put on that little charade earlier. In case, you know..."

"In case I wasn't gay?"

"Yeah."

"So what's on the agenda now you've discovered I am?"

"Now I'm gonna fuck you, baby." And as if to prove his point he had already selected a condom from those on the bedside table and was rolling it along his cock. "Get on the bed!"

I greased my ass with the lube as best I could because I was worried about a monster the size of Kev's. He lubricated the condom then began pushing his fingers up my ass. I'd been fucked before, but never like this. I wanted it bad, real bad.

He was gentle at first, but excitement got the better of him. He shoved the entire length into my hole in one thrust and let his body fall flat against mine. He reached under and pinched my nipples. That took my mind off the pain for a while, and then he bit into my shoulder.

He ordered me to turn my head to the side, which I did, and he bent over and kissed me hard on the lips.

"Just get used to it. Don't fight it. Relax. You're gonna love it. I'm gonna fuck you easy."

I felt his body pressing down on mine, with his cock inside me. We were joined. The thought of that alone was enough to blow my mind. With his hungry mouth whispering obscenities into my ear, I clamped my ass muscles and felt his cock jerk. Then he pulled back a bit and his monster shaft moved, sending shivers up my spine.

He worked his feverish cock in and out, slowly, gradually, doing it the way he promised—taking it easy.

"Like it, mate? Like my hard cock up your asshole?"

I gasped. "I love it."

I did love it. I'd never felt so full in my life. There was something special about it. I moaned, groaned and humped my hips. He started to move faster, harder, bracing his body with his arms on the bed, working his hips expertly, quickly.

"Kev!" Suddenly I was being stimulated by the movement of the bed against the tip of my cock. I was going to come. "Kev!"

"That's okay, mate, come. Come on the bed. Let me feel you come while I'm deep inside you." He smashed his long, thick cock deep inside my asshole. His head banged against my shoulder and lay still.

My cock exploded.

"Kev, fuck, I'm coming!" I muffled my shouts into the pillow as my hot, sticky sperm shot onto the sheets. With each squirt, each contraction, each spurt, I felt my ass muscles gripping Kev's cock. It was the most incredible orgasm I'd ever had.

"I feel it! I'm shooting again!" He was delirious, feeling my jerking orgasm stimulating his prick head, driving him mad with pleasure. I let out a sigh and knew it was over.

Then, faster than I could realize, he withdrew his slippery prick just about completely from my asshole and slammed it back in again. He did it half a dozen times.

I squeezed my ass to meet his cock.

"Oh, Christ," Kev wailed. He pushed his spitting weapon into my asshole so hard I thought we were going to break through the fucking bed. "You're fucking beautiful."

He rolled over on his side and pulled me with him.

"My cock's gonna slip out..."

"No, not yet!"

"Your ass is so tight, but I'm losing my hard on." And sure enough, in a few seconds his fat, wet cum-stained rubber-coated cock slipped from my asshole with a gush of lube.

We stayed like that, glued together in our cum and sweat 'til we both fell soundly asleep.

The next morning I dreaded Kev would try the old "God, was I drunk last night" routine or else he would just forget any of it had ever happened. But no, I woke to feel the hot wetness of a hungry mouth gobbling on my joint.

"Hi, baby," he said with a wink. "Just getting a little early breakfast."

I ruffled his hair as he swallowed my cock.

"Be my guest." I purred and stretched. "What we gonna do today, Kev?"

He gave me that beautiful cheeky smile of his. "I was kinda hoping that you'd wanna fuck me."

Kev's a real team player.

Davy Jones' Locker

*I*t was like the buzz of four hundred excited human cicadas amplified throughout the gymnasium complex. The students had been waiting expectantly for the return of one of the high school's most illustrious alumni. It wasn't often one of them went on to bigger and better things, especially not a student who had been as scholastically challenged but athletically endowed as Davy Jones who'd gone on to win gold medals at two Olympics bringing glory to his country and a lucrative endorsement career to himself. A little reflected glory had also rubbed off on the school, as well as a little cash, enough to refurbish the school gymnasium and build a covered half-size Olympic pool for students: The Davy Jones Aquatic Centre as the pool and gym complex had been so grandiosely rebranded.

I had been responsible in a large part for the concept and the raising of the capital after the idea had been warmly embraced by the school board. Davy was still a hero to the lower working class area from which the school took its pupils. The teachers were a dedicated bunch but they fought daily against apathy and poverty so any little local triumph was embraced as if it were of global importance because, honestly, there was so little to be proud of.

Davy was late. I was hoping the headmaster would allow me to pick up the returning hero from the airport but he reserved that honor for himself even though he had initially been opposed to the idea; adamantly so. He was an out-of-towner after all. However, when he'd gauged the community interest he did a back flip that of itself would have won Olympic gold. He thought it would do his profile no harm to be seen, and especially photographed, beside the sporting wunderkind.

Admittedly, Davy had been out of the limelight for a number of years, his premature retirement brought about by a very messy and very public divorce which saw the public siding with his 'long-suffering wife', as the scandal sheets described her, after the leak of hundreds of personal messages between Davy and a number of high profile young women with whom he had obviously been sharing sexual favors.

The public's smirking admiration of working class Davy's ability to attract the world's most desirable women melted away faster than an ice cube on a hot summer's footpath when he admitted to 'more sinister sexual shenanigans', again the newspapers' words. Of course, it's easy for journalists to drop hints of kink and perversion without being specific allowing the public to conjure up fantasies of the most bizarre sexual predilections without a skerrick of proof.

I was as inquisitive as the next guy or gal in wanting more details but the media that were so quick to scream 'pervert' were remarkably reticent about the detail. Perhaps they were frightened of a libel action. I had my fantasy scenario, however, but it had more to do with my lust for Davy Jones than from any insider knowledge. The man was a god. Is a god, although the deity is slightly tarnished these days. Not because of his womanizing but because he had a few problems with drink and drugs. He did the celebrity grovel in which he apologized, teary-eyed, to his friends and supporters on a prime-time talk show and checked himself into celebrity rehab where he emerged a week later, miraculously cured.

Unfortunately for Davy and the rehab center, he was stopped by the cops five minutes after release and found to have a high level of alcohol and cocaine in his blood. Try explaining that away when the paparazzi had photographed every moment of his freedom. It was obvious he had to have indulged on the rehab premises. Thus he managed to destroy two reputations in one moment of stupidity. Another round of talk shows and another round of crocodile tears and the public turned their backs on him. Davy Jones was as good as dead. He couldn't even get a spot on *Celebrity Survivor* as a Z-rate contestant.

Enter one Brett Morgan, an idealistic young man determined to see Davy Jones 'saved' from his demons and given his rightful place among the pantheon of this country's sporting champions. That's me, in case you haven't guessed. I stood proudly in front of the school faithful, their popular Phys Ed instructor, awaiting the entrance of our hero. Dimity Connor stood beside me, smirking because I'd put so much effort into Davy Jones' rehabilitation and she was about to reap the rewards that I was so anxious to claim for myself.

"You don't have a snowball's chance in hell," she whispered just loudly enough for me to hear above the din. "He's into pussy. Big time. Anyone who can read a newspaper or a blog can see that. Why would he toss that all away for an asshole?"

There was no mistaking the double meaning of her final word.

It was no secret that Dimity and I detested each other. We'd been students at the school at the same time, vaguely aware of each other's lowly status as nerds. We'd both blossomed: me courtesy of the gym and she courtesy of good bone structure and sympathetic makeup. We had both had a gigantic crush on Davy, neither successful in requiting it with the man of our dreams. Dimity was in a loving, monogamous relationship, by all accounts, that had produced two young children, cared for by her mother while she worked at the school which meant her ardent desire to stir the flames had more to do with besting me than genuine desire.

I, on the other hand, was still embarrassingly uncoupled, not through lack of trying, still pining for my teenage Lancelot.

My obsessive promotion of Davy Jones may not have been entirely altruistic, I must admit, although I did see it as a small step toward the rehabilitation of his reputation. You see, I owed Davy my life.

Back then I was new to the school, my dad having put down temporary roots in the town after carting us around the country as part of his duties for the military. I hated having to up anchor every few years after I'd finally managed to overcome my shyness and started to make friends only to have to repeat the process. I was not gregarious like some. Like Davy, for instance.

I was allocated the locker next to his. Normally it would have gone to someone in the same class as him, he was two years my senior, but the school was running short of the hideous grey metallic monstrosities that lined the hallways, and I'd arrived on a day on which patience was in short supply and I'd been given the first empty locker the school secretary had come across. It was both my doing and my undoing.

I had no idea why the locker next to mine was painted black as there were signs throughout the school and, in fact, pinned on the board right next to the offending black compartment itself, stressing there was to be no adornment to the natural battleship color that dominated the hallway and the students' futures.

"Yo, new kid."

I looked up and went weak at my fifteen-year-old knees. His hair was wet and hung across his face, his eyes shone, his lips curved in a smile, and he had proffered me his hand to shake. I took it, more to touch this student god, than through any politeness. He shook it heartily.

"You got the locker next to mine?"

I nodded my head, my throat so dry I didn't dare speak.

He leaned over to me conspiratorially. "Just between you and me, you're gonna piss off a lot of people. That locker of yours is prime real estate. Guys will think you're getting above your station."

"What should I do?" I croaked.

"Stay right where you are," he advised. "You won't hassle me like some of the others. You won't, will you?"

"No," I said honestly. "Why would I?"

"You'll have your reasons once you get to know me."

Then he winked at me and walked off. A little way along the corridor he turned and called, "If you do want to move, let me know. We could probably sell that locker to some wanker for a lot of money. Cheers"

Davy always treated me like a mate, sometimes grabbing me in a head-lock and roughing up my hair. I loved it when he did that, the feel of his warm body against mine. My dick got hard in my shorts and I'd stand with my body hidden as much as possible by my locker door. Sometimes I wondered if he got as much pleasure out of it as I did. He surprised me with this intimacy because otherwise he gave me a wide berth, only speaking to me if we ended up at our respective lockers together.

I asked him once about the black and he said that he couldn't stand being the same as everyone else so he painted it.

"There was hell to pay," he told me. "Threats of expulsion, blah, blah, blah. I gave it 'em straight. I keep me black locker, no punishment, and I stay on the swimming team. I have to paint it conformity grey or I get punishment you can stick your swim team up your jacksy. It was the first time anyone from this shithole of a school ever got close to winning sports medals or anyfink. You can see for yourself, they backed down. Now no-one dares touch it."

I couldn't say that about mine for just a short time later Davy found me in tears facing my locker which had 'fag' scrawled across it in bright red spray paint. I'd tried spit to wipe it off to no avail. I turned away from Davy; I didn't want him to see my humiliation. He pushed me aside, the vile word glaring at me accusingly.

"Hmmm," he said. "I admire the fact someone has tried to brighten up an otherwise shitty locker but I question their choice of color. Now, let me see."

I didn't dare look at him in case I saw disgust in his eyes but also because he would see the accusation was true. There was an odd rattle behind me; followed by a hiss, then the obvious odor of...I spun around. Davy handed me a second aerosol can. We had the fucker painted over in no time. A nice gloss black. I was not harassed from that moment on. In fact, his act protected me all through high school, my black locker alongside his a sign to leave Brett Morgan alone or you'd answer to Davy Jones.

As soon as we'd covered the entire grey surface, I knew as surely as gravity causes hemorrhoids, that I *was* different to other people but, more importantly, I loved Davy Jones with all the passion a fifteen-year-old could muster.

I began to follow him around, at a distance, like an adoring puppy. If I became too much of a distraction he'd yell 'Piss orf' and I'd scurry out of his sight. I never took it personally, because he always yelled it with a smile. When I look back on it now, my presence must have been a constant irritation.

Swimming and athletic pursuits had never attracted me up until then, but in order to be close to Davy on Wednesday afternoons when the school made a minimal effort to instil team spirit into us, I took swimming in summer. He was in a class all his own and two lanes were set aside especially for him to practise for sports meets where he blitzed the opposition. His times were becoming so good he had attracted the attention of major sporting bodies. He took the adulation in his stride, not for a moment believing it would lead to anything that would drag him and his parents out the economic mire.

I used to run alongside the pool as he swam his distances, shouting encouragement. Sometimes, in a playful mood, he would wave as he thrashed through the water. I was his biggest fan. It was this behavior on my part that led to his saving my life. I knew his times better than the Phys Ed teacher who was supposed to be coaching him but he'd give me the stop watch in order to retire to his office to sleep or drink or whatever bored teachers get up to.

Running alongside the pool, not taking my eyes off the stopwatch because Davy was about to beat his best time, I didn't see the towel that someone had dropped carelessly, so ass over tit I went into the pool, knocking my head against the tiled edge as I somersaulted in. I couldn't have been unconscious long for I remember suddenly finding myself in this calm wet blueness, the sounds of shouting and frantic activity above me as if it were being filtered through glue, my breath caught in my chest, my heart beating fit to burst...for a moment I was at peace. My watery gaze saw Davy swimming toward me, panic deforming his handsome face.

Then I was yanked back to reality by the neck. Davy had heard the commotion and swam back, dragging me to the surface before manhandling me onto the concrete surrounding the pool. I lay still because I felt such a fool. Davy, mistaking this for drowning, went into overdrive in an attempt to bring me round. After ensuring that I hadn't swallowed too much chlorinated water he held my nose and clamped his mouth over mine. He was, of course, giving me mouth to mouth resuscitation. My eyes flew open and he saw that. He relaxed and expelled his breath. He hesitated for a moment and then brought his mouth back to mine but instead of blowing air into my lungs he pressed his tongue gently into my mouth.

Davy Jones was kissing me. What's more, I could feel his cock hardening and sticking into my side. He removed his mouth again to gulp in air before returning to the tongue wrestling. I had never kissed anyone like this before, let alone another boy so my technique probably lacked finesse. He didn't seem to mind.

There was no chance of faking it any longer. After we broke apart, I sat up and coughed as brazenly theatrically as I could. It was enough to convince the Phys Ed teacher who suggested I wrap up warmly and went off to call my parents. There was much back slapping for Davy who was soon escorted off by a sea of admirers while I sat shivering under an old army blanket outside the coach's office.

My parents kept me out of school for the remainder of the week and I went back the following Monday, full of excitement that Davy Jones must like me a little bit because he kissed me in public although, strictly speaking, it wasn't a kiss to those who'd been watching so it wasn't really in public. My mind was doing cartwheels, confident that life was about to become like those movies I went to every Saturday afternoon.

Fate loves to kick young love in the gonads, so you won't be surprised to read that Davy was gone. Offered a scholarship at a swimming academy that was too good to refuse, he had left that weekend. I tried his locker but it was stuck tight and no amount of forcing it would get it open. It was like he'd shut himself off from my friendship.

The next two years passed slowly. I concentrated on my studies to get a good grade to make my parents proud and because I knew now what I wanted to do. I wasn't the brightest globe in the lamp so I cut my cloth to suit by abilities. I would become a Phys Ed teacher, try to help young kids like myself through the quagmire of adolescence. If I'd had someone to talk to when I was growing up things may have been easier.

Of course, I followed Davy's career, through good times and bad. I had scrapbooks of his achievements as well as his darker periods. I experimented with other men when I left school but no matter how pleasurable, it was always Davy making love to me, which was the reason none of them ever lasted. I'd never attempted to contact him as I felt betrayed that he'd not told me before he left. He knew where I lived. Perhaps I was being unfair. On such a slight acquaintance he really owed me nothing. But, damn it, he kissed me!

The buzz grew more excited as the headmaster walked into the gym, Dimity craning her neck for a better view. Then all hell broke loose as the Man himself appeared, immaculately dressed, only slightly fuller in the face, his smile as warm and welcoming as I remembered, although it seemed just a little too mechanical. While Dimity preened to impress, I shrank into my body. I hadn't thought this through. What was I expecting? To impress with my witty repartee in the four seconds or so that he would shake my hand? That he would even remember me? What a bloody fool I was. There was no way I could sneak out now.

He played up to Dimity, kissing her hand, the headmaster reminding him of her name. He flattered by saying, "What a pretty girl you must have been in school, because you've grown into one helluva woman. I kick myself I never dated you."

"There's still time," she said breathlessly.

The headmaster ushered him along the line of well-wishers. "And this is…"

Davy let out such a whoop the entire school looked at us.

"Brett Morgan. How the fuck are you?"

He ignored the hand I proffered and I found myself in a bear hug. Not that I was complaining.

I could feel Dimity's envy boring into the side of my head, particularly when the headmaster had to almost physically prize the two of us apart. I liked to think our reconciliation had something to do with the change in his demeanor, for he bounded through the dedication full of charm and bonhomie, captivating teachers and students alike. He was gracious in his speech of acknowledgment, singling out many of the great teachers the school had been home to, as well as some teachers who still trudged the halls not yet broken by their thankless task.

At the conclusion of his speech, it all felt a bit of an anticlimax.

"Show us your budgie smugglers!" one of the shit stirrers from the upper grades yelled.

Pandemonium ensued. Davy turned to me, a broad smirk on his face. "Should I?" he mouthed.

I nodded my head.

Davy went into an impromptu strip routine, flinging his coat and tie over his shoulder. Dimity ran to pick them up and brush the dirt from them. I let her; I was not prepared to pick up after Davy Jones. Finally, he was stripped to the waist, his shoes and socks discarded. Everyone held their breath as he undid his belt, slid down his zip, and slowly peeled down his trousers. I'm sure I wasn't the only one wet from the performance. My cock was leaking like a tap with a faulty washer. I had to remind Dimity to breathe.

It's all very well watching someone on television, or seeing their photos in the newspaper or on the net, but Davy Jones, for all his problems with booze and drugs and marital infidelities was a magnificent specimen. At twenty-eight his body was buff though much thicker than it was when he'd been a half-starved student. His butt was a work of art, his Speedos clinging like a desperate lover to the curve and the crack. And what they didn't hide of his package was not worth worrying about.

"Couldn't he be arrested for obscenity?" Dimity whispered.

Perhaps not him, but I probably could have been for what I was thinking.

The whistles of admiration and the stamping of feet drowned out the attempt by the headmaster to regain control. Davy held his hands up and the audience fell quiet. He walked to the end of the pool and with a dive, to which he gave an extra theatrical flourish, tore off down its length. I clocked him, an automatic response I suppose. As he rounded the first end he was ahead of his personal best. The man had lost none of it. The crowd went berserk as he reached the other end and stood to thrust a triumphant fist into the air.

As he clambered from the pool, students and teachers alike surrounded him for autographs, Dimity clutching his clothes to her breast as if she were about to expire. That was the way I wanted to feel, but I didn't. While he was receiving backslaps and, I suspect, a few gratuitous gropes from students and teachers alike, he looked up as if searching for someone, his face clouded with concern.

I walked away, pleased for Davy that his homecoming had been a triumph, saddened for myself that it had opened wounds that I had long believed sutured. It was the lunch break and I was not on duty so I wandered the halls until I found them. The lockers were still there, still painted black albeit now scratched and battered, a bit like I felt and a lot like Davy's life had been.

I mentally slapped myself for being so self-indulgent. I was a young man, not unattractive though I could never hope to match Davy's charisma. Okay, so I had made a mistake. Don't they say you learn from your errors: they make you stronger? I must have been living so much in my head at that moment I didn't notice him until he spoke.

"They're still here, eh?"

"You startled me."

"I thought they would have chucked them out years ago."

"Nah," I said. "I've persuaded a local museum to take them as a national treasure. Davy Jones' Locker."

He stepped forward, producing a small key which he inserted in the rusting door. It screamed its reluctance to open.

"You still have your key?"

He yanked harder and it gave but not without a screech as if in pain. It was empty. Or so I thought.

"Better remove this then. Don't want people in a hundred years stumbling on it," he said as he scooped up a small sheet of paper almost adhered to the base of the locker.

I was puzzled why it would be so important after all these years.

"I left it for you," he said and handed it to me, averting his eyes.

It contained only a few words in an immature teenage hand, complete with incorrect spelling.

I'm such a cowerd. Forgive me.

"But it was locked. I would never have seen it if you hadn't come back."

He shrugged. "As I wrote, I'm chicken shit."

"About what?"

I guess somewhere deep down I wanted it to be what I was thinking but...

He turned me toward him; I saw the look of hope in his face. I smiled. He leaned in and kissed me, his hair still damp, hugging me to his body so I could feel his erection through his suit trousers, matching mine. He was tentative at first, until I opened my mouth to welcome his tongue. His hands moved down to massage my butt provocatively to the whistles, cheers and catcalls of the students passing in the hallway. Still he did not release me. I would be in deep shit with the headmaster.

He broke the kiss and without letting me go, whispered. "Don't say anything now except you'll let me pick you up after work. Okay?"

I managed a weak, "Uh huh" and nodded.

He strode away, turning once to wink, while I tried to get my legs, now turned to jelly, to move. A few people were standing gawking, and one young boy had such a look of stunned disbelief on his face I knew he'd be reappraising his future shortly. I chuckled as I returned to the staff room where a chilly voiced Dimity led the attack. She and one or two of her supporters got stuck into me with such vehemence it had to have come from envy.

But nothing would dampen my spirits today. Davy Jones was picking me up after school. No matter the letdown that was inevitable later, at least I'd have this time with him. Dimity blathered on in the background growing increasingly hysterical because I shut off listening to her, ignoring her provocations.

I simply smiled at the headmaster when he carpeted me, accepting his admonishment while reminding him that hetero teachers had occasionally behaved similarly in the corridors to no punishment, telling him in the sweetest possible manner that if that was permitted to continue after my dressing down then I would have no choice but to seek redress under the anti-discrimination laws. That took the wind out of his sails.

At the end of the school day, I was confronted by a gaggle of students at the gate. Yes, he had turned up, dressed in leathers riding a friend's Harley. God, he looked hot, and more than a few female students were pressing against him in the hopes of a ride – in all senses of the word. The group parted to allow me through. Davy looked up from showing some of the boys the mechanics of the bike. I wanted to bury myself in his smile. He hugged me in greeting, then kissed me deeply to a chorus of 'gross' from the students, although it sounded less than deeply entrenched. That was a start.

He handed me a spare helmet and I got on behind him, holding his waist tightly. Motor bikes are not my favorite mode of transport.

"Will we see you again, Mr. Jones?" one of the boys asked, eyeing the bike with little short of lust.

"That depends on Mr. Morgan here."

I was startled, really startled by that statement.

I shrugged. "If it's up to me, you'll be seeing an awful lot of Mr. Jones in the future."

Just before we roared off down the road, he turned to the group. "In that case you better call me Davy."

He must have felt my cock pressing against his ass, as surely as I felt his when I squeezed his crotch. The traffic noise and the muffling effect of the helmets meant our conversation was limited to his asking if I still lived at the old address. I did, my parents had left the house to me when they moved to warmer climes up north. Twenty minutes' later we pulled up in the front yard of the single level brick bungalow I called home.

We were barely inside the front door before he had me in his embrace, kissing me all over my face and neck before settling on my lips.

"You have no idea how much I've wanted this," he panted.

"I think I do," I managed before he took my breath away.

When he allowed me to breathe again, I shoved him in the chest pushing him backwards until he flopped down in the lounge. Then I straddled his lap and ground my ass into his leathers. He went to speak but I put my finger to his lips.

"Let me enjoy this, Davy. No matter what you say afterwards, let me enjoy this. I've waited more than ten years for it. If I'm to be disappointed afterwards, I don't care. Not if I can have you just once."

He complied, allowing me to unzip his jacket, naked beneath it, so I could run my hands across his hard pecs flicking his nipples with my fingers, stinging him. He shuddered but made no complaint. I stood up to remove the jacket before turning my attention to his trousers. Playfully licking his boots, although I would do it for real any time he demanded, I pulled them off and removed his heavy woolen socks, sniffing the heady odor.

Rubbing my face into his leather covered crotch, I felt the heat from his cock, drawing the zipper down with my teeth. He groaned as he watched me fumble for his prick to finally free it so that it jutted straight and proud. I blew my warm breath over the head and licked it quickly with my tongue.

"Don't tease me, Brett. Not when I've waited so long."

I gave it a few quick licks, enough to make him jump. "Whose fault is that?" I asked.

I pulled his trousers down over his legs until he sat tantalizingly naked. Shucking my own clothes, I sat back down on his lap rubbing my belly and my hard on against his chest. He reached round to my butt, tentatively spreading my cheeks apart so he could finger my warm hole, damp with sweat and expectation, until I gave him permission to enter me by pushing back against his hand. I'd wanted this for so long I didn't dare prolong it. I hoped there would be more, and Davy's comments outside the school suggested there might be, or maybe he was just after friendship.

I leaned over to the side table and found the strip of condoms, tossing them to him, and the lube which

I uncapped and squirted on my fingers before rubbing them into my hole. The foreplay could come later; I wanted to get to the main event. Davy seemed surprised by how quickly we'd progressed to this point but I didn't hear any better offers. My only regret was that we couldn't film it so I could give a copy to Dimity in the staff room the following week.

Davy sheathed his cock in the rubber and I lathered it, holding it steady as I lowered my ass until I felt it squeeze into my hole, spreading me open with short bolts of pain. I didn't care. I eased down slowly until the head broke through, such an amazing moment I almost blew my load. With intense concentration I thought only of the pleasure I was giving Davy and sank down to his balls.

He sighed, eager to continue but allowing me to get comfortable with the formidable cock wedged in my ass. I bent my body to bite at his nipples, obviously a highly erogenous zone from the heavy breathing that greeted my ministrations. I'd had to lift my butt off his thighs to reach allowing him short thrusts in and out of my slick chute. He took his time, obviously enjoying the feeling as he scratched his nails down my spine, making me wriggle with the ticklish sensation.

"Your ass is so hot, Brett," he whispered. "It's even better than I imagined."

It was no lie to repay the compliment. "I could die happy with your cock wedged in my butt, Davy."

"I never want to take it out."

I milked his cock, squeezing my muscles as I slithered up and down the shaft, until I had him thrashing beneath me, but it was not the way I wanted him.

"Get on top of me, Davy. I want to watch your face while you fuck me."

He lifted me up, to lay me along the lounge, pushing my legs back until my feet were against his chest. He positioned himself comfortably on his knees and drove his dick home. He watched my reaction as he began to pick up pace. I held him at bay with my feet but now I allowed him to push them over his shoulders to give him greater entry to my tunnel.

He kissed me as he sped up.

"Fuck me hard, Davy. I want to feel it."

"You'll feel it, baby. No doubt about that."

True to his word, he varied his technique, keeping me on the edge as he went from a slow slide to a frantic ramming motion through a slow fuck that picked up speed and battered my ass in the last few inches. I had no idea how much time had elapsed while he banged me into submission but no matter how long it was it would never be enough.

"Fuck, Davy. I can't hold on much longer."

"Me either. Let's come together."

I held off as he picked up pace but his cock felt so good, so at home in my asshole I grunted and my spunk spewed onto my stomach, my ass clenching his prick. That brought him to the edge and, with a roar, he squirted, pushing his cock in hard, short thrusts until he'd totally unloaded.

He fell on top of me, our bodies sticky with sweat and slime, and I wrapped my legs around him. Neither of us spoke for a few moments until we got our breath back and then he slowly moved off me for which I was grateful as my legs were getting pins and needles. He pulled out, sliding the condom off his dick holding it aloft.

"How much you reckon I'd get for this little lot on eBay?"

I slapped him across the back of the head. He laughed, breaking the embarrassment that threatened us.

"You hungry?" I asked.

"Ravenous. I haven't eaten since the plane and that wasn't fit for man or beast."

"There's not much in the house..."

"Let me take you out."

I jumped at the chance because my cooking skills would have failed miserably to impress.

We jumped in the shower together to wash off the smell of sex and testosterone, scarcely able to keep our hands off each other. Davy was insistent, "Let me take care of your needs, Brett," he begged.

"You've already fucked me into the middle of next week. What more can you possibly do?"

He sank to his knees and engulfed my dick in his warm mouth. It reacted instantly and although I put up feeble resistance I braced myself against the cold tile wall, his tongue already working its magic across my slit. I held back, allowing him to control the action, shuddering at the sensitivity in the head of my cock until I was on the verge and I gripped the back of his head, ploughing gently into his throat dumping my spunk in his gullet.

After that, bed seemed like a better option than dinner but I'd promised and we had a lot to catch up on.

It pays to be with a visiting celebrity, even a tarnished one, for we were shown to the best table, other diners whispering behind their hands pretending not to notice him, especially when he took my hand after we were seated.

"You're not embarrassed are you?" he asked.

"About what in particular? You kissing me in the school corridor? You kissing me at the school gate? You holding my hand in public? No, Davy, I'm not embarrassed although I'm not sure once the rumors get around whether it will do my reputation good or ill."

"Probably a bit of both," he smiled.

"There speaks a man of experience."

"You're such a good looking man, Brett," he said, squeezing my hand. "I know you're unattached." Before I could say anything, he added, "I asked the headmaster. He thinks very highly of you."

"How long are you here for, Davy?"

I wanted to know if I could count my happiness in seconds, minutes, hours or days.

"That depends."

"On what?"

"A certain sexy man who is seated at the table opposite me."

"Don't fuck round, Davy. I couldn't stand it."

"Why's that then?"

"Do I have to spell it out? You must have guessed."

"Could it be the same reason I had to come back? Yeah," he said when he saw my scepticism. "I've been close to coming back so many times, but like the note said, I'm a coward. I ran away when I was a kid because...you know why, Davy?"

"No, I never understood that, except you got a scholarship to a swimming academy or some shit."

"It's because you made me feel things I didn't understand. For Christ's sake, I was a kid. My hormones were running riot. I didn't think it was right to have those sorts of feelings, those sorts of dreams about another boy."

I couldn't believe what I was hearing. "You dreamed about me?"

"The drugs, the booze, the divorce, and the wild behavior: they were all about you. Trying to get you out of my head. It was only when I accepted that I couldn't that I began to clean up my act. And I promised myself, when I got clean I'd come looking for you. See if you felt the same way about me."

I laughed. "It's pretty obvious, isn't it?"

"I was so scared you'd be married or have a boyfriend."

"Nah, no one ever lived up to you."

The meal was one of the best I ever had, although I don't remember tasting a morsel. And Davy was the best date I'd ever had. He was charming, witty, funny, and, above all, polite and generous, even when people from surrounding tables pressed him for his autograph or uninvited gave him advice about getting his life in order.

I panicked as the waiter brought the bill. "Where are you staying tonight?" I ventured to ask.

"The school put me up in a hotel but..."

"How about moving your stuff in with me for however long you're in town."

"I don't want to impose."

"You wouldn't be imposing."

"It makes sense, I suppose. I've got to return my mate's Harley tomorrow. He wouldn't let it out of his sight for more than a day, so it would save on travel."

"Oh, so you intend to spend a lot of time at my place, do you?"

"I'm hoping," he said smugly. "Besides, you haven't fucked me yet."

I almost choked on the last of the wine I was finishing off.

Davy slapped me on the back as wine shot out my nose.

"What, you don't want to fuck me?" he asked.

"If you think that, you're dreaming. I'll ream your ass so you won't be able to sit down for a month."

"Promises, promises."

"How long are you really staying, Davy? I need to know so I can prepare myself."

I loved the man so much.

"For what?"

"When you leave."

"As long as you'll have me, and with apologies to the immortal Dolly Levi, Davy will never go away again."

I grabbed his hand and dragged him from the restaurant.

"God, you are so gay."

HERE'S TO YOU, MR. ROBINSON

*B*loody tease!

How was I supposed to concentrate on my uni reading list if he persisted in washing his car every Saturday in a pair of hip hugging overalls peeled down to the waist to reveal his gorgeous pecs, abs and biceps? I'm a muscle queen – I love the male body. Love to rub my hands across a smooth, or hairy, muscular male body. I'm an equal opportunity man lover. Hairy, smooth, doesn't matter. What does matter is that I like my men with a certain amount of maturity. A few laugh lines around the eyes, a little earthy experience, plus an ability to plough my ass for hours on end. Maybe even return the favor sometimes and let me jab my dick up their anal chute every once in a while.

The 'He' in question was Mr. Robinson. He had moved in just across the street and down two from my family's home. The house had been vacant for about a year when I went off to university in the summer. I didn't return home for the first two-week semester break, much to my family's dismay. I used that old excuse that I was falling behind with my work and needed to concentrate to keep my assignments up to scratch. What I was really doing was socializing. Most kids who go on to higher education, especially those who are living away from home for the first time, discover a parallel world they scarcely dreamed existed. A world of sucking and fucking, of falling in love, of experimenting with their sexuality.

I was experimenting every spare moment. I had a fair idea I was 'otherly inclined' before I left home and I was determined to prove it one way or the other to my own satisfaction, if to nobody's else's, before the year was out. I guess I believed my family loved me enough to be supportive of where my proclivities lay. I knew it wasn't a 'choice,' it was the way I was programmed in the womb.

Sure, I'd had loads of girl friends in high school but no girlfriends. I'm sure my family must have noticed. My best mate, Troy, and I stuck together like the proverbial glue. We had lots of interests in common, from Japanese manga through old Steve Reeves and Gordon Scott sword and sandal movies of the 1960s to, we discovered later on, a deep and abiding sexual interest in men.

Neither of us had done much through high school. While our straight mates were busy nailing cheer leaders and erstwhile girlfriends they'd promised to marry when their economic ship came in, we were busy discussing which jocks we'd heard played around under the bleachers after football practice.

Troy and I had made a few fumbled attempts at experimentation together but we'd ended up giggling a lot, too embarrassed to touch each other and ending with a half-hearted wank. We swore it would remain our secret and we'd never try it again. We very successfully stuck to our pledge for years and it didn't look like being broken any time soon. Besides, Troy had a great new relationship that was going gangbusters and he was happier than he'd ever been, eager to introduce his mate to me, and just as eager to see me partnered.

It was a long-term goal of mine as well. I just couldn't see it occurring in my insular home town. I'd need a big city to find my heart's desire. I was convinced of that.

Mum picked me up at the airport, handing me the keys to her small car, telling me it was mine for the duration of the break. She only used it to do the shopping and to visit friends and I was more than happy for her to borrow it back when the occasion arose. I had no need of a vehicle at uni as I lived on campus and just about everything I needed was within walking distance. Occasionally, if a pick-up lived on the edge of town, I would resort to a taxi to get home but my technique was good enough he usually asked me to stay the night in order that we could repeat the exercise the following morning. If it was a weekend, we would sometimes repeat the exercise all day Saturday and well into Sunday, before he drove me back to the campus, me all fatigued and usually sore.

Not much likelihood of that in Dullsville as I liked to christen my dreary little town. It had the basics: a sex emporium which stocked gay porn DVDs, as well as having porno booths with glory holes. If I was desperate I could always get my rocks off anonymously. Dullsville also boasted a gay bar of sorts. By day it was a working men's bar, catering to the factory workers in the area. At night, it transformed, like Cinderella, into a magic fairyland that, unfortunately, was more likely to attract the ugly sisters than Cinderella herself. It was a friendly haven for the same-sex attracted plus any number of variations that had been labeled perverted by psychiatry until well into the twentieth century.

The small population, of course, did not allow for individual premises for each and every fetish and predilection so on any given night you were likely to see drag queens mixing with leather fetishists, and those into BDSM. I think the town ran to one or two of each sexual variation, which meant there was always someone to chat to, acceptance being the core value rather than moral outrage if you suddenly stumbled upon someone lying in the urinal waiting to be watered.

Any new face in town was immediately the center of attention, especially if he was a local boy returning. Strangers passing through were easy pickings, while kids just experimenting or coming to terms with their attraction were mentored through the lonely process by a number of older men in the town who saw it as their duty to ensure a happy transition into the brotherhood. It was a strictly hands off mentorship and the men were scrupulous in their dealings. It was one of the things I did admire about the town.

It was always a shock on my return to feel a smile creep across my face and my pulse quicken as the familiar streets beckoned to me. My own street, in particular, made...

Whoa, what was that?

I was so busy craning my neck I almost ran into the gutter near our home.

I pulled over, my heart racing, managing to croak out. "Who was that?"

I thought it must have been God, he was so gorgeous.

Mum turned to look. "Oh, that's the Robinsons. They moved into the house across the street from us. I thought I'd emailed you about that."

If she had, she had failed to mention that Mr. Robinson was a gay boy's walking wet dream.

"Robinsons? Plural?" I asked.

"Lovely couple. Two children, about eight and ten."

Damn. There was the word I didn't want to hear: *couple.*

Oh well, eye candy was useful to fuel my fantasies and, by the looks of it, Mr. Robinson was going to feature heavily in my dreams.

"They've been here about five months now. Keep very much to themselves. Not exactly hermits but not exactly gregarious either. Enough to smile and say hello."

"Maybe they're just shy," I said as I restarted the car and drove into the garage.

My old room had been left as a shrine to my adolescence. The posters, the books, the Japanese manga all neatly stacked awaiting my return. One day soon all trace of me will be packed away and the room denuded of my existence as I cut the ties with home and head out into the bigger, scarier, and more exciting world. The thought depressed me for a moment, but I shook it off when I got a text message from Troy inviting me over to meet his new beau that evening.

Mum was disappointed, but forgiving, as long as I stayed home long enough to greet my dad before I went out. I intended taking a nap as I find homecomings tiring. It's the reactivating of old synapses in the brain that have hibernated during my absence from the town. After a cup of tea with mum who asked too many leading questions about my social life, although I think I successfully fielded them, I excused myself and went to my room where my bed welcomed me like an old friend. If I could bottle the feeling of warmth and security I get when I slip under the familiar covers, I'd be a wealthy man.

The sound of kids play screaming woke me an hour or so later. It was an unfamiliar sound in this neighborhood and I sat up in bed. A deep masculine voice shouted, "Don't go on the road, you hear me?" I'd never heard that voice before but I sensed immediately to whom it belonged: Mr. Robinson. Luckily, my upstairs bedroom faced the street and I was at the window in seconds. Pulling the curtains aside, I peered over the road and down a few houses.

I was right. Mr. Robinson had obviously picked up his son and daughter from school. He chased around after them making them laugh and shout, enough to disturb the whole area. He must have realized because he stopped suddenly and looked about as if guilty. Then he raised his eyes and looked directly at my window. I gasped. Even from this distance I could see his eyes flutter wide revealing their intense blue. He seemed surprised, as if he weren't expecting to see anyone watching him, and then his face broke into a wide smile. He clapped his hands and gathered the boy and girl to take them into the house all the way keeping his eyes on my window where I was paralyzed with desire, too excited even to swallow.

I drove mum mad with questions about the neighbors, hoping that I covered my tracks concerning my throbbing desire for Mr. Robinson by asking about the children and his wife as well. She could tell me frustratingly little and attempted several times to change the subject. My dad turned up with my younger sister, Terri, and the subject was mothballed for the time being. He asked polite questions about my studies, skirting the personal, and lauded my scholarly success. My little sister merely grumped that I'd come home to usurp her position as favored child. She would have to share the accolade for the duration of my stay. It would be an uneasy truce.

I excused myself to shower and head out to see Troy who welcomed me with a hug as welcoming as my old bed and a chaste kiss on the cheek. I kept my inquisitiveness on a leash as I listened to him rave about his partner, Vince, who would be joining us later for dinner. I could read the love and affection he harbored for his boyfriend but it became mawkish and repetitive. In the midst of yet another long paean to his mate's perfection, I interrupted.

"What can you tell me about Mr. Robinson?"

I thought he would be pissed off, but he smiled indulgently. "Sorry, I do go on a bit. Mr. Robinson? So, you've seen him then?"

"He's hard to miss."

"That he is. And knowing your attraction to older men I knew you wouldn't miss him."

"Come on, spill."

"He's gorgeous. Built like a brick shithouse. Gay guys drive up the street on a Saturday morning just to ogle his body as he washes his car."

"What?"

"He does it stripped to the waist. Vince has driven past and says the street is a bottle neck around eleven in the morning. He has washboard abs, pecs of steel, although how anybody knows without touching them I'm not sure, biceps like outsize walnuts, and speaking of his nuts...well, no one knows because they've never seen them."

"Shit," I pouted.

"He's married with two kids. Never turns up at the bar, has never been seen at that toilet beat in the park, and absolutely nobody has snared him in one of the local gay social groups on the net. His kids are happy and well-adjusted while his wife is, I have it on good authority as I'm no expert, as appealing to heterosexual men and lesbians as he is to gay men and straight women."

When Vince arrived I warmed to him immediately, although he could add little to unraveling the Mr. Robinson mystique. The meal was top notch, Troy has a real flair in the kitchen, and we adjourned to the lounge room where Vince was content to sit back and listen as we two old friends waxed nostalgic about our years growing up together. When Vince started to get a little frisky I knew it was time to leave.

Over the next few days, impatient for Saturday to arrive and praying that the weather would be sunny, I sank back into the town's slower pace, meeting up with Troy and other old friends for lunch and gossip, most of which revolved around the fact I lived opposite the town's new sex god. It was probably just as well the poor guy knew nothing of his status among the gay mafia in town, let alone among the single women and not a few married ones. He would have run screaming for anonymity in a big city.

My fourteen-year-old sister, Terri, and her shrieking friends drove me insane in the afternoon with their ceaseless chatter and loud music, especially as I propped myself at the window to watch the subject of my unrequited lust drive up with his kids in tow after school. I had lectured myself severely on the morality or otherwise of desiring a married man with kids, especially a seemingly happily married man but, what the hell, it didn't hurt to look. If he was out of reach, I was only window shopping.

Each morning I would sit at the kitchen table, morosely attempting to get my poor over-heated fantasies to leave my sleep-clogged mind, as my sister rabbited on about the sorts of inanities that occupy the undeveloped mind of a young female teenager.

"My girlfriend, Jenny, thinks you're cute," Terri said during a lull in the conversation.

"That's nice," I said, munching on my breakfast muesli. I meant it sarcastically because Terri was obviously spoiling for a fight.

"Don't you try anything with her," Terri pouted in a way which suggested she felt betrayed by Jenny's obviously keen interest in me.

"I won't," I grunted. "She's too young for me." *And the wrong gender,* I felt like adding.

Terri wasn't about to let it go. "She's my best friend in the whole world and I don't want my icky brother trying to get into her pants."

She'd been baiting me all through breakfast. I was exasperated, so I opened my mouth without thinking.

"No worries there, kiddo." She hates being called a kid. "I'm not interested in pimply adolescent girls. My taste runs to older men with experience who know what they're doing."

I had the spoon half way to my mouth when my brain suddenly flashed an alert on what I'd just said. There was a thunderous silence around the table. I screwed up my face in disbelief I'd just outed myself, before opening my eyes to look at my parents. Was that shock I saw on their faces? Disgust? I didn't have a chance to think about it because my sister, oblivious to my faux pas, sailed on. "You better keep your hands off my boyfriend then, too."

Stalling for time, I said, "You've got a boyfriend?"

"Of course," she said smugly. "I bet you don't."

As I had no reply to that I continued eating, waiting for the kitchen to cave in around me.

There was a long silence before mum said, "Well?"

"Well what?" I mumbled without looking up.

"Do you have a boyfriend?"

"No," I admitted.

Terri began a singsong chant, "My brother's a loser. He doesn't have a boyfriend. I've got a boyfriend and he doesn't."

"You're excused, Terri," dad said sharply.

"I haven't finished my toast," she pouted.

"Take your toast with you, and run outside," mum said.

"You just want to have a grown up conversation. I'm going but I can't guarantee I won't listen at the door."

"You do that, honey," mum replied, knowing full well if she gave permission it took away all desire to do so.

After she'd left, dad turned to me. "So, Troy is not your boyfriend."

My mother interjected. "No, sweetheart. That nice Vince Slater from the farmer's market is Troy's boyfriend. They've been together for months now."

"Oh?"

"You never listen when I tell you anything—"

"Gossip," he humphed.

Mum ignored him. "Is that nice Mr. Robinson across the street more your type then?"

"Mu-um!"

She put her hands up in defense. "Just asking."

I put my spoon down. "Okay. Get it over with."

"What, dear?" My mum was all smiles.

"The tears. The accusations. The threats. The warnings about dying sad and alone."

"Whatever gave you those ideas?" mum asked.

"We're just a little upset," dad added, "that you've taken so long to tell us. I emphasize the words 'a little'."

I was gobsmacked. "You knew all along?"

"I may not be the brightest at math," mum said, "but even I can put two and two together."

Dad ticked the points off on his fingers. "No girlfriends through high school. Always mooning over the latest boy band. Do you know how excruciating it is for a grown man to have to listen to all that saccharin music? No, I guess youthful hormones don't necessarily instill an appreciation of good music..."

"Dear." Mum attempted to steer him back to the point.

"Troy. Nice kid but as obvious as glitter on a giggle. You and him holed up in your bedroom locked in private conversations for hours on end. The only girls you ever mentioned, and then it was only rare and in passing, were those fag hags that hung around the two of you at school. The posters you hung on your bedroom wall were always male jocks without shirts yet you never showed the slightest interest in sports. The way you took no interest in television programs unless the star was what you kids call a 'hot male number' and then you'd squirm on the lounge as if adjusting yourself constantly."

"Da-ad!"

"Need more?"

"Was I really that obvious?"

Mum was more placatory. "We wondered. We knew you'd tell us when you'd worked it out for yourself. We were always here if you needed us."

I suddenly got a little teary eyed.

"So, you're okay with this?"

"Of course. With IVF we can still look forward to grandchildren," mum smirked. "And they'll legalize gay marriage any day now and I can look forward to planning a big wedding and—"

"Whoa," I cried. "Way too early. I'm still finding my feet."

Dad stuttered for a moment, coughed, then launched into his embarrassing question. "By mature, you don't mean like my age? There's this one chap at work, unmarried, a bit anally retentive if you ask me, but—"

"Ewww. I do not want my parents trying to set up blind dates for me in an attempt to show how accepting they are. Let me make my own mistakes please." I'm afraid I raised my voice. I wondered whether it would have made it easier if they had been less accepting.

A bit stunned by everything that had transpired at breakfast I returned to the bedroom. It was just about the time Mr. Robinson would appear in his fashionable suit, gather the children and strap them in the back seat of his Jeep and head off down the street toward the local school. Every morning I sat at the window to ogle and sigh at the short glimpse I got of the unattainable man of my wet dreams.

Just as I set myself up for a comfortable perv, there was a knock at the door. I sprinted back to the bed just as mum opened the door.

"I'm just heading off to the mall. Would you like to come with me?"

"Not today, mum, I have a lot of studying to catch up on."

"You used to like going shopping with me."

Before I could answer, there was the sound of a car being backed out of a garage opposite. Mum moved to the window, pulling aside the curtain. I was mortified, for the binoculars were still on the sill aimed directly at the Robinson house. She saw them, and then looked out at the view.

"Oh, I see. Well, I can see it's nothing your father or I can help you study so I'd best leave you to it."

I mumbled, "Thanks mum" as she quietly closed the door.

I scooted over to the window quickly. Mr. Robinson was going about his usual routine when I heard his name called and he looked around.

Shit, no! It was my mother crossing the road to speak to him. What was she up to? No matter how hard I strained I was unable to hear their conversation. At one stage, Mr. Robinson looked up at my window, smiling. I was hiding behind the curtain and hoped he couldn't see me. I was beetroot with embarrassment.

The following day was my first Saturday at home. I was a nervous wreck waiting for eleven o'clock to roll around. I told mum I didn't want to be disturbed under any circumstances for at least an hour as I would be working on a particularly difficult assignment that needed my utmost concentration.

The traffic did seem to get heavier as the hour approached. It was a hot day so everything looked set for quite a show. The garage door opened and Mr. Robinson drove his car out onto the street. Yes, he was dressed in old overalls. As he began to suds the vehicle, the water and soap wet his outfit so that it clung to his body. It did not appear he was wearing underwear.

My cock was hard and I'd taken the precaution of having lube nearby so I could stroke without my knob getting hand burn. Men in cars not normally seen in the neighborhood honked their horns as they passed and Mr. Robinson waved happily. He was either very friendly and gregarious or totally oblivious to the sexual connotations of what was occurring. One adventurous individual went as far as pulling up alongside my adored one and spoke to him after lowering his window. Mr. Robinson seemed quite amiable enough in conversation even looking toward my house from time to time and pointing once while nodding his head.

Then the car pulled into our driveway. It was Vince and Troy. They'd interrupted my road to orgasm. Although my cock was still leaking pre-cum I quickly put it away and threw on baggy clothes that would disguise my excitement, and ran downstairs. Mum had already answered the door and was happily chatting to my best friend and his lover.

I invited them up to my room but mum suggested, "It's too hot and stuffy inside today why don't you boys go out and sit on the front porch. I'll bring you something nice and cold to drink."

What could be better? A front row seat.

"Your mum is so cool," Troy said as we lounged on the chairs and the love seat while ogling our neighbor. He waved as we came out of the house and we all waved back although me more eagerly than the others.

"You think my mum knows I fancy him?" I asked.

Vince snorted.

"That man is god," Troy said and Vince biffed him on the shoulder.

Troy pretended to pout. "I can look, can't I?"

"But don't touch."

Troy snuggled into his boyfriend, pecking him adoringly on the cheek. Mum brought out the cans of soft drink at that moment: Troy and Vince sprang apart guiltily.

"We're all adults here," she said. "Just don't scare the neighbors."

We all helped ourselves to the icy cold drinks as mum waved to Mr. Robinson who called out a greeting.

"I can see what all the fuss is about now," she said dreamily. "If I were thirty years younger I think I'd make a play for him myself. Hmm, I wonder if he likes older women."

"Mu-um!"

"Just saying. You know desire doesn't automatically dry up when you turn fifty, young man." She flounced back inside the house putting on quite a show for the man over the road.

Troy said it again. "Your mum is so cool."

Vince had been watching me. "You really like him, don't you?"

"Who wouldn't?" Troy asked.

"No, I don't mean in that superficial kid in a lolly shop way."

"Yeah, as much as I can without knowing the man," I admitted.

Vince stood up, grabbed a cold can, taking it across the street. Mr. Robinson wiped his forehead before popping the can and putting it to his lips. Some of the liquid spilled out the corners of his mouth and ran down his chin. My tongue inched out as if attempting to lick up the residue. They talked for a few moments, glancing our way from time to time, then shook hands, and Vince strolled back to join us.

"Why do I get the idea you're up to something?" I asked.

Vince's smug looks merely confirmed my suspicions.

"Just make sure you're showered and in your best finery at eight o'clock when we call for you," Troy said.

"And it wouldn't hurt to douche," Vince added mischievously. "Just in case."

"Ewww," I said.

Just in case, I did shower, shit and shave and was ready half an hour early, getting very antsy while I waited impatiently. About five minutes later I got a call on my mobile from Troy. He was running late.

"Not to worry," he said chirpily. "We've asked a friend of ours to pick you up. We'll meet you at *The Back Door* a little after eight-thirty."

He hung up before I could tell him I'd changed my mind and intended staying home.

The town's gay bar was called *The Back Door* not because of some silly attempt at innuendo but because in its early years in a homophobic town it remained unnamed and unsignposted, its only identification in the town's down-market area being a hand-painted sign with an arrow and *Enter by the Back Door*. The name stuck and no attempt to give the venue a classier name ever took. The locals always referred to it as *The Back Door*.

It wasn't a bad spot. It had loud, thumping music upstairs for the younger crowd or the younger-at-heart vulture dressed up as chicken, while the downstairs bar was more conducive to chatting and enjoying a drink. It was for cruising. I know Troy and Vince were well intentioned but I didn't feel like it. I began to rehearse my excuses for not going: a terrible headache, a prolapsed sphincter, an attack of crabs. None of them seemed even remotely plausible.

I was still deciding between excuses when the doorbell rang. I sucked in my breath hoping the first thing that popped out of my mouth wouldn't be too stupid for words. I knew the guy at the door was a blind date Troy and Vince had obviously set up and I didn't want to be rude. Chances are he wouldn't be a dog but he'd be unrelentingly average and I just didn't feel like average that night.

I was already apologizing profusely as the door swung open, the words catching in my throat.

"Hi," he said. "You ready? Vince rang to say I should pick you up, he's running late."

I'm afraid I just gaped at him, unable to speak.

He seemed concerned. "Are you okay? You look a bit feverish."

"Who is it, sweetheart?" Mum called from the kitchen before walking in on my total paralysis. "Oh, Mr. Robinson. Jayson, you didn't tell me you were going on a date with Mr. Robinson."

That brought me around quick smart. "Mu-um, I'm not going on a date. I'm going out with Troy and Vince. Mr. Robinson is just giving me a lift."

"Okay, if you say so."

I knew she wasn't buying it for a minute.

Then, just like a mother, she added, "Don't get too drunk. And don't be home too late."

Way to put down your son in front of a man he's trying to impress. I shoved him out the door, closing it behind me before she could belittle me any further.

"Cool lady, your mum," he said.

"If anyone else tells me how cool my mum is, I think I'll scream," I said churlishly, wondering whether he fancied her. That would be just my luck.

Mr. Robinson walked ahead of me, giving me the opportunity to admire his perfect round butt encased to perfection in his tight jeans. He was good enough to eat. He wore a T-shirt, two sizes too small to contain his massive arms and chest, the fabric straining not to burst at the seams. I felt weak in the sphincter just looking at him. My mind was only just beginning to join the dots. Mr. Robinson is gay? Nah, there were lots of straight men who went to *The Back Door* for a drink, although I couldn't think of any just at that precise moment.

"Debbie's taken the kids away for the weekend, so I had a free night."

I hopped into the vehicle, still unable to speak.

"Buckle up and we'll be underway."

I clicked my seatbelt into place and turned to stare at him. The first thing out of my mouth was the excruciatingly embarrassing, "You can't be gay."

He merely chuckled as he started the car. "This body says otherwise, Chiquita. How many straight guys you know built like me, eh?"

I knew it was a joke rather than conceit.

"But everyone thinks you're married with kids."

"Debbie's my little sis. The kids are hers. She's taken them to visit her asshole of a husband to see if there's anything left to salvage of their relationship. She still loves the bastard. I don't know what she sees in him. She's better off staying with me so I can take care of them."

"Stifles any chance of a relationship, or even sex," I suggested.

"I'm over relationships. Big time."

I filed that away for later because the bitter way he said it brooked no discussion at the moment.

"As for sex," he continued. "A much over-rated commodity in my book."

I'm such a klutz, my mouth is always flapping. "Easy for you to say. You're gorgeous and can obviously have any man you want—"

"Then how come the man I wanted didn't want me," he snapped.

Change the subject, Jayson.

"All I'm saying is, I'm just starting out and I'm a bit on the homely side so sex is a really big deal for me at the moment. When I'm old and jaded like you are, then maybe I won't care so much."

He looked over at me and lifted my face toward him, keeping his other hand firmly on the wheel. If he was insulted he didn't show it.

"Who told you that you were homely, kid?"

"Don't ever call a grown man 'kid', even in jest."

"Sorry. I forget how sensitive you young guys are. When you're my age you'd do anything to be called 'kid' again. And you didn't answer the question."

"Dunno what it was like in your era, granddad, but we young 'uns have this new-fangled invention in our log cabins. We call it a mirror," I joked. "Shows us young folk what we really look like without fear or favor."

He let my face go, saying simply, "Then your mirror is lying if it tells you you're homely."

That comment took my breath away and we spent the remainder of the journey in silence. The car park was crowded, not unusual for a Saturday night, and I saw Troy's car was already here.

As we walked toward the bar, Mr. Robinson – shit, I still didn't know his name – said, "Sorry about calling you a kid earlier. I'm not much good around young guys. Not my scene. All they have between their ears is party, drugs and loud music." I went to interject. "Yeah, I know I shouldn't tarnish all you young guys with the same brush but, well, experience has taught me otherwise."

I would have to seriously reappraise my attraction to this man. "You know, Mr. Robinson, for someone who is so goddam physically perfect, you're a real downer. Maybe you should get yourself a personality to go with the body."

With that I strode away from him and into the bar where I was engulfed in a flurry of activity as the entire bar screamed "Surprise!"

I beamed at Troy and Vince who had draped a banner proclaiming 'Welcome Home Jayson' across a corner of the room, setting up party central around a number of the booths. Even patrons who didn't know me joined in the revelry. I was backslapped and congratulated across the room to where Troy was beaming. I hugged him and Vince and was genuine in my thanks.

"What a nice welcome," I choked.

"Where's your date?" Vince asked.

"You mean the guy with the muscles and the fun bypass?" I said sarcastically.

Troy looked stricken. "You didn't?"

I nodded that, yes, I had. "Both barrels"

Troy sighed. "Vince, go see if you can find him."

He pulled me aside. "I told Vince we should have warned you. You'll have to cut him some slack, Jay. He's hurting. Short version is he was in a relationship for fifteen years. He and his boyfriend bought the house opposite you together and just before they were about to move in, the bastard boyfriend ran off with a younger man. That was less than six months ago. Since then he's thrown all his energy into paying the bastard off for his half of the house and helping his sister and her two kids through their messy problems."

"You told me you didn't know if he was gay."

"Vince got the story out of him earlier today when he originally turned down our invitation to join us tonight. This is his first time out since his break-up. It's a big deal for him."

The crowd hushed as Vince dragged the obviously reluctant Mr. Robinson into the bar. Patrons gaped or buzzed with gossip so that by the time he reached me half the men had claimed prior knowledge of his gayness or else maintained they had slept with him.

Vince shoved him in one side of the booth while Troy did the same to me from the other end. Mr. Robinson and I met in the center, hemmed in by our two well-wishers.

"I think you two should talk," Vince said.

"Be good," Troy added.

"If you two promise not to move, we'll be right back with drinks."

He took our order, leaving us alone.

"Sorry," I said. "I didn't know."

"He told you?"

"Yep."

"Shit."

"That's exactly what I feel like."

He laughed.

"I can't call you Mr. Robinson all night," I said. "Sounds like I'm back in high school."

"Where are my manners?" he said. "Oh, I remember. I left them with my personality."

"Ouch."

"Scott," he said.

"Jayson."

"I know. I knew your name the day you came home."

"You stalking me?"

"I'm not the one staring through binoculars."

"You saw me?" I reddened.

"The sun glints off the lens in the morning."

"You must think I'm some sort of pervert."

"That makes two of us then," he said kindly. "I borrowed my nephew Ty's telescope one night, he's mad keen on astronomy, to see what you were up to. You know you can see straight through those flimsy curtains of yours at night when you have that little Snoopy lamp on beside your bed?"

"Oh, fuckin' shit!"

"That's a nice piece of meat you're carrying."

"You watched me jerk off?"

"There was nothing of interest on TV that night so..." he shrugged.

I smiled. "And what did you do?"

"Joined you, of course. You should see the hot expression you get on your face when you're about to come."

I snuggled up against him. "Maybe you'd like to see it up close and personal."

I felt him tense. Disappointed, I moved away.

Troy brought our drinks over and I downed mine in one gulp.

"Steady on," Scott said. "If you get drunk too early, someone will take advantage of you."

I stood up to go buy a second vodka and bitter lemon, sneering, "That's what I was hoping."

Okay, I was being a jerk, but the prospect of consummation with the man of my dreams was receding faster than the hairline on the older – much older – man who sidled up to me at the bar.

"This one's on me," he said, adding before I could refuse, "I work with your dad."

I looked at him more closely. Attractive in a seedy sort of way. Body still in good nick. I arched an eyebrow.

"Of course, should anything occur between us I would be discretion itself," he added.

"That goes double for me..."

"Nigel," he said.

"Thank you, Nigel. I'm sure I'll be seeing you again before the night is through."

I wandered off, flirting outrageously with anyone half attractive in the bar. I needed to get laid. Obviously, I had been fantasizing over the wrong man. If I couldn't have Mr. Perfect, I'd settle for Mr. Second Best. Or even lower down the scale if necessary. I should have stopped at three drinks but I didn't. I was horny and I was obnoxious. I wandered back to Scott who was busy beating off a number of persistent admirers and plonked myself next to him. Troy shook his head in exasperation at my behavior.

I didn't care. Leaning over, I attempted to kiss Scott on the lips but he pulled away.

"I can't," he said.

"Am I that ugly?"

"Stop saying that. You're not ugly at all. If I was twenty years younger..."

"I like older men. Just ask Troy."

Troy nodded his agreement.

"I'm not ready for another commitment."

"I'm not asking for a picket fence and three puppies. All I want is a fuck."

Scott recoiled.

I stood up shakily and squeezed past Troy. I turned to the bar and in my loudest voice shrieked, "I'm not looking for a lifetime commitment. All I want is a fuck. What does a guy have to do to get a fuck around here?"

That brought them out of the woodwork. I headed to the toilet in embarrassment as well as to get away from Scott in case I lost my temper even further. I went into the nearest cubicle and sat fully dressed on the bowl. Foolishly I had neglected to lock the door. It was pushed open by none other than Nigel, dad's work colleague, who took the opportunity to bolt the door behind him while attempting to disguise it with concern for my health.

"Are you feeling all right now?"

"Never felt better," I lied.

"Good," he said, lowering his fly. "I have an early start tomorrow so I thought this an opportune time to collect on my investment."

He had his pants down around his ankles and was massaging his cock to its full potential before my brain even registered that his investment was the drink he'd bought me earlier.

"I knew you were a slut the moment I set eyes on you. I bet you suck like it's second nature."

I began to object, "Just a minute—" but I couldn't finish as he slid his very eager prick into my mouth. I attempted to push him off but he held firm to the back of my head and was poking into my throat before I could stop him. The quick glimpse I'd had of his cock showed it to be far more prepossessing than the man it belonged to. If I could just blot him out and concentrate on the rather nice slab of meat filling my craw I might get through this without throwing up. Nigel wasn't going to take no for an answer.

He kept up his barrage of slut talk even after I heard the toilet door open and someone enter the men's room. It registered that the newcomer stopped close by the cubicle in which we were ensconced and was probably listening to our sexual activity.

"Suck it good slut. I'm sure you'll have as many men as you want lined up to get a sample of your blow job skills. Oh, yeah, get your tongue round my knob, boy. I knew you'd be good, little fucker."

It was turning me on, except Nigel's whiny voice was not the one I wanted to hear saying these things to me. I don't mind role playing a slut but I need someone much more aggressive and powerful than Nigel.

He let me come up for air, my lips spilling drool down my chin. I sucked it in. "Come on, Nigel, you can do better than that. Pound my slut face, choke me on your big, hard cock so I'll never forget how good you are."

"Good slut faggot boy! Suck it."

I gagged, almost puking around the dick that filled my mouth. He was getting into it now and I held his flabby butt cheeks to keep him as far down my throat as I could so as not to taste his nasty seed when he blew. I used all my expertise to bring him off while his string of expletives became less coherent as he raced toward ejaculation. I heard the door open and our eavesdropper leave.

I took my mouth off and tried one last ruse, "Feed me, daddy. Feed me all your hot spunk."

That did it. No sooner had he rammed as far into my gullet as he could possibly go he stood stock still, his body juddering as he shot his cock phlegm deep inside me. I tasted none of it, clearing my throat as he pulled out to keep it down. He wiped his residual jizz on my lips, pulled up his trousers, and then patted me on the head like a favored pet. "We must do this again."

I waited a few minutes before I staggered to my feet, making sure the door was securely fastened lest some other horny man decide I was easy prey, and then I made my uneasy way back to the bar. Flashing my ID, I ordered a double bourbon.

"Here, let me pay for that," a deep resonant voice just near my left ear said, slapping a fifty on the counter.

That's what you've got to do to get a fuck, I thought. *Make a total fool of yourself in the town's only gay bar. Still, if it works...*

The barman scooped up the cash before I had a chance to say 'no'. I turned to thank my benefactor.

"Get it into you before you make a bigger fool of yourself than you already have. Then I'm taking you home."

"Promise," I said, realizing I was slurring my words.

I went to pick up the drink but Scott beat me to it, downing it in one gulp. He slammed the glass back on the counter and held the bar for a moment.

He grabbed me, hustling me to the front door.

"Wait. I have to say good-night to Troy and Vince."

"They left ages ago," he said, not letting go for a moment.

Out in the cool night air, my legs buckled. Scott scooped me up in his arms. I snuggled into his chest as he carried me to his Jeep. He plonked me in the passenger's seat, securing me tightly before getting in to drive off.

I was in a playful mood and tried tickling him, running my fingers along his thigh, playing with his hair, but each time Scott forcefully removed my hand without saying a word. I gave up and sulked until he pulled up outside my house.

"Boy, are you drunk," I slurred. "Your house is on the other side of the street."

He got out and came around to my side, dragging me from the seat and hoisting me over his shoulder. It wasn't a good idea as it put pressure on my stomach and I puked all down his back. Scott was impressive. It didn't faze him. Nor did he hesitate in his intended task. He lowered me off his shoulder and propped me upright as he rang the bell.

"I thought we were going back to your place. You promised."

Mum opened the door, took one look at me, shot daggers at Scott and slapped him rather hard across the cheek. Dragging me inside, she slammed the door in his face. I was rather pleased until she began to curse me in a voice much too loud for this hour of the morning. She managed to get me up the stairs and into my bedroom, content to just cover me with a blanket to sleep it off.

The whole family was waiting around the breakfast table when I finally emerged the next day, feeling like the sludge at the bottom of a toilet bowl. My head throbbed, my mouth was dry, my eyesight blurred. My sister looked self-satisfied, mum looked like thunder, and dad was more bemused.

"No lectures necessary," I whispered. "I've learned my lesson. Never again. Black coffee and dry toast please."

I sat with my head in my hands until my meager breakfast was served. My sister began with her chatter but dad shooshed her. She wanted to know why.

"You'll understand, love, the morning after you first come home in the state your brother did last night."

She didn't understand but she kept quiet for which I was grateful.

I looked at mum. "Thanks for getting me up to my room last night. Most parents would have left me on the front doorstep."

"When I see that Mr. Robinson—" she exploded.

"Mum. It had nothing to do with him. In fact, he stopped me, otherwise I'd be in a much worse mess today. He dragged me out of the bar."

She turned sheepishly to my dad. "I slapped him across the face."

I crawled back to bed after I'd had my carbohydrate and caffeine, not even getting up when I heard mum cross the road and knock on the front door of Scott's house. There was a lot of mumbling then the sound of a door closing. Either Scott was so pissed off he'd closed the door in her face or else she'd gone inside. It didn't matter, I just wanted to die.

Troy rang to enquire after me but I was too far gone to take the call. In fact, it was Monday lunch time before I'd even recovered enough to get out of bed. I stank. I needed to clean my teeth and have a shower. I felt marginally better, and later in the afternoon when I heard the Jeep pull up, I glanced out the window. Scott was looking up at my bedroom, concern written all over his face.

I kept a low profile for the remainder of the week, refusing even to see Scott when he called in on Tuesday evening to ask after my health. I did manage to get myself over to Troy and Vince's for a debrief, telling them everything that happened. They listened patiently and without recrimination.

By Friday night I missed him. Or rather, I missed my little voyeuristic activities and I daringly left my curtains parted just enough that if he wanted to he could watch while I brought myself off to fantasies of our passionate lovemaking. Hoping he was watching, I even blew a kiss in his direction. I slept soundly for the first time in a week.

The next morning was Saturday and I was up bright and early for the car-washing ritual. Just before Scott opened his garage door and emerged driving his Jeep to the side of the road, I was already at work on mum's car. I had on the tightest pair of shorts I could melt my body into. They hugged my ass so tightly you could see my tight puckered hole outlined if I bent over, and I intended doing a lot of bending over. The endless parade of cars wending their way along the street now had two prize gay men to ogle. Scott and I got wolf whistles and outrageous propositions that I must admit were quite tempting if I hadn't been after bigger game. In the midday heat, Scott peeled his overalls down to just above his butt. That was the opportunity I was waiting for.

Turning the hose on full bore I aimed at Scott and let fly. He got soaked, his hair dripping and his overalls clinging to his legs and groin like a wet T-shirt competition. But he was laughing.

"You bastard," he called, picking up his bucket of sudsy water and racing across the road toward me. I was too slow, taking the soapy water full on, slipping over on the wet grass of the nature strip. Scott was on top of me before I had a chance to regain my footing, pinning me down.

He sat on my chest, just staring at me. I tweaked his nipples which were hard as stone and dared to place my hand on his crotch. I wasn't imagining things. He slid down my body until he felt my cock pressing into his groin. His face was inches from mine, his mouth quivering with desire but unprepared to make the final move. Placing my hand on the back of his head, I pulled him down to me.

His kiss was the sweetest, gentlest and most passionate I had ever encountered. I melted into him and he reciprocated. There was none of the mad competitive thrusting I was used to. This was a kiss to get lost in, to take your time over, like a fine wine or the smoothest Swiss chocolate. I never wanted the feeling to end, especially as he ground his hard muscular body against mine, but a cry of 'Either come inside or get yourselves a room' from my dad broke the spell.

Scott broke away mumbling an apology and fled back home. I looked up at my sister's wide-eyed amazement at what she'd just witnessed.

"Sorry, son," dad said as he helped me up. "But you two were creating so much heat I thought you'd scorch the grass. Either that or you'd be arrested."

For another kiss like that I'd gladly brave arrest. I raced upstairs to my bedroom, locked the door and watched the window across the street. Scott was naked, caressing his beautiful cock, thrashing about on his bed. I was hard in seconds and although it was difficult doing it while balancing binoculars I matched Scott's strokes until we both blew our loads within seconds of each other.

There was no repeat of the previous Saturday night as I was forced to spend the night at home entertaining my aunt and uncle and their Terri-aged daughter who were unable to attend my birthday barbecue the next afternoon. It was a family tradition that friends and neighbors were always welcome at the family Sunday afternoon birthday barbecues.

I'd given mum a few names, Troy and Vince at the top, of people I'd like to invite, but that had been before Scott and I had even met, let alone kissed. I hoped she'd had the good sense to invite him. The next day, however, it looked as if she hadn't or else he didn't want to come. I put on a cheerful face during the party and both Troy and Vince rallied around to keep my spirits up, even going so far as to pop over to Scott's place to see if he was home. He wasn't. His beloved Jeep was gone from the garage.

He'd made it painfully clear in so many ways that I wasn't his type. I'd humiliated him, I'd shown him what a tramp I was, so what did I expect? That night I went to bed saddened that in a week or so I would be back at university and I could put all memories of Scott in the fantasy basket. I didn't bother going to the window when I heard his Jeep pull up, and the delighted squeals of the kids. Yeah, I blubbered a bit, got all teenager angsty. So, sue me. I reckoned I had feelings for the mongrel. Sure, I was wallowing a bit as well, but...

I heard a tap at the window. I sat up, wiping my eyes. I almost cried out in fright when I caught a glimpse of a man's face pressed against the glass. I opened the window, dragging him inside before he fell.

"What the fuck are you doing?" I whispered. "You could have killed yourself."

"I didn't want to miss your birthday."

"Well, you did," I said, turning my back on him, going to lie on top of my bed.

"I know. I'm sorry. I intended being there. Was it good?"

"Great," I lied. "No, it was pleasant but someone very special didn't show."

"I brought you a present."

"Really?"

"I hope you like it because I can't take it back."

"Where is it?"

He shucked off his jeans and T-shirt, standing naked in front of me with a cute little red bow tied around his cock.

"I hope you like it."

"I don't know," I said. "I haven't tried it yet."

"Be my guest," he said, lying down next to me on the bed.

"I want another one of those kisses first."

He obliged and again I was putty in his arms. He undressed me slowly, we were in no hurry.

"I couldn't stop thinking about you," he admitted as he peeled off my PJ top.

"Me either."

"I was so jealous when I heard you in the toilet with that guy."

"That makes it all worthwhile then, because he forced himself on me."

"I wanted to rip his cock off for touching you."

I kissed him to show him how much I appreciated what he was saying.

"Then that week when I didn't see you at the window. It was like someone had ripped part of my soul out. If you hadn't come out to play yesterday, I was going to come after you. But that kiss. I knew then I was in way over my head. I was going to tell you at the party today how I felt but an emergency sprang up with my sis, and family comes first."

"I understand," I lied.

He kissed my nose. "Look. I don't know what I'm doing. It's been fifteen years since I had to date anyone. I'm out of practice. I don't know what young guys today are looking for. I'm awkward, a bull in a china shop. All I know is, I like you a real lot, Jayson. I'd like to spend time with you, see how we get on. I'm older than you..."

"That really doesn't matter to me."

"You say that now. But I love for keeps, Jayson. I wish I could just settle for a tumble in the grass. Okay, maybe that's what this might be, but I'm looking for something steadier. You know what I mean?"

"I've got feelings for you, too. Stronger than I ever felt for any guy before. I want to spend time with you. Get to know you better. If you'll let me."

I pulled him closer to me, raising his arms above his head and buried my nose in his arm pit. I licked and sucked the hair tasting the salty flavor of his sweat, working my way along his arm until my tongue brushed over his nuggetty bicep and then down to his hand, tracing my tongue over the webbing between his fingers. I slowly licked up his abs, feeling the power of the man's body as it surrendered to me, until I reached his pert hard nipple, running my teeth over it before sucking it into my mouth.

Scott writhed beneath me as I repeated the teasing on his other arm. I kneeled and burrowed my nose between his legs, sniffing his balls as my tongue darted out to lure first one and then the other into my mouth where I sucked them gently until Scott moaned and shifted in the bed. I lapped up the underside of his cock until I reached the head, holding it steady as it throbbed in my hand, peeling back the foreskin to run my tongue across the slit. He groaned loudly enough that I had to put my hand over his mouth in case it woke my parents.

"I can't help it, babe, you're so good. I can't believe anyone so young could be so expert."

I wrapped my lips around the entire head and sucked while drawing patterns on the crown with my tongue. His body arched as he tried to escape but I was not about to let him go. I slid my mouth down to the base of his cock, licking and sucking as I slowly descended, until I had my nose in his pubic hairs. I opened my throat and swallowed him.

"Holy fuck!" he croaked. "No more. I can't take it. You'll make me come."

I was counting on it.

Picking up the pace I moved my head in a circular motion as I caressed his cock with my tongue for a few seconds and then pushed my face down to engulf him, sliding the last few inches into my throat. It was hard not to gag but I did my darnedest and was rewarded with Scott placing both hands on my head and beginning to fuck my mouth. He did it with a gentle rhythm that was easy to match as I wanted this to be good for him. I had never enjoyed having a man in my mouth as much as Scott. I wanted to worship every square inch of his body.

He began thrusting faster so I concentrated, hoping more than anything to taste him. I wanted his spunk on my tongue so I could savor him. I took him down my throat and kept him there until I felt his balls clench, then moved my lips up the shaft capturing his jets of man juice in my mouth. I sucked him dry, running my tongue across the last drools that oozed from his cock head.

"You fuckin' swallowed?" he said in awe.

I wondered just what his former boyfriend used to do for him.

"You've worn me out," he sighed. He gazed sleepily at me before he said, "I guess I should get going." But it didn't sound like his heart was in it.

"Please stay the night," I begged.

He ran his fingers through my hair, then around my eyes which were still a little bloodshot.

"You've been crying," he said.

"A little."

"Because of me?"

I didn't answer him. He kissed me with such tenderness he almost brought on another jag of weeping.

"I never want to hurt you, Jay. Forgive a stupid old fart."

"Fuck me, Scott. I need you inside me."

He turned me over, slipping a pillow under me to elevate my ass, then spread my cheeks for access to push his tongue against my hole. I wanted so much to moan out loud, scream my appreciation of what he was doing, but contented myself with little gasps of pleasure. He flicked around my asshole lubricating me with saliva before aiming for the center and pushing through. His mouth action almost made me come and I had to ask him to stop for a moment as it was too much.

He spat in my ass and slowly slid a finger inside me. It was so pleasurable I felt no pain at all, begging him to add another finger. Then another.

"Your ass is amazing," he said. "The way it grabs my fingers and sucks them in. The way the rim of your hole is drawn out as I withdraw."

He finger fucked me languidly until my asshole was on fire.

"I need you so bad," I whimpered.

Rolling me over onto my back, he raised my legs. I was glad as I wanted to watch his face as he entered me. He rubbed the head of his prick against my hole, lubricating it with his pre-cum, and then pressed gently. I sighed as he sank in slowly, inch by inch, never rushing, until he was finally embedded all the way inside. I held him in place.

"Let me feel you like this for a moment."

It was sheer perfection. When I released his ass he began a slow grinding motion that shot pleasure to every part of my body. He sawed his cock in and out of me with enough force that I felt it deep in my bowels but also with such tenderness I wanted to love this man forever. He was giving me more pleasure than I ever thought possible from having a cock inside me.

"Yours is the hottest ass I have ever fucked, Jay. And that's no bull. I could fuck you forever like this. The things you do to me."

He wrapped his hand around my cock, milking it in time to his thrusts so that it was a leisurely process as if we had all the time in the world. But we didn't, and he picked up the pace as we both felt our balls churning. He still fucked with a slow, sensual rhythm that had me squealing. None of the jagged rutting that I was used to and put up with because I'd never had better.

"I never knew sex could be like this," I panted.

"Me either."

His heavy breathing matched my own. His pace picked up, as did his hand on my cock. I pulled him down to kiss me as I felt the spunk shoot out all over our stomachs. My asshole spasmed in the throes of orgasm until he couldn't control himself any longer and I felt him shoot up my ass. He collapsed on top of me and I held him tightly then he shifted so he didn't crush me, allowing me to lower my legs once his cock popped out of my ass.

"Happy birthday, Jay," he smiled.

"The best ever," I replied, even though it hadn't been a question.

We slept on and off during the night, waking to do other things to each other's bodies. Scott got me to fuck him even though I'm inexperienced in that department. He made me feel like I was better than anyone who'd ever fucked him before. I didn't believe him but I was grateful for his consideration. We finally fell asleep about five o'clock in the morning. I didn't want to because I knew when I woke up he'd be gone. I wrapped my arms around him as if that would be enough to keep him by my side. He reciprocated and much to my surprise we were in the same position when there was a knock on the bedroom door the next morning. Fortunately, I'd taken the precaution of locking it the previous night.

"Time to get up, Jay. Breakfast is ready."

"Okay, mum. I'll be down in a second." I put my finger to Scott's mouth so he'd not make a sound. He was searching for his clothes in order to make his escape.

"And, Jay?"

"Yes, mum."

"Will it be just you, sweetheart, or is Scott staying for breakfast?"

Gay Dungeon For The Straight Boy

I cursed myself that I wasn't better with tools.

Let me rephrase that: the right sort of tools. You know what I mean, hammers, wrenches, screwdrivers, monkey grips. Those other types I handle expertly. But when you're attempting to demolish a backyard dungeon, then it's building equipment you need. I had none. I had no prospect of getting any. It was Sunday. And I was running out of time.

Peter and his family were due later that day, I hate people who give a few days' notice of a visit, especially if it's your extremely jealous boyfriend and his parents, so I was in my council-approved and architect-designed fibro dungeon. Okay, dungeon implies underground, dark, dank, and damp. This one was light, airy, and fibro-thin. It was so many meters from the neighbor's fence, was sound-proofed, was etc. etc. etc., oh, and had to be painted a heritage color to blend in with the surrounding houses even though it could not be seen from the street. That was the local Council regulations for you. They and their regulations had stopped work on the construction of this edifice for more than nine months. The gestation of the dungeon was almost as long as that of the child I'd fathered – well, I'd donated a jar of sperm, if you can call that fathering – with a local lesbian couple. It was a competition to see who would see completion first. When a boy was born, I suggested they name him Dungeon in tribute to the fact council regulations and approvals took longer and were more arduous than child birth.

The lesbians slapped me and called the boy Hank. And where were the lesbians when you needed them? Sure, they wanted my sperm but they weren't too eager to muck in and help with the really heavy labor. That's why I was thumbing through the city's two gay bar rags looking for someone who might charge less than the gross domestic product of a minor European principality for a little Sunday demolition. Those that didn't laugh at the prospect of working on a day they usually spent recovering from the night before did, indeed, quote a price that would have necessitated my taking out a second mortgage on my own home.

In frustration, physical and mental not sexual, I was going through the local business directory, having as much luck as I had with the rainbow fraternity. The price wasn't the problem this time, after all these carpenters and handymen were married men and women with children and a spouse to support, not an expensive drug habit and top-of-the-range overseas holidays. No, the problem was the actual task. Simple enough except when it got down to the nitty-gritty. "A dungeon, mate? What was it used for?" And because I believed honesty would net me the least squeamish tradesman I was upfront. "Nah, don't think so, mate. Not my line." A few of them referred me on to gay tradesmen I'd already called.

I was toying with the idea of hiring a bulldozer to just smash the whole edifice down when an advertising flyer fell out of the gay papers. It had to be an omen. Either that or my mind was becoming dangerously disturbed. The heading attracted my attention immediately. Good advertising copy always has that effect. It read: *Our handymen have all the right tools.* Then it went on even more suggestively: *No job is too big – the BIGGER the BETTER.* And then in a miniscule type face: *Or too small.* Impressed by their use of double entendre and exotic but masculine typefaces, I found I was getting hard. The flyer promised, after teasing with the phone number, *Full service and satisfaction guaranteed.* I had to read it again to ensure it was really an advertisement for a handyman, not a rent boy.

Imagination is a wonderful thing but the voice who answered the phone brought up visions of fat hairy butt cracks and beer guts. Still, his quote was reasonable – if reasonable is missing the next three payments on my car – and he didn't quibble when I explained the...um...details of what was required. "I'll send my son over within the hour. I'd come meself but the wife wants some doing around the house." He was about to launch into a long spiel about his wife's more demanding attributes when I found myself interrupting tersely, "I just want a dungeon demolished not your fucking family history."

Shit, I'd blown it. There was a long pause during which I considered my options: I was in this situation because I had constructed my monastical retreat in my backyard so I could whip/fist/flail without fear of my housemate stumbling across a half beaten submissive slave lapping up my warm piss from a dog bowl. The dungeon fortress contained all the paraphernalia necessary for the execution of my proclivities. And I had one afternoon in which to remove and destroy the evidence before Peter and his dad and mum arrived.

The loud laughter on the other end of the phone line brought me back. "Yeah, right mate, sometimes I get too carried away." He took down the address and, still chuckling, said, "I'll get Joe over straight away." Joe? Joe! What sort of name is Joe! That was my grandfather's name for fuck's sake. I was picturing a Shane or a Justin or a Stig or…Maybe I should spend the waiting time giving myself a little hand relief. My mind really was out of control.

I put the mobile away, sighing as I looked around the leather floggers, the silicon dildos, the shiny metallic cock rings and tit clamps, the face mask, oh fuck, why was I getting rid of all these memories even if they were covered with the dust of neglect?

Love was the reason. It makes us do some silly things. Things, oft-times, we live to regret. I hoped this wasn't one of them.

I'd met Peter quite a few months prior to panic Sunday. He was a cute fucker. His body was just my type, slim but firmly muscled, his face handsome and chiseled, the usual good-looking, trim, fit gay man in his thirties. But, oh, that bubble butt. I couldn't wait to get him home and in my sling, to bury my fist up his hot pliant ass.

I'm afraid I'm an ass man. Show me a gorgeous rounded gluteus Maximus or two and my cock's as hard as corrugated cardboard. So it was with Peter. I smiled at him across a crowded bar where he was talking with a group of suited admin types after work one Friday evening. I suspect, like most of the patrons in the trendy city watering hole, he was winding down from a busy week and probably debriefing with his office mates.

My smile did the trick because he raised his glass in acknowledgement. A few of his mates turned to give me the once over but seeing I was male immediately turned back to their conversation. This wasn't a gay pub although there was a peppering of closeted gay men throughout the predominantly male business suits. Some I'd even had.

Peter, I learned his name later, broke away from his group and headed to the men's room, looking back over his shoulder to smile an invitation. I downed my beer then gave it about thirty seconds before following him. There was a guy at the urinal but it wasn't Peter, so I checked the cubicles, only one was occupied. That, at least narrowed it down for me. Arithmetic is not one of my strong suits.

The guy at the urinal shook his dick, zipped up, and was out the door. Dirty bugger didn't even wash his hands. I pushed at the cubicle door and it swung open. Peter had his trousers and underwear off and was slowly milking the juiciest cock I had seen in a long while. He smiled dreamily as I stepped in, locking the door behind me. Fortunately, the walls went almost to the floor, although anyone who got down on all fours would be able to see two sets of feet sharing a stall meant for one person.

It was unlikely any of the patrons would do any such thing because management, leery of losing their lucrative punters, turned a blind eye to the activities that went on in the privacy of a toilet stall. Admittedly, most of that activity was the abuse of recreational substances rather than self or fellow man abuse.

I could see no reason why, if Peter had stripped for the occasion I should not follow suit. I shucked off my trousers and briefs, hanging them on the wall peg on top of his. Not a word was spoken as our activity was accompanied by the soundtrack of automatic flushing urinals, the men's room door squeaking open and closed, the splash of taps, and the hum of the wall hand dryer, plus the tinny piped music from the PA system that was so monstrously saccharine it would make anyone shit.

This was not the occasion for foreplay or formal introductions. We were both consenting adults who knew what we wanted, although a one-on-one session in my well-provided suburban torture chamber would have been preferable, I'd settle for that pink butthole that was oozing liquid soap lube as Peter lay back on the toilet seat and hoisted his legs up and over his head. God, the man was supple.

I do like a guy who comes prepared and even though I knew that soap would probably sting like buggery around my knob, I was too horny to pass up a sweet opportunity like this one. Rubbing my cock head around the makeshift lube at the entrance to his guts, I pushed my way in slowly. His hole was hotter than hell as it closed around my glans. I saw no signs of discomfort on his eager face, pushed farther inside and he rewarded me with a satisfied sigh. He was an accomplished bottom, squeezing his ass muscles as I slid inside him.

Neither of us expected this to last long, it was one of those hot and hard spur-of-the-moment encounters that would leave us both satisfied, and produce a lingering smile if we ever thought back on it. As his sphincter gripped my cock, I knew I would be blowing my wad sooner rather than later, so I grabbed his stiff prick to beat it in time to my pelvic rhythm and hoped to get him to drop his load round about the same time I did.

We both headed for the final lap, oblivious to the constant slap of the door closing and the hand dryer's lament, until a voice echoed through the tiled toilet

"Hey, Peter, you still in here?"

We were both so close it was hard to stop now.

"Yeah, mate," he croaked. "Won't be long."

"Me and the guys are heading off. So see you at the office on Monday. Okay?"

"See you," he panted as he blew his spunk between us, spattering both our stomachs with his slime. "Oh, shit!"

"You okay, mate. You sound funny," the voice said.

Peter caught his breath as I held him tightly and blew a load into his guts. "Never better," Peter called back. "See you Monday."

I collapsed onto his body and we both broke out in a fit of giggles as we heard the door flap shut.

That near mishap cemented our friendship and over the following weeks and months we spent more time with each other until our friends just assumed we were a couple. Neither of us had said anything, it just felt natural although occasionally I had the itch, putting the paddles and the sling to good use with some opportune stranger. Peter and I had never discussed our relationship let alone fidelity so I felt little guilt although I knew he was probably monogamous from the things he'd said during our countless discussions around the subject.

I also knew that his tastes were conventional. I'd frightened him in the weeks following our initial meeting by introducing him to the dungeon and although he'd eagerly hoisted himself into the sling to see if it was the right height for my cock to penetrate his ass, the whole set-up turned him off and I had to backtrack, pretending it had been created by a previous flat mate who'd moved out, leaving it for me to dismantle.

That day I'd disavowed a part of my personality. That did bring on a huge bout of guilt. I don't like secrets, so not being able to share an important part of my sexual life, albeit one I was phasing out for the sake of our relationship, did not sit easy with me. Every time I attempted to broach the subject, he screwed his face up in distaste, telling me the subject distressed him and he didn't wish to know about 'such people.'

Warning enough, you would have thought, but infatuation and the grip of Pete's superb back passage were enough to distract me. Plus the fact, at thirty-five, I was beginning to feel my age. Perhaps vanilla was the way to go. Peter had begun introducing me as 'my new boyfriend,' hinting strongly that 'those perverted items in the back shed' should be disposed of as expeditiously as possible. I bristled at his description of my toys, knowing I wasn't ready to give up my covert lifestyle no matter how little I indulged, rejecting his suggestion on the false grounds that my mysterious ex-flat mate would one day turn up to claim his property.

Peter insisted on calling it a Play Pen, to call it a Dungeon would legitimize the alternative sexual gymnastics that occurred therein. While it sat dark and under-utilized in the back yard, visible from the kitchen window, it was a source of constant irritation, like a grain of sand to an oyster, except in our case, it was producing something less beautiful than a pearl.

The festering sore in my case led to a wariness of committing fully to the relationship which, in turn, aggravated Peter. So much so, it seems, he unilaterally declared he had invited his parents over the following Sunday afternoon to meet the man with whom he had decided to spend the remainder of his life. A man who had gone to considerable trouble and expense to build a small cabin at the back of his property as a haven for Pete's parents should they ever stay over.

"You'd better put your skates on because I can't see mum and dad sharing a cosy evening in the same sling, can you?"

I ran my hands longingly over my accumulated gear wondering if I could pries up the floor boards and hide it there. If I was thinking like that then there was no way I was ready to banish the Dom/sub in me. Trouble was I'd agonized over it for so long it was now Sunday lunch-time and, even though I had assured Pete via phone that the interior demolition was progressing well, in truth I had done nothing. Hence the panic. He and his parents, whom he'd gone to bring down from the country, would be here in a matter of hours.

I could burn it down, I suppose. Lock the door and say I'd lost the key. If I hadn't procrastinated, I could have demolished the dungeon and put the contents in storage until I was comfortable that part of my life was truly over. I was wallowing in my own stupidity when I heard a van pull up out the front.

I hastened down the side passage to show the newly arrived handyman the direct access to the dungeon I was now regretting I had promised to dismantle. It wasn't until I heard the slam of a door caught by a sudden breeze that I remembered I'd left the key to the dungeon door inside. I cursed my stupidity. I cursed that I'd got myself in this situation.

I didn't curse for long. When Joe stepped out of his van, the company's brightly stenciled tag along the side, and waved as he opened the back to get his tools, I almost lost it. From the top of his buzz cut to his thick work boots, the man was a god. His clothing barely contained his body which seemed to ripple with muscle beneath the fabric of his shirt and jeans, and his package was enough to make the fishes and loaves envious. I'm afraid I slobbered.

Fortunately, he had his back turned as I ambled over to the van to help him. When he turned his dazzling sneer to me, it was so masculine I felt his testosterone smack me in the face.

"What's so important it couldn't wait till Monday?" he said, with enough aggravation in his voice I thought about paying him off and telling him to go away. This guy wasn't gay friendly; he was a snarling ball of surliness ready to snap my head off, reminding me too much of the bullies at school.

I stood my ground. The reality was he was such a stud, even to a Dom like me that I'd gladly pay anything to keep him around just to ogle for an hour or so. Stupid, huh?

"Well...ah...I have to get my dungeon demolished before my boyfriend gets here with his parents in a couple of hours." There, I'd blurted it out. I tensed in case of physical or verbal abuse.

He smirked. No, he smiled.

"Yeah, dad said he was gonna advertise in the gay papers. Says you guys have a lot of disposable income and there's no reason why we shouldn't get some of it." He pulled his sunglasses down his nose and looked me up and down. "Hmm. Don't go getting any ideas. Me straight, you gay. No fuckin' way mate."

Even the fact he could crush my neck in his powerful fist didn't curtail my tongue. I saw red at his assumption, even though there might have been just the tiniest grain of truth to it, and launched a barrage of abuse. "Okay, listen here Tarzan of the Apes. Don't know why all you straight guys think us gay guys are panting over your bodies. Your girlfriends may like the Neanderthal look but some of us like a bit of brain with our brawn. Got it?"

He actually laughed in my face. "Well said. That would sure put me in my place if that thing didn't betray the lie to what you're saying." He nodded in the direction of my crotch where my super hard cock was tenting my shorts.

"Oh, shit!" I muttered, straightening myself up as best I could.

"This the way?" he said, heading off down the side of the house.

I followed meekly; embarrassed I'd made such a fool of myself.

"Sorry," I mumbled. It wouldn't do to antagonize the guy. He was doing me a favor coming out on a Sunday although I'd pay handsomely for his trouble.

"Yeah, me too. You're doing me a favor. My chick was rabbiting on about weddings and all that shit. I couldn't take much more of it. I don't see myself as marriage material, do you?"

I guess my brain didn't get to my mouth in time because I said, "If you were gay I'd marry you in a minute."

He snorted, whether in contempt or amusement I couldn't tell.

"Shit. I said that out loud, didn't I?"

Ignoring the question, he asked, "You think you could handle what I got to offer?"

Conceited prick.

I decided to give as good as he gave, after all I was no slouch in the looks department either although when it came to alpha males I was a W to his A. "More like can you handle what I've got to dish out?"

He turned to me, his eyebrow raised questioningly.

"This is the dungeon," I said, shuddering at the heat from his body as I grazed his chest pushing past him.

He snickered loud enough to be annoying. "I thought dungeons were supposed to be underground, not some fibro shack with fuck all ambience."

"Look dick-for-brains, you try getting a below ground swimming pool approved by the stupid bloody local council we've got here with their kilometers of red tape let alone an underground dungeon."

He didn't seem fazed by my outburst, kneeling to examine the earth, scoping out the surroundings.

"As long as you don't have any nosy biddies for neighbors, you could dig this up and sink a pretty good dungeon under your back lawn. It would take a couple of men, but it'd be worth it. Just bypass the council. Once the lawn grows back no-one'd even know it was here."

"What are you, some sort of serial killer?"

He shrugged. "Just trying to help out."

"Anyway, it's beside the point now. The boyfriend wants it gone. Converted into a granny flat for his parents."

"Oh, mate. Big mistake. I've seen it so many times before. Wife insists they build a granny flat for the parents, usually above the garage. First, they visit for public holidays. Then they start staying a few weeks at a time. Before long, they move in permanently. Always to save money, you understand, and help out the young couple."

That thought had crossed my mind because Pete was very attached to his parents. I didn't fancy the idea of them as permanent guests.

I groaned at the scenario.

"Just saying," he said. "Now, let's get this show on the road."

I told him the key to the 'shed,' as he insisted on calling it, was locked inside. Thank God he didn't ask how it happened, he just squatted to find the necessary implements in his tool box, revealing the most exquisite butt crack I had ever seen. It was tanned olive perfection not the usual visual pollution.

He flexed his cheeks, I suspect to give me a bit of a show. At least he wasn't the rabid homophobe I'd thought when he first arrived. Fiddling with a few bits of metal in the lock of the shed, he had it open in record time.

"You want to get that lock changed, mate, a good swift kick and anyone could have got inside."

He pushed the door open, standing aside for me to enter first. The place initially smelled stale and dusty, then of leather and silicon, finally of long ago poppers, sweat, and sex. Too long ago, I realized and sighed. I opened up the two windows, council regulations, to let in light and fresh air, bringing the accoutrements into sharp focus.

Joe, who'd followed me in, stood gaping. "I've heard about this SM shit, but I've never seen anything like this before. Man, this is some set-up. You mind?"

"Go for it," I said, admiring the way he moved about the room testing the paddles and floggers, the restraints, spreaders, manacles...

He fingered one of the studded leather collars, placing it loosely about his neck, admiring himself in the full-length mirror I'd installed so subs could watch as I worked them over. It looked good on him, confining his bulging neck, but he obviously didn't understand the significance.

"You put that on and it signifies you're my bitch," I warned.

"Your bitch?"

I nodded.

He hurriedly returned the collar to its spot. "Shit!"

"I've never found anyone I wanted to wear it."

"I guess your boyfriend is not into this shit, that's why you're tearing it down."

That's just it, we weren't tearing it down. The clock was ticking. It was getting late and he'd have to make a move shortly, even though I liked to watch him playing with my gear. I had other gear he could play with if he were bi curious, although I'd bet my ass it would be me getting my furrow ploughed, not Mr Butch.

He examined the cock rings, metal and leather, and was examining the dildos without actually touching them, whistling his disbelief, when his mobile broke the near silence.

"I can't believe the size of those things," he said as he pulled the phone from his jeans pocket. "Guys really put them up their butt?"

I nodded. He groaned before answering his mobile. "Yes, Heather, what is it?"

I gave him a commiserating grimace; he smiled by way of reply then stepped outside for privacy although I could hear him.

"It's not a woman, it's a gay guy. Heather, I told you, this is my job. When I finish uni, then I can give it up, meanwhile I help dad so I can pay to take you out and buy you presents. What do you mean, 'Is he cute?' He's a guy. Yeah, he's good looking, I suppose. Works out, got a good body by the looks of it. No, he hasn't made a pass at me. Heather, how many times do I have to tell you: I'm not gay."

Interesting. Heather was worried about his hetero bona fides, plus he thought I was good looking. Still not enough to work on. And my Neanderthal man was a uni student.

Joe was getting terse with Heather. "Look, I'll ring you when I finish up here. It won't be for hours yet. Heather!"

He cursed. She'd obviously hung up on him. His mood was black as he shucked off his plaid shirt, his torso clad in a navy singlet, his chest barely constrained by the cotton fabric, his arms slabs of muscle that mountaineers would baulk at climbing. Now, if only he'd remove his jeans. That was too much to ask.

"Bloody girlfriends," he spat as he came back inside the cabin. "Sorry about that. Bitch doesn't trust me. She thinks I'm out fucking everything that moves: animal, vegetable or mineral."

"If I looked like you, I guess I would be."

"Not my style, mate. Love me home comforts. Did all me tom catting when I was younger, got it out of me system. Must admit though, me balls turn blue pretty quick if I'm deprived, and sure as eggs, Heather will get her revenge tonight that way. Besides, she doesn't like it all that much. Says I'm too big in that department."

I almost choked. God, could Joe get any more desirable? He slapped me on the back to get me breathing again.

I mumbled my thanks.

While I recovered from his rather frank admission, Joe surveyed the dungeon, pushing and prodding at the items he was to dismantle.

"Decent enough job, whoever did it. No crap here. Won't take all that long to get down though. You want the shelves left?"

I nodded.

"So mainly the stuff that would look out of place in your boyfriend's parents' bedroom."

"You got it," I said.

"Seems a pity. You've gone to a lot of trouble to get it just right."

"Yeah. It's had plenty of use. Fuck buddies and one-night stands. All great." I smiled sheepishly. "Well, a couple not-so-great."

He winked. "I know what you mean. Chicks, that is." He hesitated a little before asking, "You never want just one guy?"

"Hell, yeah," I said too eagerly. As if he was offering. I slapped myself mentally.

"You live it twenty-four/seven or just for fun and games?"

"Not sure. Never had the choice."

He shrugged. "I guess you'll never know."

He went outside to bring in more tools for the job then got to work loosening some of the wall brackets while I set about storing the toys in cardboard boxes. Those I'd keep in the attic until I found a way of disposing of them to sympathetic homes. Every now and then, Joe would tug his singlet up to wipe away the perspiration allowing me a glimpse of his washboard abs.

It took about fifteen minutes to box the dildos and cock rings and I was getting started on the paddles and other shit when Joe spoke up.

"Mate, I don't know how you could stand it in here in summer. Especially in all that leather. I thought dungeons were supposed to be cold and damp, this one's like a fuckin' sauna."

"It gets the afternoon sun. Council wouldn't let me install air conditioning. Too close to the house next door. They thought it'd be too noisy."

He wiped his forehead with the back of his hand. "I thought dungeons were meant to be uncomfortable. Just not so hot." He lifted the singlet over his head and mopped his chest which glistened with beads of sweat that trickled down to his belt. Swabbing himself down like that was one of the most erotic things I had ever seen and I was hard in seconds. I did wonder whether he was doing it deliberately: give the queer some eye candy. Prick tease.

He went to the door and flung his top onto the lawn.

"Mind if I have a fag break." He looked at me for confirmation he'd not said something wrong.

I ran off at the mouth again. "It's not offensive when you mean a cigarette," I laughed. "Unless of course you meant something entirely different."

"Like I said mate—"

"Yeah, I know. You want a beer as well?"

"Yeah. Might cool me down."

Normally I don't let anyone smoke inside but, in this case, I was happy to make an exception if only to keep him in eye's reach. I'm a pragmatist. My genuinely held beliefs are very flexible, especially when confronted by such a truly magnificent specimen. So magnificent I was in danger of forgetting all about Peter.

"Look mate," his cheeks reddened slightly. "The next bit is gonna get real dirty and I came here straight from a party so," he shrugged, "no overalls. We're both blokes, so you mind if I work in me undies."

If I believed in a deity, I would have fallen to my knees and given thanks. He must have seen the look of delight on my face because he warned, "Don't go getting any ideas. It's strictly a comfort issue."

I thought quickly. "If you're gonna be embarrassed, I'll go inside. I don't want you feeling uncomfortable," I said, thinking of ways I could hide my erection.

"Nah. I know you're cool."

He stripped his jeans off, flinging them out to join his singlet. He wore a pair of briefs that scarcely covered his delicious butt, and his slumbering cock dozed cozily behind thin fabric, its outline giving the truth to Heather's concern about its size.

I handed him the beer from the bar fridge I kept stocked. "Thanks mate. That should help cool me down. He placed his tools on the floor, popping the lid and swigging a good mouthful, before burping his satisfaction. "Let me just get settled and I'll start work on this." He looked around for somewhere to park his ass but I'd already taken the only stool. He shrugged and hoisted his butt into the sling, his legs dangling, his body swaying sexily.

"What's this thing for?"

"That's a sling. Really comfortable for the guy getting fucked. Supports his weight while it gives me easy access to his ass, and the rest of his body. You can raise it or lower it so the guy's ass is at the right level for your cock."

"Could a chick use it?"

"Yeah, it works for either sex."

"Maybe Heather could take me easier with one of these things." He stretched around to tug on various pieces and looked at the bolts securing it to the wooden beams in the ceiling. "How's it work then?"

"The person in the sling lays back and you strap them in."

He threw the butt of his cigarette on the floor and leaned over to place his empty beer bottle on a nearby shelf, wriggling his butt back in the sling. "Show me how it works. I'll buy it off you if you don't want it. Might liven up Heather's sex drive a bit."

Much as I wanted to, I didn't dare touch him, but I did move closer. "Lay back so your butt is on the edge."

"Where do I put my head?"

"Let's just pretend it's Heather in the sling. She could put her head here in the rest so she can watch you pounding her. Or she could hang it over the end here to give you better access to fuck her face. Deep throat fucking."

"If only." He lolled his head back over the edge. "Heather doesn't like doing that."

"Yeah, well I'm sure there'll be lots of other chicks out there eager to suck on that monster between your legs." I could have bitten my tongue off when that slipped out.

Fortunately, he was too engrossed in this new experience to notice. It was like he was discussing something with a professional. My sexuality didn't enter the equation.

"Right, so she puts her head here. What about her hands?"

I shrugged. "She can keep them free on her stomach or play with her tits."

He tried that but found gravity kept dragging them off his torso.

"What I find best is to put them in the cuffs above your head."

He noticed the padded cuffs and swung his arms up, keeping them there for a few moments.

"That would leave her vulnerable, wouldn't it?" he smirked.

I gulped, barely able to nod my head.

"Okay, let's try it. If I'm gonna buy the fucker, I gotta know how to use it."

I croaked, "Are you sure?"

"Course I'm sure. I'm bigger than you."

He raised two hands toward the cuffs. When I touched him, I felt a jolt of the dirtiest desire course through my body. His face had this quizzical look as if he'd felt it too. I quickly confined him. He tugged at the restraints and his hands popped free.

"That's not very good," he complained.

"I was just demonstrating," I explained.

"No, come on, do it for real. I gotta get a feel for it."

Okay, if that's what he wanted. I locked the restraints over his wrists. He wriggled fiercely but couldn't get free. He smiled his satisfaction. "Bugger me. Imagine if I got Heather like this. I could do anything I wanted." He looked at me. "Now what?"

"If it's Heather, I guess you'd want to have her pussy or her ass on display so you can fuck either."

"In your dreams. She doesn't do anal. Barely does pussy."

His relationship was obviously not one made in heaven. Why was he allowing her to set the marriage agenda?

"I'll need to get a real feel for the apparatus. I can't really tell with my undies on. Feels good against my back but what's it like against her butt? She's real fussy like that. Could you just slip em down at the back so it's skin against the leather? Just at the back. I don't wanna scare the horses eh?"

I tried not to stare at the sleeping giant in his briefs as I tugged his briefs down over his thick muscular ass. My throat was dry, my heart was thumping, my cock was screaming. When I'd finished, he wiggled his cheeks about on the sling, finding it to his satisfaction. "I'm fuckin' twenty-six, why have I never come across something like this before?"

Because you mix with the wrong people.

"What about me feet? You'd better strap them in so I get the whole kit and caboodle. Then I got a favour to ask."

Please god, please god, please god.

"Can we swap places so I can see what it will be like from my point of view? You play Heather."

"Sure," I said, wondering if he'd want me to strip down to my briefs as well.

I lifted his legs, removed his boots which I was so tempted to shove in my mouth toe first, then his socks before confining his feet to the manacles, exposing his ass cheeks to my view. I cheated a little and spread them wide so I could just get a glimpse of his sweaty crack.

He laughed. "You sure could take advantage of someone trussed up like this."

Was that a wink, or did I imagine it?

"You use those paddle things when you got someone cuffed in this position?"

"Paddling is mainly on the cross over there."

"How about you show me while I'm here."

Shrugging, I got one of the smaller leather paddles, slapping it against the palm of my hand. I gave his butt cheek a bit of a tap, careful to avoid his balls.

"That the best you can do?"

It sounded like a challenge so I gave him a good swat, still far short of what I'd usually give one of my subs. His breath caught as the sting hit home. He throat sounded croaky. "Not much better."

Did I dare? The sound of a paddle cutting through the air became the thwack of the instrument against butt, albeit covered to a large extent by undies. Joe gasped, but his cock shifted. I didn't give him time to catch his breath and swatted the other cheek. I don't know what possessed me but I kept at it until my arm was sore and Joe's ass cheeks were red. He'd struggled through most of the beating, his cock stretching to its full length so the head peeked through the waist band of his briefs. He rattled his cuffs in an obvious attempt to either cover it or jerk it.

I wasn't about to set him free until he'd calmed down. I still had a few good years of life I wanted to live.

"Shit, that was intense mate," he said.

"Sorry if I hurt you." It was best I apologise in case he flew off the handle when I loosened him.

"Don't spoil it mate," he said. He was silent for a long while. I was about to take the cuffs off when he said quietly, "I'm so defenseless you could probably cut my undies off with those scissors over there and play with my cock. Absolutely nothing I could do about it."

I snorted. "And get myself arrested."

We locked eyes. "Nah, it's my own fault I got myself in this situation. Let it be a lesson learned."

That was all the permission I needed. I collected the scissors and carefully cut his briefs from his body, pulling them off to reveal his cock in all its glory, oozing pre-cum. He bucked his hips as an invitation. It really was a magnificent cock. As I ran my hands across his stomach muscles, as solid as a grooved asphalt highway, I leaned in to lick the pearl of pre-cum in the slit, running my tongue around the underside of his glans before flicking the eye and swallowing. He closed his eyes and sighed. If this was the only way he could get off on gay sex then I wasn't going to be the one to deny him. I trusted him that he wouldn't beat me up but I've known guys who enjoyed a walk on the gay side only to regret it once they blew a load.

This was going to be a one-off so I knew to make the most of it. I clasped his balls in my hand as I swirled my tongue around the crown of his cock and then slid my mouth down its length. It was almost too much, but I was determined to milk a load out of him. I bobbed my head up and down the shaft, sucking, licking, anything to turn him on, then plunged down until his prick was embedded in my throat, keeping it there just shy of gagging. Joe thrashed about in the sling, probably desperate to get his hands on my head to force me down until he blew. I wasn't going to let him get away so quickly.

Bringing him to a peak where he was about to lose it, I took my mouth from his cock and licked my way up his stomach to his chest and those massive pecs. I licked them clean of his salty sweat before I turned my attention to the hard brown nipples, nipping and sucking each in turn until he was groaning. But I had my ambitions set on something far more succulent. Farther up his chest I licked, then across to his biceps on to my ultimate destination. I breathed in the delicious odor of his wet pungent arm pits before attaching my mouth leech-like to his pit and sucked.

It was the taste of heaven, salty, man sweat. It's how testosterone would taste if it had a flavor. I nibbled at the hairs, pulling a few loose with my teeth, then sucking and licking the skin until it was all clean. I turned my attention to the second, repeating the routine as Joe struggled, exclaiming "Shit. Holy fuck," until I thought he would twist inside out. But, I knew all good things must come to an end, and time was running out. I moved back to his groin and began licking at his balls.

"Aw," he cried, "I love that."

As far as I was concerned, that was an open invitation to continue. I worked over his balls, sucking, licking, chewing lightly, until I could resist no longer. His asshole was tantalizingly close. I licked down his perineum getting closer and closer to that little pink hole. I felt his body tense but I wasn't going to give up this close to the prize. I'd get one shot and I had to take it. My tongue reached the outer ring and Joe was rigid with fear.

Placing my mouth over his hole, I stroked my tongue around the muscle feeling it relax and his body slump back in the sling. I licked softly, daring to suck every now and then before, emboldened by his passivity, I chewed his sphincter. Back to the tongue work, I prodded against his hole until he opened up allowing me a little way in. He began to grind his ass back against my invasion until I was in danger of losing my tongue to the clamp of his sphincter muscles.

Reluctantly, I went back to his cock, realizing it was time to get him off, but before I did I kicked a bottle of lube under the sling, squatting to pick it up without his discovering what I was doing. To deflect his attention, as soon as I'd slicked my middle finger, I forced my lips down to his stomach and his fragrant pubes. As he bucked against the feeling of my throat constricting around his rock hard cock, I slid a finger deep inside his ass.

For a moment, his body paused as if to ascertain what the new feeling was but whatever his decision it did not include demanding I pull it out. I swept his chute with my digit until I felt the little knob that would make this one of his most memorable blow jobs ever. Or so I hoped. I sawed my finger in and out, rubbing his prostate every second or third insertion until I had him gasping, all the while sucking and tonguing his prick.

"I can't take much more, I'm gonna come."

That was the signal for me to work him over in earnest. I inserted a second finger that he fought against until it hit his pleasure button then he relaxed and I sucked his brains out. He screamed, "Don't say I didn't warn you" just before he blasted a salty load against the back of my throat. I swallowed as fast as I could but he just kept shooting, his ass contracting around my fingers.

Finally, he collapsed into the sling, wrung out, as I extracted my fingers from his hole and took my mouth reluctantly from his cock which was now at half-mast.

"You fuckin' swallowed?" He sounded surprised. "Oh man, that is so hot."

Obviously, Heather's taste didn't extend to man sauce.

I waited, expecting some sort of outburst about the liberties I'd taken.

"And you sucked my pits. No one has ever done that before." There was a sense of amazement in his voice. He watched as I wet a cloth, the dungeon had all the mod cons such as a sink and hot and cold running water, to clean his cock and his ass that was slimy with lubrication.

I could tell he was enjoying the attention and if this were anything other than gay sex in a dungeon, he'd be laying back, an arm behind his head smoking as if this worship was his due.

He nodded at my obvious arousal. "It looks like you could sure use some attention yourself."

Until that moment it hadn't occurred to me I was still dressed, my cock poking against my shorts in an attempt to attract my attention.

"I dunno," he continued, "but you could probably force me to suck your cock. It looks like it needs it."

"And have you rip it off with your teeth," I laughed. Sorely tempted as I was, I was nobody's fool.

Joe thought it over for a moment. "I guess you'd probably threaten me with dismemberment and a burial underneath your floor boards if I was stupid enough to try anything like that while you've got me at your mercy."

"I guess I probably would," I agreed as I shucked off my shirt and shorts, my cock eager for a good blow job although how good Joe would be on his first try was anyone's guess. As it transpired, he was pretty damn good. Against my Dom nature, I was gentle with him. There was no force involved for as soon as I approached, his head slid over the edge of the sling and he opened his mouth. I would have loved nothing more than to skull fuck the pretty straight boy, coat his throat with spunk and throw him out in the street, but I was getting to like the guy. In fact, I was even cooing softly, telling him how to improve his technique as if this was going to happen again.

You know the funny part? He actually started to do as I instructed so that by the time I was ready to come he was taking it farther down his throat. He was no expert but he wasn't a novice any more either. This guy had real potential. As much as I wanted to make the guy a cocksucking whore, I really wanted to plug his ass, but I guessed that was a step too far.

As I was close to coming, I pulled my cock out of his mouth and beat his face with the spit covered shaft. He opened his mouth in an attempt to capture it again to continue his oral technique.

"Let's give this place a bit of ambience," I said as I closed the door and pulled the blinds down on the windows. I alleviated the gloom with a shaded lamp in the corner which gave off an eerie red glow.

"Better?" I asked.

"Makes me nervous about what you're gonna force me to do next," he said without a hint of nervousness to his voice.

"What do you think I'm gonna do, fucker," I snarled at him.

His cock twitched to life when I spoke to him in that fashion.

"Please don't hurt me," he begged in the least sincere tone I'd ever heard. "Please don't rape my virgin ass. Please."

So that's what he wanted. I smiled, only too happy to oblige. But I wanted to tease him first.

"And get my head beaten in. I'd have to be insane to chance that," I said.

"I might be tempted to beat the shit out of you for raping my ass with that big cock of yours..."

Might?

"Except for the fact you'd probably film it on the camera in your mobile phone and threaten to put it on the net for my mates to see if I laid a hand on you."

He had it all worked out. I wondered at his ability to justify his deflowering in his own mind.

I picked up the lube and greased my fingers, plunging them straight into his ass without any preliminaries. It was only two fingers but he bucked with the pain of the sudden invasion. I slowed down after the initial assault to allow him time to relax, to get used to the fullness in his ass. His initial snorts of pain gave way to slow, heavy breaths that belied his excitement.

By adding a third finger, increasing the thrust into his butthole, he was soon loose enough for me to get my cock inside. I ran the head of my prick up and down his ass crack, stopping at the puckered entrance that was slimy with lubrication.

"I wanted to fuck your hot, straight ass from the moment I saw you, straight boy," I spat, tugging his dick swollen with blood and excitement, before slamming into his guts. It winded him momentarily but I wasn't about to wait for him to recover. I buggered his ass like a man starving for sex and this was the last butt on earth. I pistoned into him, forcing the sling back on its chains, screwing my face up with the intensity of the fuck, feeling nothing but his hot, wet ass clutching my prick as it invaded virgin territory. His oomphs of discomfort slowly gave way to his thrusting backwards as best he could to sink his ass against my cock, forcing me inside him as deep as I could go.

"You like my cock inside your straight boycunt, fucker? You like what I'm doing to you? Making you my slut? Tell me you like it boy."

I pinched his nipples as I leaned in to kiss him. That was a step too far and he turned his face away. I saw red, grabbed his face in one hand, forcing him to face front, squeezing his cheeks.

"You look at me when I'm fucking you, boy. Don't turn away from me you cocksucking piece of trash." I spat in his face, rewarded with a groan.

"Tell me you want my cock in your boy pussy. Tell me!" I shouted at him.

"Yeah, I want you to fuck me till I can't stand up."

"You like that? You like cock in your ass?"

"I fuckin' love it," he cried out, thrashing his head from side to side. "Holy shit. This is the best fuck I ever had."

I was so close to climax but I wanted him to come with me. I stroked his cock, hoping it would squirt about the same time I did.

"Oh God, I'm so close," he sobbed. "It's so fuckin' good, I can't stand it."

"Come for me, baby. Let me see how much you like it."

I slowed down as I pounded his prick. I felt the clutch in his balls and then his spunk gushed out in long spurts, hitting his chest and his chin. I leaned over to lick it up as I grunted; pushing my dick into him as far as it would go and spewed out enough cream to fill his ass to overflowing. I howled like a banshee which is probably why neither of us heard the door to the dungeon open until light flooded in and a female voice screamed, "What the fuck is going on here?"

"I thought that would have been quite obvious," a deep masculine voice chuckled.

"Dad? Heather?"

"I think we should leave," I heard Peter mutter as my eyes adjusted and I saw the shadows of two elderly people escape quickly through the door, followed by a figure who spat out, "You bastard!" as his exit line.

Now came the awkward part. Heather raised the blinds to reveal me and Joe in all our glory. I was wedged up his ass, his cock was rapidly deflating while his chest was a pool of his own cum, and I had the remains of his semen around my mouth.

Heather turned on me. "You fuckin' pervert. You raped my boyfriend. Handcuffed him in this pervert machine and raped him. I'm fuckin' calling the police."

She snapped open her mobile but had trouble focusing because of her anger. I saw Joe's dad give him a look and stand ready to snatch the phone out of her hands.

"Heather," Joe said quietly. When it had no effect, he shouted. "Heather! Put the phone down."

She dropped it and Joe's dad scooped it up. We all turned our attention to Joe. He extracted his hands from the cuffs, a little too easily for my liking, he'd been faking the extent of his restraint. When he attempted clumsily to sit up in the sling, my cock popped out of his ass, followed by a small stream of my cum. Not the best position for a girl to see her boyfriend in.

"You devious bastard," I laughed.

"What's he mean?" Heather looked confused.

"Why don't I take you out for a meal and a drink or two and explain it to you?" Joe's dad said.

"Okay," she said, a little unsurely.

She turned to look at Joe. "Honey?"

"Don't wait up tonight," he smiled a little unkindly.

Joe's dad put his arm around Heather, ushering her out of the dungeon but, before he disappeared, he winked at both of us.

"Dad?" Joe said, his whole body slouched in helplessness.

"It's fine son. I've watched you struggle with it for years now. Glad it's all out in the open." Turning to me, he said. "You take real good care of him."

"I will," I replied then turned back to the handsomest man I had ever known. He was grinning fit to burst.

"I feel so cheap, so used," I mocked.

We both roared.

"You wanna go after your boyfriend?" Joe asked.

I knew I should. "Nah." Joe looked relieved. "I feel such a huge sense of relief. It wasn't the kindest way to tell Pete it's over..."

"No, me either with Heather." He shook his head. "Though I wasn't expecting her to turn up here."

I scooped the bottle of lube off the floor and handed it to him. "Besides, you have some catching up to do." He was more than eager to give me some of my own medicine.

OMG!
*S*ANTA'S *G*OT *A* *S*IX-PACK!

"*I*'ve been watching you. You're really wonderful with children."

Holy Bat toast with Robin jam. Mr Perfect is talking to me!

I snapped my lips together knowing that if I opened my mouth, I would make a total fool of myself. See above reaction. My mouth always engaged before my brain even woke up to what it was saying. 'Juvenile' is the word most of my boyfriends used to describe my childish reaction to everything around me. I say boyfriends but most of them didn't hang around longer than the two-and-a-half minutes it took them to blow up my ass.

Those that did last longer usually ended up braying, "When are you gonna grow up?" before making their exit, inevitably after a break-up fuck.

But it's not me you want to read about, is it? If I'd called the story of my life *Santa's got a Skinny Butt*, you wouldn't even have put it on your Wish List let alone bought it. So let's get to the selling point: Mr

Perfect. Not his real name. I guess you've already sussed that out for yourself. No one's ever accused me of being the brightest bulb in the ceiling.

He looks very patrician. At least I thought so. I was going to call him Patricia, but that seemed a bit insulting somehow. So I settled for Mr Perfect because he looked like my comic book superhero of the same name. But I'm getting ahead of myself.

You see, me and Thelma have names for all the people who line up with their children. Helps pass the time. Usually it's some tic or habit or facial feature we zone in on and then we give them a moniker like the villains in Dick Tracy. We even had a Pruneface. Not that he looked like a prune in this case, it's just his tone and personality gave us the shits. He was the sort of character who spoke in capital letters.

He attracted our attention by snapping his fingers at us, "You There! My Child Has Been Waiting Absolutely Ages To See Santa. How Long Will It Take?" His attitude got him the animosity of the people in front of him in the line and the sympathy of those behind him, except for Mr Perfect who gave me a sympathetic smile.

Pruneface's daughter clutched his trousers, trying to hide among the pin-stripes, obviously terrified of meeting the jolly fat man in the red suit, but he'd missed that salient point.

"I Can't Afford To Waste My Time With This Nonsense. I Have Important Meetings To Attend," he added.

Keeping my voice level, although I would have dearly loved to shout at him, I told him, "It's not all about you, sir, it's about the children. If you can't spare the time now, then may I suggest you come back at a time more convenient to yourself when you will be able to wait your turn again."

A few people snickered; a few others gave me what I like to think were grins of appreciation.

See what I mean, though? I can't help myself.

Thelma's the same, but much older. She must be close to a million years old but she says she's closer to fifty-five. I think she's injecting monkey glands because she knows so much stuff, she has to be way older, or else she's somehow transplanted Google into her head instead of a brain.

There I go again. You'd never know I was nineteen and studying to be a graphic artist. Ultimate aim? To rule the universe! I say that but it's not true. I'm not the ruler type. More the set square or compass. *LOL* Maybe not. Real ultimate aim, not fooling around? To draw the best comic book ever. That's the ultimate dream, but I won't be too unhappy if I end up drawing the best comic I can.

It's a bit personal. At the moment, I'm doing it for myself, not for publication. See, I'm just starting out, so it's practice. I showed it to Thel and she said I was 'really talented.' She's just being nice. She did say, though, that Mr Perfect is not a real good name for a superhero and that if her hubby had been as packed in the underpants department as my cartoon Mr

Perfect she never would've left him. I stopped showing her after that. She knows I'm gay, I'm not ashamed or embarrassed by that, but I was scared she might think I was an unsuitable candidate for this job.

Both Thel and me are elves. Not real elves. All we get to wear is the hat and booties. Green felt rubbish that makes my hair hot. The real elves get to wear the total green outfit which is even bigger rubbish. But they get more money and have to stay in character all day. They tried me out on that but I was as crap as their costume. They thought my sense of humor was better served looking after the kiddies while they lined up to sit on Santa's knee. Our job is to keep them in line so they don't get too noisy or rambunctious, entertaining them with simple party tricks or jokes while they wait their turn. Parents seem to appreciate it.

So do the Santas. There are a half dozen of them because no one could stand the racket or the unruly behavior for eight hours without a lot of breaks. It's hot and tiring work and sometimes a Santa gets a bit emotional. Or drunk. Then management will dismiss him and find a replacement. A couple of them want me to sit on their laps – when they're naked. I'm polite. It's Mr Perfect I want sliding down my chimney. Actually, up my chimney.

That's enough background. You're probably eager to get back to Mr P. who's still waiting for some sort of response from me whose jaw has dropped to the floor in cartoon surprise at being addressed. Without thinking, I bend down to mime picking it up. He looked at me kinda strange.

"What are you doing?" he asked.

"Picking up my jaw," I said.

At least he laughed. "You're a queer one."

"Queer as in 'oddball' or queer as in 'gay'? Or both. And is it a bad thing?"

Yep, I did say it out loud. I squeezed my eyes shut and screwed up my face at my stupidity, waiting for him to call my supervisor to complain.

Instead, he introduced me to the young boy who clutched his hand timidly. "This is Damien, he's here to see Santa."

"Hello, Damien." I shook hands with the little fellow who seemed delighted that an adult was treating him with all seriousness.

I turned back to Mr P. "You haven't answered my question."

Mr P. did not have a chance right then because a young boy tugged at his coat and in a most severe manner as only a six-year-old can, said, "Mister, bugger off, he was telling us a joke and he hasn't finished."

Apologizing profusely to the young audience, Mr P. backed off, smiling broadly at the reprimand. Just before I got back to the joke which required all my skills mimicking various woodland animals, Mr P. whispered, "I liked the way you handled Pruneface. Well done."

I couldn't believe it; he nicknamed him Pruneface as well.

You ever get a buzz so powerful you seem to float through the day? Without drugs, I mean. Everything goes so right it's the moment you want to last forever. Or else, you just want to die then and there because life will never get any better. That moment was mine.

After work, when I got back to my bedsit, it looked like a palace not the cockroach infested dump it really was. The vermin became horses carting me off to the ball where I'd dance with the handsome prince and...

I grabbed my draft paper and my pencils; the work flowing out of me like my body was a conduit to that big library of ideas in the sky. I was so happy, I forgot to eat, almost forgetting to sleep until fatigue overtook me and my head flopped onto my drawing board.

I would have probably remained in that position all night except the knock to my head woke me enough that I staggered to bed. I was so tired I slept in the next morning and was almost late for work. No time for breakfast, I just grabbed my sketches and ran down the stairs. I got through store security and was at my locker with five minutes to spare, enough time to ram the stupid hat on my head so I looked like a stick of asparagus, but not enough to grab a muffin from the canteen.

You might wonder why I'd want a job like this. Well, I actually enjoyed entertaining the kids. They could be little brats, sure, but I identified with their wide-eyed wonder at a world still full of possibilities. Too many of them would grow into the Prunefaces of the future. If I could help just one or two of them avoid that fate. I think the word you're looking for is 'naïve.' Hell, I've been called worse.

The main reason for liking this job is that I don't have to scrub the stink of fried fat off my clothes and my body and out of my hair when I get home at night like I do the other ten months of the year to pay for my tuition and my rent and my paper and ink and pencils. It's great there are fast food outlets that employ young guys like me, dreamers I mean, otherwise I don't know what I'd do.

It's not like my parents would or could help me out financially. I put 'would' first because dad wanted me to work on the roads like him. "Good solid, dependable work, boy," he often told me as I was growing up, there's those words again, floundering about searching for something I wanted to do. "It's not all about you, you know," was his favorite expression. I guess that's why I used it on Pruneface.

Dad would then say something like, "Dreams are all very well in the bedroom late at night, but best to leave them there when you wake up to the real world in the morning. What you need is something dependable. Something that will pay the bills and put the food on the table."

When he said that, I'd think about what was in the fridge: cheap cuts of meat on the turn so they'd inevitably be cut up and disguised in stews, vegetables so flaccid and pock-marked it was a wonder mum could cut enough nutrition from around the spoiled bits to make them worthwhile, and, let's not forget his beer.

Food was a necessary evil to dad. He hated spending money on it. And his ill-fitting dentures didn't help the cause of better dietary habits either. Most of his food was mushy because it hurt him to chew. Beer was an entirely different matter. He was praying for the day nutritionists declared it a 'food.' Until then, he had to have the best. Well, why not? You don't have to chew beer.

It wasn't until I left home that I realized what a bang-up job mum did with the little she had. Still, it came as a bit of a shock to discover that food actually had taste, individual tastes, not just some glutinous generic taste of mush.

Oh, hell. I'm rabbiting on about me again, aren't I? Where was I? That's it, almost late for work because...never mind, you've read that bit already. I raced into Santa's Cave to stand beside Thel as security counted down to opening time. There was always an initial rush of parents and offspring, mums and dads not averse to using a bit of elbow power to get to the front of the queue.

Our attempts at crowd control were always short lived. The best we could do was attempt to funnel the enthusiasm, I would have called it the melee if I'd been honest, away from the adult shoppers who were buying exorbitantly expensive decorations, wrapping paper, and the other bib bobs that go with the holiday season, at the counters adjacent to Santa's Cave.

I wasn't going home for Christmas this year. Mum and dad didn't need me freeloading and it's not like we were all that close anyway. Not since they'd found certain drawings of mine which revealed it was as unlikely I'd ever settle down and marry that nice Kylie girl from down the road as it was I'd end up with a job on the roads. As a result there was a minimum of fuss when I declared my intention of moving to the city to study graphic arts for a career in advertising, apart from dad declaring that "No good will come of it, you mark my words," and a slight moistening of the eyes when mum came to see me off at the station.

I sent gifts and received a card from mum with a ten dollar note inside plus instructions to 'buy yourself something nice.' I loved my parents; I just didn't want to be them. So, even though my stomach rumbled its rebellion as I marshaled kids like sheep to the Santa, I was happy. Okay, my bed-sit was crap, I had a lousy paid job, but I still, with pretty strict economizing, had time and a little cash to do what I loved – drawing. And the absolute blue icing on a green cake: I'd met my model for Mr Perfect which is why I was so bloody tired and hungry right at this moment.

My head rang with the shrieks and screams of young children demanding rewards from Santa for being good for the whole year. It really was the wrong way to go about it. I never believed you should bribe children into good behavior. What did I know? I would never have any of my own.

My stomach gave a volcanic rumble, enough to startle the kids standing near me, bringing to mind the old adage that breakfast is the most important meal of the day, and therefore I should not have been surprised when I could scarcely concentrate on what I was doing. One minute I was turning my hunger grumblings into a creature attempting to claw its way out of my belly to the delight of my young audience as well as the stunned disbelief of some of the more staid parents, the next I was lying on my ass among the plastic bunting that surrounded Santa's Castle, a young worried face hovering over me, asking, "Mister, are you all right?"

Holy Batcrap, I must have fainted.

Parents pulled their children away lest I have some contagious disease before Thel was kneeling beside me, her face a mask of concern. "Are you all right, love?"

I didn't have time to answer before an authoritative voice broke through the confusion. "Stand aside please, I'm a doctor."

"I don't need a doctor," I whined, until I saw who the voice belonged to. Mr Perfect kneeled beside me, placing the palm of his hand on my forehead. Mmm, maybe I did just need to lie here like Sleeping Beauty waiting for my prince to kiss me better.

"I just didn't have any breakfast," I hissed at him. "I'm fine."

I didn't want to attract an audience as it might mean my job.

"If you're a doctor, where's your scalpel?" one smart little girl asked.

"I can see you're going to be a detective when you grow up," Mr Perfect smiled at her. "You don't miss anything, do you?"

She beamed at the praise. He leaned into the crowd of children and said in a stage whisper, "I didn't want to scare the patient, but his condition is serious. If I don't operate soon, the monster in his stomach will eat its way out and then we're all doomed."

His audience giggled nervously as Mr P. swept me up in his arms and carried me toward the staff canteen like a prince carrying off his princess. I knew I would never feel like this again as long as I lived so I breathed in, storing his masculine aroma mixed with soap and a citrus after shave for later fantasies. Surreptitiously I snuggled against his chest, wondering what mountain they'd carved him from.

Kicking open the canteen door marked STAFF ONLY, he carried me to an empty table and poured me into one of the chairs. He seemed as reluctant to let me go as I was to leave the safety of his brawny arms.

"Sit!" he commanded as the few late morning shift personnel sipping their heart starting beverages of choice stared open mouthed at my superhero striding to the counter to order my breakfast. None of the soggy Bain Marie slush for him. He demanded freshly made eggs and sausage and when the cook went to refuse, he kept his tone quiet which was infinitely more authoritative than if he'd shouted.

Brad Levard, the floor manager, strode in, making a beeline in my direction, his face so thunderous I imagined lightning strikes emanating from his head. "What sort of shit are you pulling?" He'd never liked me since I'd ignored his very obvious attempt to hit on me the day I began work on his floor. Mistakenly, I'd believed his feelings would be less hurt if I'd ignored him instead of giving him the brush off or a polite refusal. My belief was wrong.

I jumped up as he approached my table, earning a stern rebuke from the canteen counter. I was commanded, "Sit!" Mr P. intercepted Levard before he even reached me, holding out his hand in a warm greeting. Peering at his name tag, he said, "Mr Levard...Brad. I'm Dr Crichton. Fortunately, I was in the store shopping when this young man collapsed. I know an organization such as yours would not want any fuss so I brought him in here." Placing his arm across Levard's shoulder in a comradely gesture, Mr P. steered him away from me as Curried Pearl delivered my breakfast with a flourish. We called her that because she always smelled of whatever was on the lunch menu. Usually curry. She gave me a wink and a nudge, adding "He's a real keeper that one, eh?"

I must have blushed because she went back to the till cackling like a hen about to lay the golden egg.

Mr P. spoke confidentially to Levard, but loudly enough that I could make out what he was saying. "You know how litigious people are these days and I thought it prudent to short circuit that possibility, that's why I brought him in here out of the public gaze. You don't want Health and Safety throwing their weight around."

"Quite right, Dr Crichton. The management appreciates your diligence."

"If I may make a suggestion..."

I wanted to make a suggestion myself. Get your arm away from Levard, who seemed to be enjoying the intimacy far too much for my liking, and put it around me.

Please.

"Suggest away," Levard replied with just a hint of flirtation, obviously hoping the suggestion might include the chance of getting to know the doctor a little better.

"The young chap's blood sugar seems to be abnormally low which is why I took the liberty of ordering him a few carbs to get it back up to within normal range..."

"Very good idea," Levard clucked as if he knew fuck all about medicine.

"I think if he may be permitted to stay off the floor for about half an hour to recoup his strength—"

Levard drew breath to reply, but Mr P. added quickly, "I know, I know what you are about to say. It's a very busy period for you and the young lad is one of your very best workers..."

I almost choked. My superpowers don't include the ability to read thoughts but I can absolutely guarantee that my being a good worker didn't feature anywhere in Levard's mind.

The floor manager was vacillating in his concern.

Mr P. easily persuaded him back on side. "I'll tell you what. I'll stay here with the lad until he's fit to return to work and then I'll come to your office, with your permission of course, and give you a full debrief. If you like, I could pop in each day and, if you have time from your very busy schedule, we could perhaps have a coffee and discuss his progress."

Oh, Happy Homos, Robin. I'll get to see him every day. I wonder does that include weekends.

He was laying it on a bit thick. I wasn't sure Levard would fall for it, but a manly squeeze of his shoulders and the floor manager capitulated.

"That sounds like an excellent solution to me. I'll be in my office when you're through here."

Said the spider to the fly.

Levard gave me a cheery wave as he left the canteen, while Mr P. slid into a chair opposite me. I held out my hand. He looked at me, his handsome features screwed up with confusion.

"Well, Dr Crichton, aren't you going to take my pulse?"

Discover for yourself, it's racing.

He laughed. "I'm not a doctor."

There goes my chance to impress the parents by marrying a medico.

"No shit, Sherlock," I said. It came out a bit snarkier than I intended. "Look, I'd better get back to work; Thel can't handle all those kids on her own."

"You stay right where you are."

He was so authoritative, I got hard.

"If I have to put up with half an hour of that slimy Levard then the least you can do is make it up to me by having breakfast with me first."

"And that would make it all worthwhile?"

"Oh, yes. Very worthwhile."

Shiver me timbers and call me Shirley, I do believe the man is flirting with me.

"What are you doing this weekend?" The smile that accompanied his question made me lose my sense of decorum.

"Why? Are you asking me out on a date?"

"I've never asked a man out on a date before."

Don't say it, Kaz.

But I did. "Why not?"

"You want me to ask you out on a date?"

Is the sky blue? Does bacon on a string pass straight through a goose?

"It would sure do wonders for my image."

"Not sure what it would do for mine."

Ouch.

At least he was still smiling.

"But seriously, what are you doing on the weekend?"

"I was serious," I muttered to myself, but the look of surprise on his face suggested he just might have heard me. If he did, he let it pass.

"I'd like to make you a proposition. I'll make it worth your while."

I was taken aback. "When people proposition me, money is usually not involved, unless it's taxi fare home."

He seemed genuinely perplexed, and then blushed to the roots of his hair. "What? Oh god, no. Sorry, don't misunderstand me. I am an awkward klutz sometimes. Not that sort of proposition. I mean a real job." He looked at the expression on my face. "I've just made it worse, haven't I?"

I nodded my head, my feelings fighting for space among my toes in my elf boots.

He took a deep breath. "Hi, my name is Patric Charles Crichton, no k on the Patric. What can I say, my parents were pretentious. I'm thirty-three years old and I'm offering you employment at a children's Christmas party this coming weekend because I admire the way you handle the little bastards in large numbers."

Effective way to get me onside then offside in the same breath.

"No thanks," I said, turning my back on his attitude. "I'd better get back to work."

I'd only taken a few steps when he stopped me in my tracks with, "The job pays..." then mentioned a figure so high it took my breath away.

"Exactly who do I have to kill?" I asked.

His laugh echoed around the canteen, causing Curried Pearl to drop a metal tray which clanged to the tiled floor. Laughter was not exactly an everyday occurrence among the nondescript plates and cutlery and the warmed up remnants of what once passed as edible sustenance.

"You obviously don't know your own worth," he said. "That's the going rate for what I'm asking you to do."

I swallowed, both the lump in my throat and my pride. "Upper or lower end of the going rate?"

"It's about the middle."

"What do I have to do?"

"A car will call for you on Saturday morning, bring you to the party where you'll entertain about two dozen kids from mid-afternoon until the early evening, that's when Santa will arrive. You just have to help him cope with the crowds. Then you can join us for dinner and stay the night, take advantage of the facilities, and a car will take you back home the next day. Or, if you wish, the car can take you back after your job is finished on Saturday night."

"And there's no surrendering of body parts to keep alive an ageing patriarch or the slow extraction of all my blood?"

"Now there's a thought," he said.

I didn't want this job under false pretenses. "You must know it would take me six weeks to earn that sort of money here."

"That's because your skills are under-valued."

"Or other people are taking advantage of your gullible nature," I suggested. "I'll tell you what, I'll do it for half what you're offering, and we'll call it a deal. That's how much it's really worth."

"I can afford to pay you," he said, puzzled by my attitude.

"No, we'll do it my way or not at all."

"All right, we'll do it your way."

He got me to jot down my address, suggesting a time that I should be ready, although I immediately wished I had suggested making my own way or having the car pick me up on the corner somewhere far away from my depressed neighborhood.

I felt that even more keenly when the following Saturday a limo arrived. I heard a vehicle pull up in an area that usually rang to the sound of clapped-out bombs that wheezed down the road at snail's pace held together with hope and the leftovers of last year's pay packet, or else rocked to the beat of loud techno music as they boasted their alpha superiority by performing wheelies, leaving a wake of smoke and particulate rubber on the asphalt. I thought Patric, Mr P., might call personally but he obviously had a party to organize.

Calling to the driver from my window, I told him to wait, I would be right down. That was no lie as I'd

been up and ready since daybreak, nervous as the
Bride of Frankenstein before she met her mate. I
feared, too, that if the driver strayed too far from his
vehicle we might turn up at the party in transport
minus its hub caps. They were an official currency in
these parts.

The trip itself was uneventful, taking a little over
an hour to the outskirts of the city where a large
Victorian mansion awaited my presence. It was just
dilapidated enough that I found it fascinating, full of
character, and an ideal model for the villa I was having
problems with in my Mr Perfect comic. I was pleased
with my prescience in bringing paper and art
materials. Perhaps Patric would let me sketch him,
provided his wife didn't mind. I was under no illusions
in that department. I knew I was here to entertain
Damien and his friends and that there were no sexual
overtones connected with my visit.

I could live with that. I'd take the cash and run,
after doing my darnedest to make the Christmas party
the best I could. Mr P. came out to meet the car when
it pulled up on the gravel driveway outside the main
weathered wooden door that had all the cracked and
flaky majesty of an ageing diva.

He was all smiles. "Welcome, glad you could make
it."

His greeting puzzled me. "You sent a car. Were
you expecting it to break down on the way?"

"No, sorry. You'll have to forgive me if I'm a little
distracted. Here, let me carry your bags up to your

room." He picked up my canvas bags, straining to lift the larger of the two. "What have you got in here? An elephant?"

"I never travel anywhere without all the necessaries. Sorry, it's heavy."

Once he'd shown me into the vast tiled foyer and closed the front door, plunging us into the gloom of dark wood paneling and heavy velvet curtains so redolent of Victorian fussiness I expected to see maids and manservants bustling about to keep the mansion functioning, he put the bag down.

"Listen, there's something I must tell you about this afternoon. But not here. Come with me."

Wanting nothing better than to open the curtains and windows to let in light and air, I knew my place, following him down the corridor like the governess in Henry James's ghost story, *The Turn of the Screw*. Melodramatic? Certainly, but with that ounce of truth as Mr P. explained once we were in the book-lined library. I refrained from that old cliché, "Have you read all these?", because the leather bindings revealed they were inherited rather than purchased recently. I was pleased to see a few books on an antique side table alongside a comfortable old grandfather of an armchair situated beneath a reading lamp.

He hesitated between the armchair and the more modern chrome and leather seat behind his desk. Professionalism won over friendliness and he sat behind the large wooden desk, reinforcing the gap between us. I took a seat situated conveniently to give Mr P. dominance. As it was on wheels, I moved it so that he had to turn to address me. He was irritated at my impertinence but, what the hell, I wasn't here to play games. Well, not with him anyway.

Whether he was wrestling with what he wanted to say or whether he was attempting to control his temper at my temerity I could not tell, but the silence became uncomfortable. I had examined the bookshelves a number of times from my seat and was about to start on the ceiling when he finally spoke.

"I may have lured you here under false pretenses," he said at last.

I certainly hope so. And, yes, I will marry you.

He obviously didn't hear my thoughts because he continued in a totally irrelevant vein.

"To put it frankly, Damien is not exactly the most popular pea in the pod."

He seemed relieved to have unburdened himself of that piece of news. I did wonder, though, how the kid could possibly have inherited a charisma bypass with Mr P. as his dad.

"The other children tolerate him because their parents tell them to. He's even more morose this year because his mother is away on assignment and won't be coming home for the celebration although she's managed to organize a hook-up from wherever it is in the world she is."

My look of surprise must have galvanized him into explaining further.

"Sorry. There's no reason you would know his mother is Endive Veroche."

My mouth dropped open in surprise. And admiration. Mr P. was married to the most important war photographer of the modern age? I was stunned. Everyone knew her work. I understood now, too, why Mr P. and Damien may not know the exact location of their nearest and dearest. She worked undercover, never embedded with allied troops because, she maintained, they just fed her bullshit. She preferred to branch out on her own recording the day-to-day atrocities of a war zone. She was probably on the hit list of both sides.

"I'm impressed," I managed to say.

"Well, Damien's not. Of course, he's too young to understand and he's becoming more and more withdrawn as the days go by, therefore alienating further those few acquaintances that he does have. So today's party is of the utmost importance if not to him, then to me. It has to turn around the other children's perceptions of him."

"Oh, good, make it easy for me," I said sarcastically. "Don't pile on the pressure."

"I don't expect miracles," he said.

"Not like raising someone from the dead, just a minor loaves-and-fishes style of rabbit-out-of-hat miracle."

"No, the party's catered."

I laughed at his little joke but failed to find anything about this situation amusing.

"I'll show you to your room. It's yours for as long as you stay. It may look as if the house should have a lot of servants but those days are long gone. There's a cook comes in to make breakfast and she's a stickler for punctuality. If you want a hot breakfast, you must be at table before 8am or it's leftovers for you. For today, there will be ample food catered, so just help yourself. By all means, set a plate aside in the refrigerator if you wish. Ah, here's your room."

He showed me into a magnificently furnished boudoir the bathroom of which would have contained my entire bedsit. "Oh, my," I sighed. "It's magnificent. I feel like Norma Shearer in *Marie Antoinette*. I love it."

He seemed surprised by my enthusiasm.

Hustling me out, he pointed out his room at the end of the hallway, before climbing up a flight of stairs to what looked as if it had once been servants' quarters although now converted into a nursery-cum-play area. "Of course, you have the run of the house and the grounds," he explained, "but as best you can keep the children away from the kitchen and the library. If you need anything, that's where you'll find me. Any questions?"

"What time is Santa arriving?"

"About 4 o'clock. See if you can get them to have a nap before he arrives. Their parents will pick them up around six."

I accompanied him downstairs to grab my bag and haul it to my room where I spilled the contents all over the bed in a flurry of activity. I had requested that Mr P. buy a few items to which he readily agreed and I took them up to the Secret Room as I renamed it and set about my preparations, occasionally popping back to my bedroom when I needed further inspiration.

I was in the middle of transforming the upstairs room when I heard a little voice behind me. "What are you doing?"

I turned to study the forlorn little figure. "I'm getting everything ready for your party."

"They don't like me, you know." Such a sad little boy, and only six years old. Time enough to be disappointed when you reach adulthood. Still, I wouldn't lie to him and hope that would make everything better.

"Then we'll just have to get them to change their minds, won't we?"

"How?"

He was inquisitive, so there was still hope.

"See that packet over there?" He nodded. "Can you write your name?"

"Of course." He was indignant that I would even doubt it for a moment.

"In that case, I want you to pick out one of the T-shirts in the packet, they're all the same, and then I want you to write your name in really big letters on the front and the back. Think you can do that?"

I handed him a black marker pen, watching as he chose his shirt carefully then sat on the floor, his tongue poking out of the corner of his mouth in concentration as he laboriously wrote his name. When he completed the task, he held it up proudly.

"Good boy. Now hand me the shirt and you take a seat just over there and try not to move for a few minutes. Got that?"

"I'm not stupid," he admonished me.

"Sorry," I said.

He took a seat looking very stern. I searched his face for traces of Mr P., but could see none. He must take after his mother. With a few quick strokes of the pen, I had drawn his likeness, holding it up for his approval.

"Is that me?" he asked.

"Uh huh. Try it on and go and have a look at yourself in the mirror over there."

I helped him pull the T-shirt over his head; it was adult sized so it fitted him like a smock, which was my intention. He stood admiring himself and his drawn likeness for an age, and then he said, "Cool. Can I keep it?"

"It's all yours. But take it off now because you'll need it for the party."

I helped him when he struggled to remove it by himself. He folded it, placing it over a chair.

"Can I help?" he asked, coming back to my side, definitely more involved now.

"Of course, I'd like that."

The preparation time rushed by so that I was still putting the finishing touches to everything when I heard the first cars arrive. The playroom overlooked the front of the house and we could hear none-too-excited voices complaining they didn't want to be here, begging to be taken home. I marveled at Damien's equanimity under such a barrage of negativity and attempted to save what little of his dignity remained by talking loudly enough to drown out their voices.

"It's all right," he said. "I know."

"Time to put your special shirt on. And I'll put mine on as well." Mine had a caricature of me, my features much more exaggerated than Damien's; his was as lifelike a portrait as I could make it.

I took his hand as we went downstairs to greet the guests, feeling the tension in his grip. The parents put on a brave face as they deposited their unwilling offspring. Mr P. must have heard the hubbub because he made a special guest appearance greeting the mainly mothers by first name, some of them flirting openly with him. A few asked after his wife, Endive, they and their children scrupulously avoiding Damien until one little girl pointed at his T-shirt of which he'd become inordinately proud and said sarcastically, "What is that you're wearing?"

The other boys and girls, busy until then playing games or texting on their mobile phones, looked up.

The parents all turned to stare at Damien. Mr P. looked to me for an answer.

"That's part of this afternoon's activities," I said. "Part of the games."

Some of the parents gave me a sympathetic smirk, while others smoothed out party dresses that cost more than a week's wages for me, or attempted to pat down unruly hair on the boys. The children were all between five and seven but it was the males who looked most unhappy to be there. This group was going to take some winning over, something Mr P. must have realized as he bid goodbye to the parents and fled back to the safety of the library.

When I was finally alone with the kids, I corralled them upstairs to wait outside the door to the playroom upon which I'd taped a very large sign dominated by a rough illustration of children having old-fashioned fun. No sooner had we reached the door than some of the guests recommenced playing with their mobiles.

"Right," I said to gain everyone's attention. "From this point on, all phones off!"

"What if we don't want to?" one little boy piped up.

"Let me see," I said in my most cordial manner. "You're all grown-ups here, so I'll treat you like grown-ups." A few chests thrust out in pride. "You make your own decision about your phones. If you want to come inside and play, then turn your phones off and then seal it in one of those envelopes after you write your name on it. Otherwise, you can sit out here or down in the foyer and wait for your parents to come and pick you up. Right?"

"What's inside?" one of the girls asked.

"Games," I said.

"Computer games?"

"No, old-fashioned games. Come on, who's coming in?"

Three of the boys shrugged, switched off, then sealed the phones in one of the envelopes each. As instructed, Damien led them into the room, instructing them to write their names on a T-shirt. He closed the door behind him.

"Anyone else?"

One of the girls stepped forward but her best friend stamped her foot impatiently and squealed, "Debbie!"

But Debbie was not for turning and I soon let her into the room to join the very small party indeed. There were twenty in all, including Damien, and so far, only five were inside. I had taken a calculated risk but I knew I had to separate the guests from their electronic distractions. Don't get me wrong, I have no beef with modern technology when it's used for good but when it becomes an anti-social device, then look-out kids!

It took a further twenty minutes after I closed the door on the hold-outs before they all ventured inside lured no doubt by the gales of genuine laughter from those favored few inside. They came in dribs and drabs, the final hold-out, not unexpectedly, being the rude little girl from the initial meeting at the front door. She sulked into the room and rather than make a big fuss I spirited her straight over to the T-shirts and got her to write her name then sketched the most flattering portrait I could. She baulked at wearing it as her mother had obviously gone to a lot of expense to doll her up, but when I insisted she would have to go back outside, she relented begrudgingly. She soon overcame her snit, fortunately, and joined right in.

The T-shirts served a two-fold purpose: to keep the children's good clothes from getting soiled and to give me a reminder of their name.

The games we played were fairly conventional but their newness to these children was such that they enjoyed them out of all proportion to their origins. Once they were exhausted from all their screaming and running about inside, I took them outdoors, still without their phones, in order to explore the lawns and gardens for insects and bugs from which I wove a fantasy story about fairies who lived among the flowers and elf princes who rode snails like wild water buffalo and which I illustrated on my giant draft-paper pad.

It was an absolute joy to see the kids getting their hands dirty. I marched them off to the bathroom to wash up when catering arrived. We set up trestle tables on the lawn and gave the children blankets to lay about on in the shade because the sun was scorching hot that summer. Mr P. joined us for the food which I'd insisted be healthy with a minimum of sweet, sugary biscuits and lollies. To deflect any young complaints, I'd had each of the children pick a flower or leaf from the garden, telling them that the caterers would cook it up in the big kitchen inside and bring it out for all to share.

Admittedly, there was a degree of scepticism when a rose petal re-emerged as tomato flans, and a cicada shell transformed into vol-au-vents, dandelions into small quiches, but they ate them anyway. The caterers boxed up each child's garden choice with a couple of examples of what it had transformed into to take home with them along with a piece of the delicious tiramisu birthday cake.

Mr P. sang louder than all of us when the cake appeared with its six bright sparklers instead of candles, the partygoers oohing their wonder. I told Damien to blow them out when I judged they'd just about sparkled themselves to death, and he made his wish, screwing his eyes up tightly. Then he ran back to join a group who welcomed him with a warmth that had been sadly lacking earlier in the day. Some of the girls sought him out to talk to him which was such a turn around that Mr P. looked at me as if I had some sort of magical powers.

"I knew I made the right choice," he said before heading back inside the house.

I regretted he didn't have more time for his son but many adults lack the patience for hours of exhausting game playing. After they had finished their snacks and their fruit juices it was time to head back inside for a nap. It would also give me a chance to recharge my batteries which were seriously in danger of running out of energy.

When the youngsters were all asleep, I crept out to make my way downstairs to the library where Mr P. was engrossed in paperwork when I tapped on the door and entered.

"Ah, Kaz," he said, pausing in the midst of an important pile of documents.

"They're all napping," I said by way of explanation.

"Any problems?" he asked.

"In the beginning. Nothing I couldn't handle though."

"Damien?"

"He seems to be having a ball. He's made a few friends. I think they might stick."

"That is a miracle in itself." He sat back in his chair. "I hope you'll do me the honor of joining me for dinner."

"Yes, I'd like that," I said.

"Good," he replied then went back to his paperwork signaling our little chat was over.

I went back to the play room and was soon as fast asleep as my charges only snapping out of it when I felt a small body jump on my chest. They would definitely be friskier after their sleep and I had to channel that energy or it would be the end of me. Seating them in a semi-circle, I had them call out their favorite animal, real or mythological, and then directed them to the large sheets of paper and paints, the other items I had asked Mr P. to buy, to draw the animal they'd named, explaining it should be a large picture so they could see it from the air. I thought they may have guessed they were drawing a design on what would become home-made kites, but they painted on blissfully unaware. When they finally twigged, there was a hush of disbelief that they could actually make their own playthings. They had only ever heard of store-bought toys.

With perseverance, and a lot of help from me, each child eventually created something approximating a kite, weird and wonderful though they were. It didn't matter whether they flew or not, it was the excitement of having created something themselves. In the event, they all flew even if only for a matter of seconds but no one minded as they were having too much fun running around the lawns dragging their kites behind them, making enough noise to be heard on the moon.

They were still at it when the limo came back with Santa seated regally in the back. Kites forgotten they ran after him until I managed to calm down their unruly behavior. Santa was a consummate professional, listening to each and every child's request, gently steering them away from impossible gift ideas, like the boy who wanted a real saber sword to chop up his teachers at school. He gave out a small gift to each of them after they'd solemnly sworn to him that they'd been good all year.

When he'd finished I took him down to the library where Mr P. had drinks and a little food waiting for him. I went out to the lawn to gather up the kites just as the cars started arriving to pick up the partygoers. I gave each child his or her kite plus their mobile as their parents arrived.

Damien stood proudly in the driveway saying his farewells to everyone while some of the guests bombarded their confused parents with requests that they invite Damien to their Christmas party because they'd had so much fun at his. A few of them looked at me suspiciously as if wondering what strange power I'd used on their child.

Not all of them would reciprocate, just enough that Damien would no longer be a pariah. One little girl even ran over to peck him on the cheek and although Damien made a big deal of wiping the kiss off with his sleeve there was no disguising his secret delight. I scooted him off to his bedroom after everyone had left in order that I could debrief with Mr P. but when I opened the library door, he was nowhere to be seen. Santa, still in costume, savoring an amber liquid topped with ice, waved me in.

"Sorry," I muttered. "I was looking for—"

"Come in, lad," he said. "Close the door. Mr Crichton said for you to wait for him in here. Care for a drink?"

"Uh, no thanks."

"I hear very good things about the way you handled the children before I arrived. They were very docile in comparison to some of the other groups I've had."

"Thanks," I said, warming to him.

"So what can old Santa bring you for Christmas? Is there something you want above all else?"

I snickered. If only Santa knew.

"That was a very dirty laugh, lad. Come on, spit it out!"

"As long as Santa won't be shocked," I said.

"Ha. Nothing shocks this old Santa. I've heard just about everything. If it's that shocking come and whisper it in my ear."

I found myself walking over to him. What the hell was I thinking?

"Park your butt here, young man," he said patting his knee.

I did it automatically as if I were a young child again.

"So tell me what it is you most desire in the world."

He looked so comforting I couldn't help myself.

"More than anything in the world, right now I want Mr P."

"Who's Mr P.?" he asked.

"Patric."

"Mr Crichton? Your boss?"

"Mmm."

"Why do you call him Mr P.?"

I explained about my comic hero, Mr Perfect, and how much I'd modeled him on Patric. I rambled on and on, hoping I wasn't embarrassing myself, but the old guy chuckled conspiratorially.

"Why don't you tell him?"

"He wouldn't be interested in me. A hot guy like that. I'm just a scrawny stick. He's smart..." I was going to go on and on about Patric's good points but I thought that was probably unwise.

"Is it his money you're after?"

"Has he got money? It can't be much; this old place is falling down round his ears. It's a lovely old house though."

"If it's not his money, you after an overnighter or for keeps?"

"For keeps would be nice."

"What if he doesn't do for keeps?"

"Then I'd settle for once. I can't stop thinking about what it would be like."

"Here, son, close your eyes, make a wish and put your hand in here."

I should have known. This guy was just another filthy old Santa turned on by having a young guy perched on his knee. Before I could stand up, Santa grabbed my hand and pulled it toward him, thrusting between the buttons on his jacket, through the rent in his fat suit. Okay so the guy wasn't as fat as he looked, big deal, he was still a sleaze.

I was surprised when my hand reached bare skin: hard, muscular flesh. I stopped struggling, running my fingers from the guy's muscular chest down over his hardening nipples to his abs. Oh my God! Santa's got a six-pack! But he hadn't finished with me yet, guiding my hand a little lower until it reached a very hard cock poking up toward his navel.

I withdrew my hand as if I'd been burned.

"What's the matter, you don't like?"

Santa was an old fraud. I pulled his beard off to reveal Mr P.'s laughing face.

"You bastard," I cursed. "That was a mean trick."

"It's only mean if Santa doesn't grant your wish."

I was still on his knee. He had an erection. I had an erection. What more did I need to think about? I grabbed Santa's face and planted the sloppiest, tonguiest kiss on his mouth that I could manage, while I unbuttoned his jacket to get my hands on those fabulous abs again.

It was fun playing with his muscles but I was after that jutting monster between his legs. I pulled down Santa's baggy trousers and palmed his cock which was already straining for release. He attempted to stand up to remove his pants totally but I pushed him back in his seat. I had enough leeway to suck his brains right out of his skull via his prick. That's how determined I was at that moment. I nuzzled his balls with my nose and lips, before working my way slowly up his shaft, thumbing his slit, admiring his large cut cock, happy to spend the night worshipping it.

Eager to taste him, I slid my lips over the crown, suctioning down as far I could without opening my throat just yet. That was a gift for later, once I brought him to a peak. He seemed content to sit back and watch me while I paid homage to his beauty. He wasn't arrogant, just superior as if the world owed him their sexual obedience. Who was I to argue when the object of my lascivious thoughts was within blowing distance?

"It's been so long," he groaned, as he ran his fingers through my hair.

In that case, it was time to reveal my true talent. I took a deep but silent breath before I plunged downward not stopping until his prick was pushing into my throat. Controlling my gag reflex, I bobbed in shorts arcs to keep him wedged tight until I needed to breathe. He grasped the arms of the chair as if an electric shock had surged through his body.

"That is truly spectacular," he sighed.

If that wasn't a signal to do it again, I don't know what would be. I went back to ministering to his needs, his cock constricting my throat until I thought I would burst. I didn't know how long I could keep this up but I reasoned that as he'd asked me to stay the night that this was but a preliminary round.

Giving it my all, I bobbed until his cock was buried as deep as it could go, using my tongue, my teeth, every oral trick in my armory, until he called out as if in pain and I felt his spunk squirt down my willing throat. I regretted that I didn't get to taste him but his obvious relish of my skills offset that disappointment. Plus the fact I would get to taste him later.

"That was absolutely amazing," he said.

"Would you like a repeat?"

"Later," he puffed. "Let me get my breath."

Then I was hoping he might take care of the throbbing I had between my legs.

"If you were interested, why didn't you say something before?" I asked.

"I didn't want to jeopardize Damien's party," he said. "That was the most important thing. But now that's out of the way—"

"There's nothing stopping us."

"Plus I had to be sure you were really interested—"

"Could I have made it any more obvious?"

"I thought you may have been after me for my money?"

"Why, have you got tons of the stuff?"

He stilled my wandering hands, holding my wrists together, making me look him in the eyes. "You really don't know who I am, do you?"

"Holy Batcrap, you're a serial killer or a vampire or some shit like that, aren't you? And I'm in deep trouble?"

"Nothing like that. I'm Patric Charles Crichton. Head of PCC Industries."

"OMG!" I screamed. "Not *the* Patric Charles Crichton of PCC Industries?"

I had no idea what the fuck his name meant, so I laid it on thick. His smile of satisfaction showed I'd done the right thing.

"So you can see why I'm a bit wary of getting involved with just anyone."

I let go of his cock which I'd been pumping slowly while we got the talk out of the way. His idea, not mine. The talk part of it. "Why don't you open your mouth a bit wider and insert the other foot?"

That took his breath away. I stood up, gathering my clothes.

"Just for the record, your name and the name of the company mean nothing to me so, big shot, save the self-importance for the sorts of people who are impressed by that sort of pompous priggery, like those puffed-up harridans who brought their poor kids here today. I wanted you because I liked you. Get it? I don't suppose you do. Oh, and by the way, yes, I got those none-too-subtle hints you dropped as Santa Claus that just maybe Mr Perfect was not into relationships. Still I was willing to settle for an overnighter if that's all I could get. Because I like you. Make that liked. You're so far up your own fundament, you can't see what's in front of you. No wonder Damien's so screwed up."

That was below the belt but I was angry as hell.

"And how patronizing can you be?" I was like a dog with a bone and not about to give up. "You don't want to get involved with 'just anyone'? How about I just duck home to get my vaccination certificates, my passport, my driver's licence, my employment record, my college exam results, and my criminal record so you can make an informed decision? Then, how about you do the same for me so I know I'm not sucking 'just anyone'!"

He seemed shocked. "You've got a criminal record?"

"See? No, I don't have a criminal record; I was trying to make a point. I thought you were a free spirit but you're even more timid and uptight than all the others." I was dressed by this time. "If you don't mind, I won't be staying the night. I'd like to leave."

I didn't exit grandly like Norma Desmond; I shuffled out in case I burst into tears. How could my Mr P. go from Perfect to Puerile in such a short period of time? Upstairs, I packed quickly, sitting in my room hoping he had called the limo back because there was no way I was staying under the same roof that night.

About twenty minutes later, there was a knock at the bedroom door. I dreaded facing Mr P. again but I took a deep breath, wiped my eyes, and answered. It was the limo driver.

"Seems I have another passenger going back? You about ready?"

Of course, Santa was still here. I grabbed my bags, the limo driver helping me with the heavier one, and we manhandled it down the stairs. As we passed the library, I couldn't help but call out loudly enough that he'd hear me. "Do you want to come out and search my bag, just in case I'm stealing any of the cutlery?"

I heard a crash of something breaking from inside the closed room.

"Ouch," the limo driver commented.

Santa was waiting for me in the limo, already helping himself to the alcohol for the long ride back.

His name was Colin and by the time we reached the city proper, and my place in particular, we were the best of drunken mates, so much so the limo driver had to help me up to my bedsit, leaving Santa as hubcap guard. Patting my ass, the driver lay me down on the bed fully dressed.

"Don't think I'm not tempted, mate, but I don't take advantage of the inebriated. Maybe if we run into each other under different circumstances…"

He let himself out leaving me to sweet oblivion until I woke up the next day with a Holy Batcrap of a head.

I was sick, so sick, physically and psychically. The physical demanded immediate attention, my head poised over the toilet bowl and then a long draft of seltzer to settle my stomach and a handful of aspirin for my head, the psyche having to be stored away for later. The remainder of the day was spent feeling sorry for me and wondering if I was going to die.

Here lies the body of our dear departed son, Kaz, who remained undiscovered because no one even missed him.

I couldn't believe my head was still pounding. I just wanted it to stop. Not only was my head jabbering like a jackhammer, I was now hearing voices. "Kaz, open up. If you don't open up soon I'll break the bloody door down. Come on, it's Thel."

What? The voice inside my head was a trannie named Thel?

I sat bolt upright in bed, regretting it immediately. I groaned, stumbled out of bed, and unlatched the door, letting Thel push her own way in while I collapsed again.

"What are you doing here?" I groaned.

"When you didn't turn up for work, and didn't ring in, I was worried."

"What do you mean work, it's Sunday?"

"It's late Monday afternoon and Levard is spitting chips. You'll be lucky to have a job come tomorrow." Thel went to the bathroom and turned on the shower. "Right, now you can get yourself into the bathroom and scrub up or you can give Thel a cheap thrill and make me undress you and shove you in the shower. Your choice."

I was unsteady on my feet, but determined. "Loathe as I am to deprive you of an opportunity to feast your eyes on my privates..."

"Good boy. You must be getting better if you can string a sentence together that long without stuttering. Now scoot."

The shower was the first step in my recovery, the second was going out for a cheap meal with Thel. I explained what had happened over the last few days, not sparing my own stupidity from her derision, but instead I got sympathy.

"He seemed like such a nice man, too. Not at all like I expected."

"What do you mean?"

"You really don't know who he is? That wasn't all an act?"

"Have you ever known me to act that well?"

"No, love, your feelings are always plastered all over your face."

"So, who is he?"

"Worth a fortune if the papers are to be believed. Gives a lot of it away to good causes."

"So he's a philanthropist?"

"Wouldn't know about his religion, they never mention that. He's a bit of a recluse."

"No wonder he doesn't date."

"Must be scary to have that much money," Thel sighed, probably wishing just for once in her life she could be that frightened.

The remainder of the meal was taken up with small talk while at the back of my brain, my conscience was attempting to work out whether I had wronged the man. It was a moot point as I'd never see him again to apologize whatever the outcome of the moral dilemma.

When it came time for Thel to return to her long-suffering boyfriend I went to pay the bill over her objections only to discover an envelope in my coat pocket, an envelope stuffed with cash. I saw her to the train then raced back to my bedsit not daring to count the money in public.

The limo driver must have put the envelope in my coat when he walked me up to my apartment. I couldn't believe my sudden wealth. It was the full amount that Mr P. had suggested, not my lower acceptance. I wrestled with my conscience for a few seconds until I overpowered it for the mandatory count of ten then put the money aside for a rainy day. Beneath that hot, muscular, cheating exterior, there was a heartless of gold. Besides, I had no way of returning the extra cash.

I looked vainly for a note, so I slept only fitfully that night, my dreams full of my tarnished hero and the wrong I had done him.

Levard was surprisingly sanguine about my no-show the previous day, dismissing my apology airily with the rejoinder, "It's of no importance, Kaz. Dr Crichton rang in on your behalf saying that he had seen you on the weekend and in his opinion, you were unfit for work yesterday."

My look of surprise didn't seem to register with the floor manager, but at least my job was safe. Thinking it over, that bastard limo driver must have reported back to Mr P. on my condition. Well, he could make of it whatever he wanted.

Thel welcomed me back like I'd been gone for months instead of just a day and by morning tea she's cajoled me into my normal childish, good-natured, optimistic self. Optimistic in most respects but not about Mr P. I didn't want to invest energy and emotions in a relationship with a married man, even if his wife was away most of the year. I wanted a superhero all my own. Was that selfish?

"No, love," Thel said. "That's what we all want, but there should be a rule we can trade 'em in every ten years or so for a better model."

"Ain't that the truth," Curried Pearl added. She had joined our table for her allotted ten-minute break, slurping her coffee like she was drinking it through a straw and smoking like the proverbial chimney even though there were No Smoking signs dotted on all the available wall space between the notices for staff badminton championships and the social club outing to see *Mamma Mia*.

So the days passed as I marshaled faceless children toward Santa for their three-minutes of annual greed (photograph $10 extra) until a week later a tiny hand tugged at my sleeve. "Damien?" I squatted so I was on the same level.

He was pouting. "You didn't stay for dinner."

"Oh, I'm sorry about that. I had urgent business in town. You were taking a nap when I left and I didn't want to wake you."

It was the truth. I didn't want him to think I'd just walked out on him. I'd done a quick sketch of him sleeping, leaving it on his bedside table so he knew that I cared just a little.

"I know. Patric framed your picture and it's hanging in my room. It's cool."

I didn't want to ask, I really didn't.

"Where is Patric?"

He pointed. There was no use in not turning as the object of our conversation would have noticed we were talking about him. Fortunately for me, Levard was oozing all over him, keeping him distracted.

"Don't you like Patric?" Damien asked.

I was taken aback by the forthright question. Well, yes, I did, do like Patric, k or no k.

Before I had a chance to answer, Damien added. "He misses you."

"And I miss him, too. But don't tell him."

He crossed his heart, although I noticed he had his fingers crossed.

"Did you want to see Santa again today? Did you forget to ask for something?"

"Yes," he said earnestly.

I placed him in the line before returning to my regular duties, making sure to keep an eye open for his welfare as he moved patiently forward. When at last he hopped on Santa's knee, whispering in his ear, I saw him point in my direction. I hoped he wasn't vindictive enough that he was asking Santa for a hit man to take me out.

When he'd finished, I fetched him, offering my hand which he took as I made my way over to Mr P., my heart beating until I thought I would be unable to go through with the meeting. Both he and Levard turned their beaming smiles in our direction as we approached. Damien pulled at my hand for the last few meters as my feet seemed remarkably reluctant to take the necessary steps.

Mr P.'s face was a study in neutrality as I nodded my greeting. "Thank you for ringing Mr Levard to let him know I was feeling unwell the other day."

I saw a slight curling of the corner of his mouth on my use of the word 'unwell.'

"That's what...doctors are for," he replied. My heart stopped when he paused, hoping he might say 'friend' but I guess he couldn't. That would be unprofessional. Anyway, I didn't need a common or garden variety friend, I needed a *boy*friend. Preferably one who was available.

We stood around awkwardly until I let Damien's hand go to return to my job. I saw the look of distress on Damien's face.

"Ask him Patric, go on." A little voice pleaded.

Mr P. looked mortified, speaking harshly to his son. "Not now, Damien."

That was my cue to leave and after wishing Damien an effusive goodbye which just seemed to embarrass P. further, I made a hasty exit. I had no idea what was going on there but I knew it was not a good place to be. Maybe P. had transferred his affections to the odious Levard. The guy wasn't bad looking but his personality, let's just say, if it came down to a choice between Levard and a cobra, the snake would win every time.

As I went about my shepherding task, I watched as P. shook hands with Levard, leaving the floor without so much as a backward glance although Damien gave a little wave. I waved back. It wasn't his fault his dad was such a bastard. A sweetheart of a bastard.

The afternoon was so busy I had no time to think any further on the matter until my tea break when Thel and I slumped exhausted in the canteen chairs, so over the Christmas bustle we failed to notice how putrid the coffee was.

"There you are, Kaz," one of the friendlier Santas said, plonking himself alongside. "None of my business, but I just thought you'd like to know, that little boy you were so friendly with–"

"Damien. He's a friend's son," I said to clarify my relationship.

"Well, it's just he had a mighty funny Christmas wish. You get all sorts, of course, some would just tear your heart out, but he was very specific. He even offered to give up his other Christmas presents. Most unusual for a little boy to give up presents. But, what I'm trying to say is, when I asked what he wanted for Christmas, he pointed at you and said 'I want him as my daddy.' There you go, for what it's worth."

Oh shit, I had a sudden need to run to the men's room so I could bawl my eyes out in private.

My eyes were still red when I got home in the early evening. I wasn't depressed exactly, just a little heartbroken for Damien, and feeling sorry for myself. I tried working at my drawings, wallowing sufficiently that I didn't hear the tap on the door until it became more insistent. I really was not in the mood for one of the other occupants of the building coming to me to borrow money or ask if I was selling drugs. I ignored it for as long as I could then reluctantly put down my pencil because I was in danger of scribbling all over my portrait of Mr P. in annoyance and flung open the door.

My first reaction was astonishment, which gave way to embarrassment, in turn becoming irritation, then finally lust. Mr P. stood at the door to my scummy bedsit. Although all those emotions ran through me in record time, I was still gaping.

"Are you going to invite me in?"

I so much didn't want him to see how I lived, but to have him in the same room as me over-rode my good sense. As I stood aside I was curious. "How did you get my address?"

"Your Mr Levard was most co-operative. He gave it to me."

"Against company policy. What did you give him in return? You let him suck your dick? Oh wait, you would have had to check first that he wasn't 'just anybody'." I really would need to learn to keep my mouth shut.

I wouldn't have blamed him had he walked out after that welcome but he said simply, "I deserve that. Now it's out of your system, let's move on." Taking in my room, he retaliated with, "I see accommodation for students hasn't improved much since my day." Somehow, though, I just couldn't picture P. living in such squalor.

"What do you want?"

"I came to invite you out to dinner. At a restaurant."

"You think I need fattening up? Don't let these surroundings fool you."

"No, dammit! A date."

Holy penguins in a burnt butter sauce! Me. On a date. Call the Daily Planet. *Hold the presses! Scoop of a lifetime. Kaz asked out on an actual date by the hottest man in the universe...*

Unfortunately, Mr P. chose that exact moment to find the comic book Mr Perfect, the Hottest Man in the Universe ® ™ (patent pending) who bore a remarkable likeness to his inquisitive self.

"Is this me?"

I didn't dare speak, so I nodded my head.

"What am I supposed to be?"

Clearing my throat, to give myself time to censor my thoughts and give him the family rated version about him and my libidinous superhero, all my reservations went out the door and I babbled away like some stupid kid seeking approval from grownups. In his favor, Mr P. listened patiently, didn't interrupt the more ludicrous aspects of what I was telling him, until he couldn't stand it anymore and he placed his index finger on my lips.

All he had to say was, "I missed you," and I was in his arms.

I was hoping the way I ravaged his tongue was answer enough. I still couldn't believe that he was in my bedsit, that he missed me, and that I was succumbing to a married man.

Ain't love grand?

He backed me onto the bed and began divesting me of my clothes while he shucked off his own shirt and I struggled to undo his belt. "I want you," he muttered, blotting out the few remaining reservations I had. No one had ever wanted me like this before.

He lay on top of me, both of us totally naked after the undignified wriggling to divest ourselves of our clothing, pinning my arms above my head.

He gently bathed my lips with his tongue before gently pushing his way inside, my tongue eager to greet him. There was none of the hurried exploration like the last time we'd found ourselves in this situation.

"Mmm, sweet," he murmured when he came up for air, "I should kiss you more often."

"Make a booking. My dance card is pretty empty at present."

I snacked on his tongue, sliding my lips around it as if it were a cock, rocking back and forth in a facsimile of a blow job. I've had kisses rough and kisses gentle and his was by far the most arousing I'd ever experienced. He took it to a whole new level. I couldn't get enough as he ground his hips against my body in rhythm with his tongue in my mouth. It wasn't all selfish domination because he withdrew to allow me access to his warm wet mouth when I tried so hard to imitate his technique. He was obviously more experienced than me, so I added a small playful flourish. I tickled his gums with my tongue, making him squirm.

He pulled away, disappointing me because I was in no great hurry now that I had him in my bed, but he made me gasp when he ran his lips down my throat and across to my nipple, nibbling at it until it was hard as the tip on a frozen ice cream. He repeated the exercise on the neglected one before burrowing his nose between my feeble pecs then, snorting his breath on my skin, he licked his way down to my navel where he stopped for a brief inspection before continuing farther south, past the pubic jungle, to the leaning tower that was my busting-for-action cock.

Expecting a few tugs with his hand, I was totally unprepared when he opened his mouth and swallowed my prick whole. I called out in surprise, my body bucking on the bed, as his tongue made merry with the underside of my shaft and he bobbed his head up and down to take me to the root. I watched as my dick disappeared between his lips which only made my orgasm even more perilously close. I tried to pull his head away without success so I warned him, "If you keep doing that, I'm gonna come."

He took his mouth off, which gave me a chance to recover, and said, "Can you come more than once a night?"

Does Superman need a new costume designer? Does the Green Lantern need a new color chart? For Mr P. I could come as many times as he wants.

That ran through my mind. What I said was, "Uh huh."

"Good," P. replied and went back to his expert blow job, bringing me off in record time and...

Jiminy Grasshopper, he swallows!

I moved on the bed in an attempt to grab his cock, memories of it ploughing my throat surfacing in my mind. I was keen to repeat the experience. Unless—

"Lie still," he commanded. "This is all about you tonight."

Even my mind went blank at the thought of that.

"What would you like me to do next?" he asked softly.

You mean apart from move into my bedsit and spend the rest of your life loving me, being my superhero?

"I want you to fuck me," I whimpered.

"You got...?"

I'd already leaned my arm over to the bedside table and fished the makings out of the drawer. He ripped the condom wrapper with his teeth, and then rolled it down his shaft as he asked, "How do you want it?"

This was no time for the obvious smartass answer.

"I want to watch you as you fuck me."

He smiled. "Just the way I like it."

Hoisting my legs onto his shoulders, he slicked my ass with lube, pushing his finger inside so gently I barely felt it. Then a second and a third until I was ready for him.

I was so ready, in fact, that when he aimed his cock at my entrance and pushed, there was hardly any sting at all, and I welcomed his intrusion. As he sank slowly inside me, filling me, I had never felt so at peace. He watched me intently for any signs of discomfort and when he found none he began to thrust, withdrawing until the head of his cock was just inside my sphincter, then sliding back down until he was buried up to his balls.

He fucked me like a well-oiled machine, deliberately hitting my sensitive spot every third or fourth thrust so I didn't climax too quickly for my cock was hard again. I sighed contentedly because this was so unlike most of the men I picked up who treated screwing as an event on the Spring racing calendar. I squeezed my ass muscles in appreciation and he gasped.

"Do that again and I won't be able to hold off. I want this to last."

I did it a few more times in rapid succession, holding off my natural inclination to pleasure him more. After all, I wanted him inside me forever, maybe with time off for public holidays.

Suddenly, I realized not only was sex the greatest thing ever invented, but it was actually fun. I wasn't gritting my teeth, I wasn't wondering when he would blow and go, I wasn't looking at the clock, and I wasn't even working out in my head what I was going to eat for dinner tonight. I was giving Mr P. my full attention.

He kissed me as he pumped my ass, the speed increasing, his breath coming in short, sharp bursts. I clung to his body, trying to thrust my ass back to meet his penetration, wanting him farther inside me than was humanly possible. Whimpering, I clung to him never wanting to let go as he bellowed, shuddered, and thrust his load inside me, quivering with each spurt.

I squeezed my ass as hard as I could to milk every drop out of him, until he collapsed on top of me. I caressed his hair and down his back, tracing my fingers lightly over his ass cheeks. It must have tickled because he swatted my hand away.

"I'm crushing you," he said, moving off me and onto his side. He removed the rubber, tossing it in the bin beside the bed. I missed the feel of his strength, expecting him to beat a hasty retreat now that he'd had his fun, but he scooted me over so we could spoon, my ass cheeks rubbing against his slick cock.

"I..."

"Don't talk," he said. "Let's just lie here for a spell. Then you can say whatever is on your mind. Okay?"

"Mmm," I agreed.

We fell asleep in that position, waking up cramped and uncomfortable about an hour later. Still, for all my discomfort, I didn't want to move.

"Shit, I was going to take you to dinner," he said glancing at the clock. "There's still time."

I decided to be selfish. "I'd rather stay in bed with you."

Even though his tummy rumbled, he said, "That would be my choice, too."

My cock strained at the thought of another session with Mr P. He must have read my mind because, this time, he leaned over to grab another condom from the little pile I'd left on the bedside table.

"Expecting a crowd, were you?" he asked, but he was smiling.

He ripped open the packet, I wriggled in anticipation of another good screwing, but instead of sheathing his dick, he rolled the condom down over my cock.

"What?"

"Keep still, it's your turn."

"But..."

"Don't you want a turn?"

"No one's ever asked before," I said sheepishly.

"I'm asking," he said.

"Yes please," I said, sounding a little bit too much like a kid who's just been asked if he wants an ice cream.

"Let me do it my way first, until I get used to it. Then you can do me any way you like."

I nodded, afraid if I spoke this would all prove to be a dream.

He greased his ass before squatting over my cock, guiding it toward his hole. I lay still, allowing him to do all the work, feeling the tingle as he rubbed it around the entrance to his guts. Working it in slowly, he flinched when it breached the muscle. The last thing I wanted was to hurt him, not that I'm suggesting I'm horse hung or anything, but I couldn't bear to see my Mr P. in any sort of pain.

Eventually, like all tough guys, he gritted his teeth and got on with it. He plunged down until I was as far inside his ass as I could go. My eyes opened in wonder.

So this was why guys were lining up to fuck other guys' asses. Oh, I could totally get used to this feeling.

"Nice, eh?" he grinned. "And I'm not even very good at it. Imagine what an expert, someone like you, could do."

I couldn't have been happier. "You're good enough for me."

"Start slowly," he pleaded.

I moved my hips, pushing in and out of his ass slowly, letting him get used to the feeling. Been there, done that, so I knew what he needed. I tried to keep my rhythm as fluid as possible because the worst kind of screw is from someone who pokes like his cock is stoking a fire in a grate.

Concentrating on finding his little knob of a prostate, I changed the angle of entry ever so slightly until he rewarded me with an expletive so loud they must have heard him downstairs.

"I want you on your back, the same way you did me."

With a minimum of disruption, he leaned back in the bed and held his legs apart. If you've never seen a wall of muscle with his cheeks spread open to take your prick, then you are missing one of the wonders of the world. Mr P. was offering himself to me and I was gonna take him up on his offer. I was a little less considerate this time, allowing for the fact he'd had time to get accustomed to my dick in his butt. From now on, any man who wanted my ass would have to surrender his in turn.

He grimaced a few times until I heard him expel a deep breath, signaling he had relaxed and was now enjoying the right royal buggering I was giving him.

Does anyone last long their first time? I doubt it, and I wasn't going to be the exception to the rule. P. stared into my eyes as I rode his ass, more like side-saddle than full on home on the range, but I was enjoying myself and I think he was if the way he was bucking under my inexpert fucking was any indication.

I blurted out, "Sorry," as I increased my thrust, a matter of seconds later spewing my sperm inside him, muttering 'Oh, my god,' over and over until I couldn't squirt any more.

I pulled out slowly, proud of my first effort, grinning sheepishly as I disposed of the rubber. P. lowered his legs, pulled me to him, sheltering me in his powerful arms. Neither of us needed to say anything and I fell into a contended sleep listening to his heart race in his chest.

I would have been more content if I hadn't awoken the next morning, the right side up in my bed, the sheet and blanket covering my naked body, my hero disappeared.

Too late, I remembered that he didn't do relationships.

It was exquisite agony to get myself ready for work: agony that my body felt like it had been slept in, and exquisite because for a few hours Mr P. had been mine. He'd shown me more respect than all my other lovers put together, but it galled me that he ran out rather than tell the truth: that our liaison was a one-night fling while his wife was away.

All that was before I discovered he'd stolen the portrait I'd done of him as my superhero. I'd put everything into that. Sure, I could do it again, but I wasn't sure I wanted to anymore; it would just serve to open up the wound. I'd try my hand at something else, something more down to earth, more practical.

Fortunately, by the time I got to Santa's Cave my sprits had lifted and the idea of capitulating to the mundane had so horrified me on the bus that I swore to myself I would never travel down that route no matter how appealing it seemed.

I plugged into my memories of P. whenever I needed a boost to my flagging energy in the lead-up to Christmas during which the kids seemed to become more unruly and the parents more snarling and unreasonable. Stress compounded, screaming headaches were common place, tempers flared, and I worked with the persistent nagging emptiness where my emotions should be.

Fuck it, I missed him.

Then, all too soon, Christmas Eve rolled around and the thought of the holiday period alone in my bedsit suddenly made me look like a major loser, even to myself. Thel invited me over to her place but she had a large family among whom I'd feel totally out of place. No, I'd sleep in and go to the movies at midday to watch the latest blockbuster, maybe treat myself later to a slap-up burger and fries on the way home.

After we finally saw the last children off for the year, we could have our own little celebration, just a few drinks and canapés before heading home to family. I wouldn't make the mistake this time of imbibing too much although sleeping through the entire day was not without its good points. Even Levard joined our little group complimenting us on what was likely to be the store's best Christmas ever.

"Sorry if I was a little hard on you this year," Levard slurred as he maneuvered me into a corner, placing his arm against the wall so I couldn't escape.

Don't let him proposition me. I want to work here next year.

I tried to attract someone's attention so they could come to my aid as Levard rabbited on and on about how impressed he was with my commitment which became what a good worker I was and then not-so-subtly morphed into what an attractive young man I was.

Help me!

I noticed everyone had their eyes toward the lift which was behind me, the only sound Levard's inept attempt at a pick-up, until eventually he stopped speaking, his mouth dropping open in surprise. It was Thel's squeal of delight that made me turn.

I'm afraid I gaped, too. Striding toward us was Mr Perfect. Not Mr P. but rather my superhero in full costume as I'd drawn it on the sheet that had disappeared along with Patric Charles Crichton from my apartment and my life. My mind noted a few minor adjustments I'd need to make to the costume color scheme and an important one to the cut of the fabric covering his crotch as currently it was much too revealing, especially as Mr Perfect seemed to be sporting a mammoth erection. I knew from experience it wasn't padding.

I could see determination in his eyes as he pulled me to his body and planted the most sizzling kiss to my lips, raising me off the ground in the process, with scant regard for anyone who was watching. I thought I heard Thel clap but it could just have been the bells that were pealing in my head.

"Damien wants me to bring you home for Christmas," he said simply.

I couldn't help it. "I don't look good in stockings," I replied.

"But you'll look mighty tasty in my bed."

"Once is all right, but twice makes it look like some sort of relationship is developing."

"I missed you."

"Me, too."

He scooped me up in his arms just like a superhero. He spoiled the effect somewhat by walking to the lift rather than flying from the window. I could live with that. I could live with whatever he decided. I would even be the other woman for him.

"What other woman? What are you talking about, Kaz?" He looked genuinely puzzled as the lift ascended to street level.

"Your wife. Damien's mother."

He guffawed fit to piss himself.

"I'm not married, you dickhead. Endive is my sister. Damien is my nephew. I look after him whenever sis is away on assignment."

I tweaked his nipple really hard until it hurt.

"Ow. What was that for?"

"For leading me on. Making me worry."

Deep down I knew he could lead anywhere and I'd follow.

Once we reached the street, passers-by gawped at the strange sight, until a limo pulled up and Mr P. deposited me in the back seat before wrapping me in his massive arms, planting another of those lip searing kisses on my mouth. As the car pulled out into the late Christmas Eve party-going traffic, I spied a small box stuffed in the belt of Mr P.'s costume. I could just make out the words 'Extra Sensitive,' and the number 36.

Holy Batcrap, Robin. A happy ending.

VLAD THE IMPALER

I'm a bit of a legend. Not the bona fide celebrity sort that has paparazzi chasing me. Nah, just a small pond legend. Just enough to get me laid on a regular basis even though I'm not the best looking cock of the walk. Not ugly, but not as handsome as that daytime soap opera star who came into the club about an hour ago, before the fracas started. Naturally enough, he was the cause of it all. Arrogant dickhead.

I'm trying to introduce myself but I'm ballsing it up, aren't I? Take a deep breath, like my mom always tells me when I get confused and start slap bang in the middle of a story about my job, and start again. So...deep breath. Begin at the beginning.

My name is Vladimir Zeklos. My parents were born near Braşov in the center of Romania to the north of Bucharest, near the Carpathian Mountains where Dracula lived. They show me old photographs of the town but I have no memories of it because I was born here. I tell them I will go visit some day but they know I won't and it saddens them. Maybe I will.

Who knows? They are also saddened because I don't learn the history and the culture of the country they came from. Or the language which they speak together at home when they are alone. That's the time when I see them share something I can never be a part of for I am not part of that past.

My past, what little there is of it, is here in this country. I am its citizen. I speak its language, I learned its history at school, it's where I've spent my first twenty-eight years, and it's where my future lies. All I know of my parents' homeland is that it's the home of the nasty bastard, Vlad the Impaler, a fifteenth century prince of Wallachia who was notable for impaling the bodies of the Ottoman Turks then invading the Balkans and that his name, Dracul (son of the Dragon) was used by Bram Stoker for his famous vampire. He wasn't one of the living dead any more than I am even though round these parts I'm also known as Vlad the Impaler, although my name has more to do with the stake I have between my legs.

I'm just naturally gifted like that, I guess. Dad told me it runs in the family and that one day I will pass the genes on to my own son. Being as well-endowed as I am does have its downside. Like where to put it in my pants. Unless I'm wearing something loose around my groin, it's gonna show. Especially in the tight security uniform I have to wear in my job. As a result, my cock is out there for everyone to see. And if I'm displaying, people think it's open season to grope, squeeze, and make all manner of dirty remarks.

Sure, I get lots of come-ons but just as many 'get offs' when my sexual partner realizes my rod hurts and their eyes are too big for their cunt or ass or mouth. Yeah, I swing both ways. I have to. I started with chicks because, well, that's what you're supposed to do but I discovered only sluts with bucket cunts could take me and they weren't the sort of girls I was interested in. Especially not for keeps. Then I discovered fags with bucket asses. They could take me in their mouth and their ass right down to my balls. Problem was they tended to be old fuckers. I don't mind a wrinkle or two but I prefer them on a guy's face, not his ass.

You've probably guessed by now, I ain't the world's brightest spark. No one becomes a bouncer because they've got a degree in philosophy from a major university. No, you get that job because you're big, you're bad, and you've got a body the size of Uluru. That's me. It also helps if you love smacking other guys and the occasional chick into submission. That's not me. I only use my fists when necessary: like when someone attacks me or I go to help a mate. I know my fists are lethal weapons. A bit like my cock, or so some people tell me.

That Saturday night started off no different to any other. Me and Marty, he's my best mate, were working the door, while the other guys were inside keeping an eye on the crowd. Marty and me go way back. We share just about everything…no, don't get me wrong, Marty is strictly a cunt man. He knows I like to experiment and he knows why. The first time he saw my cock, he said, "Did you use that to plough the farm back in Romania, mate?"

I laughed. Well, I thought it was funny. Most guys try to sneak to look without letting on. Marty just went for it.

"I don't think I've ever seen anything so big and so thick before," he said. "Thought my pecker was big but yours is gigantic. Mind if I have a feel?"

I thought he was coming on to me and, truth be told, I'd be more than happy for Marty to back up against it. But he wasn't, he was just curious.

"I'm no fag, mate, but that cock is a work of fuckin' art."

I gave him permission and he wrapped his fingers around it, squeezing and pumping like he was testing some new appliance or some piece of chrome he was adding to his car. I got stiff straight away.

"You poor bastard," he said as he watched me fill out. "You're gonna have a problem finding chicks that can take that all the way."

He understood. As he kept commiserating, he kept pumping until my breath got short and I finally blew enough spunk to fill a small tumbler.

"Shit," Marty said. "Chicks better wear a raincoat when you're around."

He shook my spooge off his hand while I tucked my prick away in my pants. We never mentioned the incident again and we never repeated it, although once when me and the guys were working over a couple of drunken chicks after the bar closed I 'accidentally' ran it down the crack of his butt but apologized straight away. None of the other guys saw and Marty just smiled and wiggled his index finger to tell me it wasn't gonna happen.

I didn't tell him he could plough my ass because us tough guys don't go there.

Still, life was mighty fine.

We were expecting the usual crowds, drunken teens and early twenties out prowling for a quick fuck or something more permanent, already pissed or determined to be that way by the end of the night. Chicks in skirts so short you could see their cunt hair if they bent over, guys in jeans so tight it's a wonder they didn't restrict blood flow to their dicks. Plus the inevitable old guys who hung out here in the hopes of attracting some drunken chick who couldn't distinguish turkey from rooster, or some young buck who wanted to explore his feminine side when his mates weren't looking.

We always had a hen's night or a bachelor party booked into the private rooms and they'd turn up pissed as farts, dressed like sluts or the groom in chains, stripped as naked as permissible without being arrested. Management insisted we give those groups extra leeway, unless they became violent.

Adrenaline, the club where I worked was the top spot in the city, always in the news, paparazzi hanging around to get a shot of some would-be celebrity spewing her guts out, and her career, in the gutter.

They were rarely disappointed. They paid us for info on who was inside the venue although we never let them inside, and they tipped very well if they got that one shot syndicated around the world. We hated them but it was part of the business so we tolerated the slime.

There was one person I allowed to fondle my tackle without growling at her. Nicola was one of the few people who could come and go as she pleased. We knew that the licensee of the premises was a front man because the club had obvious connections to the underworld. Nicola's dad, Big Jim Green, the real owner, used the business to launder drug money as well as other even less savory pastimes. He had an office on the top floor of the heavily secured building. He also had a private car park and entrance that none of us knew the location of. We surmised that he accessed it through one of the neighboring buildings.

For instance, Nicola always went in via the front entrance waving to the journalistic leeches but she never came out that way at the end of the night. Nor by the fire exits at the side of the building where other photographers waited. And she wasn't inside when we closed up.

I liked Nicola. She always patted my package and threatened to do me one day. I knew better than to go there. I'd end up with my dick and my balls shoved in my mouth, my body buried under meters of concrete that made up the foundations of a suburban car park. Besides, she only had eyes for Blake

Kendall, the blue-eyed wunderkind of the popular daytime vampire soap opera, Blood Lust, that rated even better when it was repeated in the evenings. The DVD of the first series sat top of the bestseller lists for ten months.

It wasn't difficult to see the appeal. Blake always removed his shirt at least once in every episode, slowly stroking his hand across his chest and down to his washboard abs, smoldering at the camera so that everyone watching at home knew exactly where that hand was headed. Inevitably, the show would cut to an ad break just before his hand reached its destination. I would always play that section in slow motion to give me enough time to whack out a load before the pitch for the latest car or investment scheme.

So sue me. I have every series box set in my bedroom. I don't watch it for the plot, I watch it for Blake. His body is almost as choice as us security guys. He revealed his butt in series one. Dropped his dacks and his tighty whities to reveal the most sculpted glutes I'd ever seen. I thought Marty was buff. Hell, Blake was buffer and I blew without touching myself, groaning as I imagined sliding my dick into that hot crevice.

He and Nicola were the celebrity couple of the day. She was a celebrity by dint of being famous. In other words, she was famous because she had an infamous dad and was seen at all the right parties. She had appeared on a number of reality TV shows dancing, singing, lost in a jungle with a group of other nonentities, and locked in a house for three months with other losers. She never won any of these 'contests', always managing to have herself voted off the shows for outrageous conduct which got her more press inches of coverage than the eventual winner. She didn't need the money, her dad was fabulously wealthy, she needed the publicity. She got it in spades when it was announced that she and Blake were dating.

Rumor was she hoped to parlay their relationship into an acting career, but when she guested as Blake's character's former girlfriend on the show the reaction was swift. She was universally reviled as having zero acting talent. Her debut was an embarrassment and the ratings for the five episodes in which she appeared were so dire the writers killed off her character so she could never return. It also led to the now notorious butt reveal which I have programmed onto the DVD so it goes straight to that sizzling scene.

Because of the ratings bonanza, a butt scene now appears in every series. I remember Blake's reaction when a sleazy journo tried to get him to rat on his fans by suggesting that gay guys the world over would be jerking off to the view.

Blake had smiled. "If it makes them happy to fantasize about my butt, then I'm happy to show it!"

You gotta love a guy like that. I would have loved him, too, but there had never been a rumor he was gay. Fuck!

Blake and Nicola were photographed everywhere together, but especially at the beach where she could show off her surgically augmented breasts which she kept insisting were real, while he was seemingly content to provide supportive background scenery although it was hard to take your eyes off him and the bulge he revealed in his tight fitting swimwear. I wasn't the only one to think so. He had almost one million friends on Facebook.

When Nicola arrived with her all-male entourage she posed for the photographers, blowing them kisses, reporting how happy she was that she and Blake were tying the knot, gushing that it was a marriage made in heaven. I heard a comment from the crowd waiting in line while Nicola did her shtick: "A marriage made in publicist's heaven." I couldn't help but agree. But it would cost me my job to say so.

After promising to give the guys a photo opportunity with her fiancé when he arrived, she swept toward the door of the club, secretly groping me with a little more passion than usual. "Make sure that's cocked and loaded, it'll be needed later tonight. And don't let any of those bastards in the door," she said, indicating the gaggle of press men. "Tonight is very private. Got it?"

"Got it," Marty and I repeated.

"What did she mean about keeping it cocked and loaded?" Marty asked. "You slipping her a bit on the side?"

"Fucked if I know what she meant," I replied. "And there's no way I'm getting involved with Nicola. I have a healthy regard for life."

"I'd fuck her brains out if I thought I could get away with it," Marty admitted.

My cock got hard wondering what it would be like to have Marty fuck my brains out.

It was about half an hour later when Blake arrived with his best man, Grant, and a couple of minor league TV stars. Small group in comparison to Nicola's. He'd never been to the club before when I'd been on duty so this was the first time I'd seen him in the flesh. If anything, his photographs did not do him justice. Sure, they captured the size and good looks, what they failed to impart was the sheer sexiness and charisma of the guy. He dazzled the crowds. Whereas Nicola played to the newspapermen, Blake played to everyone, his infectious good humor as seductive as speed.

I noticed Grant also played the fame game. He was extremely photogenic but with a hard, cold edge and although he smiled and waved to fans there was an underlying jealousy which you could tell by the way he glared at Blake's popularity when he thought no one was looking. If he was Blake's best friend then Blake had better watch his back.

That was my reading of the relationship and management paid us to 'read' the people who passed through the door in the blink of an eye. Our well-being depended on it. We were rarely wrong.

While Grant and the minor celebrities worked the crowd, Blake took the time to talk to us bouncers, something so unusual I could see Marty was shocked.

We like to keep the patrons at arm's length until the end of the night in case of trouble, although Blake was not your average patron and I thought it was pretty nice of him to stop while his mates got a little press attention. Besides, the man was so hot in close up I was in real danger of melting.

"Hi guys," he said introducing himself and shaking hands. He had a real masculine grip but not one of those that try to maim your fingers to show how alpha he is. Marty was first then he gripped my hand. The buzz of attraction shot straight up my arm. I don't know if he noticed how turned on I was but my cock began leaking attraction juice and would spread a stain across the crotch if I got any more excited.

Blake seemed puzzled as if he felt the electrical jolt as well. He looked at my biceps and then at his own.

"I'm buff," he said modestly. "But man, you're huge." I thought I saw his eyes drop to my bulge just before he said it. Nah, I must have imagined it. "Wouldn't like to get on the wrong side of those muscles. Glad you two are looking after us." Then he smiled at Marty and me before he called his mates. "Come on, guys, the party's waiting."

With a final wave to the crowd, he and his entourage disappeared inside.

"Wanker," Marty spat, although the veneer of scorn he always assumed whenever we paid host to stars couldn't disguise his admiration for the guy. "You obviously liked him."

"What do you mean?" I stuttered.

He nodded at my crotch. "That thing you keep in your pants was so happy to see him it's positively frothing at the mouth."

Marty was close enough to see the outline of my hard-on and the twenty cent-sized wet patch. I hoped no one else waiting in line could.

"Maybe you better go and...um...take yourself in hand," Marty smirked. "I can hold the fort while you get yourself straightened out."

"Thanks," I said as I pushed my way inside.

The club was humming, the muffled bass line from the music on the dance floor thumping through the walls as I made my way to the staff room on the ground floor. I was going to relieve the pressure but thought better of it; after all, I might get lucky later in the evening. In the end, I did, but not in the manner I expected. I cleaned the wet spot on my trousers, drying them under the hand dryer, packed my cock away in my briefs after it had lost its rigidity and was heading back when I heard raised voices from one of the private rooms. I recognized Nicola's voice doing the shouting. The last thing we needed was the boss's daughter engaged in a row, particularly on her purported hen's night although to date no hens, only roosters, had turned up for the official party.

Even the hubbub of loud conversation could not cover Nicola's next outburst. "Don't deny you're fucking that slut who plays your girlfriend in the show." Obviously, Blake did attempt to deny it because Nicola's voice went up several octaves when she spoke next. "How would you feel if I went out and fucked every man I fancied before the wedding?"

I smiled because rumor was that's exactly what she was doing in case she found someone who could fast track her career with more enthusiasm than Blake was showing.

When I got back to the front entrance of the club, I reported to Marty what I'd heard.

"So it's a marriage not made in heaven," he said.

"From the sounds of it, it's not likely to be a marriage at all."

No sooner were the words out of my mouth than one of the newer bouncers came out to relieve me, informing me Big Jim Green wanted me in his office asap. Marty gave me one of those looks that meant 'oh oh' in eyebrow speak. He wasn't concerned for my job because I was one of the most popular security guys at the club and a favorite of management's. This had to be something more serious.

I tapped on his door and waited for the "Enter" which meant he had tucked away the money or the broad or the drugs or the evidence he was working over when I knocked. The door buzzed and I pushed into the inner sanctum.

His huge mahogany desk and the bank of monitors which showed every room of the club, bar the toilets, dwarfed big Jim. He had a set of controls with which he could change camera angles or zoom in for a close-up. At present his eyes were fixed on his daughter's party and even without sound we could both tell she was in a rather excited state: excited as in angry, not excited as in sexually stimulated. The dumb show on the monitor was extraordinary as she seemed to turn purple with anger before our very eyes, perhaps because Blake seemed to be laughing at her, refusing to take her outburst seriously.

Big Jim didn't say a word, obviously expecting me to read his mind and watch the drama unfold. The other guests seemed bemused by Nicola's outburst as if it were a rehearsed theatrical show. Grant, Blake's Best Man, deserted his friend by moving stealthily toward his screaming adversary, stranding him on one side of the room. Blake's other buddies had obviously left the sinking ship earlier as they were not behind him in support.

"That doesn't look good, boss."

"I want you to get in there and make sure the situation doesn't get out of hand."

"Will do," I said, heading for the door.

"And Vlad..."

I turned back to Big Jim.

"Look after my little girl, will you? Do everything she tells you, no matter what. Don't worry if it seems a little extreme. We'll cover your back."

"Got it."

Striding across the foyer to the private rooms, I didn't like the situation. It smelled fishy. Like a set-up. If I had my guess, Blake Kendall was in deep shit. The whole exercise seemed much too rehearsed somehow.

I grabbed an ice bucket and a bottle of the most expensive champagne from behind the downstairs bar, draped a white serviette across my wrist, and headed for Nicola's party. Knocking briefly, I opened the door to a barrage of hurled threats from Nicola and announced, "Compliments of the management," which sucked a great deal of tension out of the air.

The raised voices died, people's attention concentrated on me as I maneuvered the cork from the bottle, careful not to spill a drop as I filled the glasses set up on the table together with the extravagant smorgasbord. I played waiter, mingling with the crowd as I offered a glass to each partygoer. Most just grabbed from the tray I was carrying so that Blake was the last to receive his.

Grant offered a half-hearted toast to which the group raised their glasses with not even a quarter heart. They turned their attention to the food with a more celebratory air. I stood aside to watch that everything ran smoothly, ready to intervene at a moment's notice. Blake had a perfunctory conversation with Grant who didn't seem keen to be seen with him, before approaching me with a plate of food which he'd originally attempted to hand to Nicola. She had rebuffed him.

I took the plate but placed it back on the table.

Blake whispered. "Can you get me out of here? Something's going on and I don't like it."

"Trust me, you need to stay." I replied, keeping my voice low. The guests were watching us but Nicola and her crew knew that no matter what Blake was saying, my loyalties were to the club.

"Why should I?" he asked.

"Because whatever it is they have planned, no matter how humiliating or painful, it will be kept in-house. You try to escape and it will be much, much worse and very public."

"What are they planning?"

"I wish I knew, but I'll be here to guard your back. Notice even your friends have changed sides."

"Grant always was a treacherous bastard."

Nicola clinked a knife against her glass to attract everyone's attention.

"Here we go," Blake sighed.

"Remember, if it gets too heavy, I'll get you out of here."

He retained his sense of humor. "As long as it's not in a box or with my body in several pieces."

Nicola looked over at me. "Lock the door, please Vlad."

I did as she requested, noticing that Blake looked decidedly uncomfortable until I stood behind him albeit to the side so that it didn't look as if I was favoring him.

"Thanks for coming to what was to be our combined bachelor and bachelorette parties but you've probably already noticed a distinct lack of my girlfriends here tonight. That's because I got some very disturbing news yesterday. Most of you know what it was. It was devastating. It tore my heart out." Her eyes misted, it was a bravura performance. "For those of you who don't know, briefly, it was brought to my attention that my husband-to-be, the man I love deeply and to whom I have remained faithful since our engagement even though I have had offers from some of the world's most handsome men..."

A few of the men behind her smirked.

"Marriage is very precious to me," she continued. "It is not to be entered into lightly. I take the marriage vows seriously, unlike, it seems, the man who was to be my partner for life. I have good reason to believe that Blake Kendall has been fucking his leading lady all through our engagement. Under the circumstances I have no alternative but to call a halt to the wedding."

There was a theatrical gasp from the guests, Nicola leaning against Grant for support.

"Why did you do it, Blake? You've broken my heart. Crushed me. Why couldn't you keep your dick in your pants? What's that slag got that I haven't?"

I crossed my fingers that he wouldn't say what everyone in the room must have been thinking: talent.

He was a gentleman, he didn't resort to sarcasm.

"Who told you that ridiculous story?"

Nicola's glance at Grant gave the game away.

"I should have guessed," Blake said. "Grant is a little gold digger. He's been trying to get my role in the soap for years, and he's been trying to get into your panties as well, Nicola. Well, you're welcome to each other. It's not been announced officially yet but I've been offered a night-time series of my own so I have to leave the soap and, as of the beginning of next season, Grant will be taking over my role. The show has been good to me but it's time to move on."

From the look on Nicola's face she already knew of Grant's forthcoming promotion. She favored him by leaning against him for support. Blake snorted.

"I don't know what Grant told you, Nicola, but what he doesn't know is that my character will be involved in a serious accident in the series final this year. Typical cliff hanger. Will he? Won't he die? I'll let you in on the secret. Yes, he does. The producers don't want to pay me my rather exorbitant fee to just lie in a hospital bed covered from head to toe in bandages so they've employed someone who just needs to lie there and expire convincingly three weeks in when the doctor pulls the plug. I think even your meager ability will be up to that, Grant. Unfortunately for you, unless people read the end credits, they'll still think it's me lying there."

Grant looked as if all the wind had been knocked out of his sails.

"As for the story my leading lady and I are getting down and dirty, well, that's impossible."

"Why's that?" Nicola asked.

"I'm sure Beth won't mind my telling as she's preparing to reveal all to the world herself. She's a dyke. She and her girlfriend are expecting a child in a few months and she intends using that happy event to come out."

Nicola looked conflicted, obviously mulling over whether to go ahead with her plan or backtrack in case Blake was telling the truth. A boyfriend in a night-time series was a much better prospect than one wrapped in bandages in a daytime soap.

"Bullshit," Grant spat. "You'd do anything to save your neck."

Blake asked to borrow my mobile. The room waited in silence while he dialed. "Hi Jack, Blake here. I'm with Nicole and I couldn't wait to tell her the good news. Yeah. Well, the thing is, she's a little skeptical. Excited, yeah, but skeptical. Can I put her on?" He handed the phone to her, mouthing the words, "My agent."

"Hi Jack," she said, clearing her throat, now clearly unsure of herself. "Uh huh. Yes. Oh, definitely a good career move. Yes, blanket coverage for both of us." She nodded a few more times before thanking Jack and disconnecting, handing me the phone in a state of shock. "It's true." Then in a performance that really was worthy of a nomination of some sort, she flung her arms around Blake and kissed him warmly. "Darling, we'll have to move the wedding forward so you can be ready for the new show."

Blake untangled her arms from around his neck. "What wedding? I heard you say it was off. Everyone in the room heard you."

"That was a mistake, darling," she whined. "Just a misunderstanding. I forgive you. Now it's your turn to forgive me."

269

"I don't remember any behavior of mine that required your forgiveness, Nicola. As for me forgiving you, I don't think so. You believed the most scurrilous accusations against me without discussing it first. You've obviously thrown your lot in with Grant and I certainly wouldn't want to be the person to stand in the way of true love."

Nicola slapped Blake across the face. Hard. "Bastard," she hissed.

Grant moved to put a protective arm around her shoulders but she shrugged him off. She wriggled her ass on to the buffet table scattering food and glasses as she made herself comfortable, her ultra-short black sheath riding up as she moved back.

She smiled sweetly at Blake as she slowly lifted the hem of her skirt, revealing she wore no panties, and unveiling her sculpted pussy, a true work of art: plump pussy lips, sweet tuft of hair pointing to the delicious opening. "If you won't miss me, honey, you'll sure miss this." She was pissed. She never could hold her grog. Plunging her fingers inside, she groaned so that I suspect every man in the room popped a boner. All eyes were on that inviting entrance between her legs. My impaler seemed to growl as it stretched to its full length. That was one mighty fine piece of pussy.

"Put it away, Nicola," Blake sneered. "We've all seen it before. And, if I'm not mistaken, we've all had it before. Well, maybe the security guy hasn't because he can't actually help further your career."

Nicola picked up a plate of small puffed pastry flans, the closest thing to hand, and flung them at Blake but he ducked and they splattered ineffectually against the wall.

"Your pussy is the most talented part of your entire body, Nicola. You could probably have a career lying flat on your back. Even then, though, you'd only be mediocre. You don't have what it takes to be a star."

I'm glad she was on the table because I suspect if Blake had been anywhere near her she would have shredded him in a matter of moments. Screaming like a banshee, she lay back on the table and spread her legs wider, giving the room an uncensored view of her love tunnel.

"You think so, eh?" she shrieked. "I'm a fucking star in the bedroom and don't you forget it. You never complained. I've never had any complaints. Right, guys?" She glared at her entourage to ensure no one disagreed. She was slowly adding more and more nails to the coffin of her relationship.

"Why don't I show you how much of a fucking star I am," she taunted. "Show you what you'll be missing for the rest of your life. No use begging, you and me are over. But let me give you a farewell present."

I didn't like where this was going.

"A break-up fuck. But not with you and your puny prick. I'll let you watch how a real man does me. Any volunteers?"

There was a stampede of zipper pulling as guys jostled to be alpha male. Blake just stood his ground with his arms folded. He seemed amused rather than upset.

"Hey, security," she yelled. "Drop your pants and get over here."

She obviously meant me but I didn't want to get involved, especially with her dad watching every move on his pervert's web security system.

"I've always wanted to know what you had curled up down there. Get over here if you know what's good for you."

Reluctantly, I headed over to the table, her entourage parting like the Red Sea. "You're the only one in the room who hasn't sampled the goodies so you can give your unbiased opinion."

I stood there gaping, Grant looking daggers at me. "Loose the pants," she demanded.

Remembering Big Jim's direction to do everything his daughter asked, no matter how bizarre it seemed, I skinned my trousers off, my cock throbbing, barely contained in my briefs.

Nicola appraised me like a prize bull at an agricultural show. "Nice," she said. "Lose all the clothes. I want to see it all."

I shucked out of my uniform and stood naked for her inspection. She whistled her appreciation. "I like a man with muscles…where it counts." She climbed down from the table in order to run her hands across my body, snagging her hand around my cock. "This is going to be a real pleasure," she smiled.

I looked across at Blake, embarrassed to be in this position but my prick always had a mind of its own and Nicola's pussy was available so...Blake's look of jealousy puzzled me. There must be more to their relationship than I gave them credit for. Perhaps she knew what she was doing. I was sorry to have been embroiled in their problems even if my cock wasn't.

"You always said you loved my blowjobs, Blake. Watch while I blow the bouncer's mind as well as his cock."

Blake did look, fascinated to see his fiancée on the floor licking at my knob. Her technique smacked too much of putting on a show but my cock and balls didn't care.

Nicola sucked a little, licked around the head, took time off to breathe and suck my balls, while I noticed Blake watch my face to see if I was faking my reaction. Then she went too far. Showing off, she impaled her mouth down my shaft in an effort to take it in its entirety. She miscalculated the size or her ability, maybe both. She gagged, her eyes watered but she held on for as long as she could. In the end, it defeated her as she'd only succeeded in taking half of it down her throat.

Her attempt felt good but she was an amateur when it came to sucking my cock. Realizing she was losing face, she turned to her audience, declaring, "I want that cock in my pussy." She made her way back to the table; lying on her back, she exposed her fine cunt to me. She fixed a smile on her face. "I'll milk you so dry you'll think you're in the fucking desert."

I hesitated. I needed my job and I really didn't know whether Big Jim meant I should fuck his daughter when he said I should do anything she asked. I imagined him in his office jerking his cock as he watched. Plus, I didn't want Nicola humiliated publicly again. Sure, I'd heard she was a bit of a slut but my cock is huge. Many a girl thought she could take it only to beg me with tears in her eyes to take it out. Nicola was trying to prove something rather than take me on for pleasure. It was the worst way to go about it.

"I don't know if I should," I said.

"Let the poor guy go, Nicola. You won't prove anything by doing this. I'm not jealous, and the relationship is over. Walk away with a little dignity." It was Blake's first comment on the direction the party had taken.

I was grateful for his intervention, my cock wasn't.

Nicola glared at me. "Don't make me ask you again. Ram that prick into me or you won't have a job tomorrow."

Grant looked uncomfortable and attempted to protest, stopped in mid-sentence by Nicola's sharp, "Shut it, Grant. Best we establish who's boss around here right from the start. You can go next. Get your cocks out boys, I feel like a slut tonight."

"Then you and Grant are ideally suited," Blake said. "Neither of you has any morals. Or any talent for that matter."

"Fuck me, damn you," Nicola screeched at me.

I ran my cock head up and down her slit in an effort to get it slick from her wetness but it remained as dry as the proverbial. "This is gonna hurt unless you let me lube up a bit."

"What's a little pain," she said cavalierly.

"This will be a lot of pain."

I saw Grant's eyes light up as he leaned over to whisper in Nicola's ear. Her smile gave her the appearance of a serpent about to devour its prey.

"Men," she said sweetly to her entourage. "Could you please help Mr Kendall to his knees. He is the solution to our lubrication needs."

A couple of the guys manhandled Blake, pushing him to a kneeling position on the floor.

"Suck his cock, Blake. Get it nice and slick for me so it slips in easy."

"You know I don't do that, Nicola."

"Now's the time to start," Grant said viciously.

Blake remained calm. "I don't think so. No offence, Vlad."

"None taken," I muttered. Indeed, I didn't take offence although I was desperate to have his lips wrapped around my monster. If it came to a choice, Nicola could close her legs and head back to her apartment. I'd rather a half-hearted blow job from Blake than a full-on fuck with Nicola. God, I had it bad.

Her voice took on an ominous quality. "I don't think you understand, Blake. If this hurts me then it's really gonna hurt you. Get my drift? So, if you want to escape with your ass intact, get slicking his cock."

He struggled to get away. "I'll have you on a charge if you try that, Nicola."

"It will only be the bouncer's slime in your ass. We'll deny everything. We can all vouch for one another. We can't be held responsible for what one of the club's security men does to you. Right, guys?"

There was general agreement along with raucous laughter.

I had no way of reassuring Blake that I'd go easy, so I gripped the back of his head gently to guide his mouth over my prick, hoping that might do the trick. I had no intention of pushing my cock all the way down his throat. If he struggled, it would only make it more unpleasant for him so I held his head firmly. I slid between his lips slowly and thought I felt the tip of a tongue work its way around my glans. Nah, couldn't be.

The sight of my weapon disappearing into my hero's mouth turned me on. I pushed just far enough that it looked convincing to Nicola and her entourage, and just enough that Blake could work it comfortably. But rather than take his time, he kept pushing his face along my stalk. Holy fuck! The guy was swallowing me whole. Very few men or women had ever been able to take me right down to the balls without gagging severely.

Grant was watching up close and his eyes widened as Blake passed Nicola's benchmark and kept right on going. You don't get that proficient without practicing.

"He's taken it almost all the way down to his balls," Grant said, sounding almost admiring. Then he reached down to squeeze Blake's cock in his trousers. "Shit! He's stiff as a board. Maybe your ex-boyfriend is a fag, Nicola."

Nicola looked startled at the concept. "Nah, I would have known. For all his faults he's a good fuck."

From the way Blake was munching on my wick, I think Grant's assumption was on the money. If so, Blake had managed to keep his secret very secret indeed.

"That's enough," Nicola snapped. "Don't wear him out. I want that prick inside me. Now."

She lay back on the table with her legs spread, much less inviting than Blake's warm, wet mouth. Reluctantly I pulled out of his throat, my cock slick with his spit and slime. I aimed at Nicola's cunt and pushed home. I should have taken more care because of her threat to Blake's anal virginity but I was beginning to think he could take care of himself and, besides, it would be my cock sliding between his muscular buns if Nicola screamed in pain.

I slowed down, pushing gently, impaling her on my shaft. She was snug and warm but far from wet, not excited at all. Gritting her teeth, breathing deeply, as I penetrated farther into her pussy, thumbing her clit in order to turn on her natural lubrication, she took me a little over half way before screaming in frustration and pain. It almost sounded like she was giving birth.

I remained still for a moment to give her time to relax.

"Keep pushing," she demanded and I began again, inching my way in. Perspiration dotted her brow from the strain, her determination faltering. I feared for Blake if she failed in this endeavor. Blake must have thought the same thing, for he interrupted her efforts, although not in a manner I would have thought conducive to flattering her.

"For god's sake, Nicola, you're such an amateur."

He pushed me aside and my cock popped out of her tight canal. He stood between her legs, stripping off his clothes until he stood naked and magnificent. I almost shot my load just looking at him.

Nicola must have believed he had forgiven her or, at the very least, was going to throw a break-up fuck into her. It transpired that neither alternative was on the cards. He swept another area of the table clean, hoisted himself up alongside Nicola, and opened his legs, holding them up and to the sides. "Let me show you how it's done. Come on, Vlad. If you wouldn't mind. Give it all you've got."

"It will be my pleasure," I said smiling.

"I think I can guarantee that," he replied immodestly, but then cutting off any negative connotations by adding quickly, "But I think most of the pleasure will be mine." He turned to his ex-girlfriend who was demanding Grant show his sexual superiority between her legs.

"This is how it should be done, Nicola," Blake said, encouraging me to sink my dick into his inviting pink hole. I placed my cock head at the entrance to his guts and his warmth almost sucked me in. Pressing slowly, my dick still slick with his spit and the small amount of pussy lube Nicola finally manufactured, I opened him up gently, fearful that I might hurt him. I sighed at my good fortune as he grabbed my ass pulling me into his superb body, my every nerve ending in awe that I was fucking Blake Kendall, although my cock was eager to slam dunk his butthole and get on with it.

I wondered at Blake's seeming unconcern for his reputation, particularly on the eve of a new night-time series. Rumors about his sexual preference would certainly not help although Adrenaline management confiscated mobile phones at the door so there would be no footage to post on YouTube. Unless, of course, Big Jim saw fit to release security footage. That, however, would warn off major celebrities who liked a place in which to relax without fear of exposure. The club's success depended on their patronage.

It wasn't until I heard one of Nicola's awestruck men mutter, "Shit, he's taken it all," that I realized I was chock-a-block inside the man of my dreams. I couldn't help myself; I leaned over him, wedging his legs over my arms, bringing my lips to his. The most he could do was reject the affection. I hated that there had been no foreplay with Blake, no 'getting-to-know-you' time.

He welcomed my kiss, opening his mouth to invite me in, my tongue probing him as eagerly as my cock. He reciprocated, no hurried coupling here, content in his ability to take me. It was as if we were on another plane and I forgot that we were in a room full of horny men who were waiting to take their turn with Nicola or Blake. Over my dead body. I was possessive of this man now that I had him, even if it was only for the next hour or so.

He whispered "Oh, Jesus," over and over, as I pushed in and out of his ass, opening it up until he was gaping. I did everything to prolong the wonderful feeling of being inside him, from pinching his nipples which made him moan to running my hands over his amazing pecs and biceps. I played with his cock, wishing I'd had time to suck it before the anal onslaught, and fingered his silken ball sack, gently squeezing his testicles between my fingers.

"Fuck me hard, Vlad," he groaned after I had kept up a steady pace for about five minutes. We were oblivious to the activity going on around us, the world existing for only the two of us. "I like it rough."

I kept the leisurely action going for a few more strokes until I thought I had frustrated him enough then, after pulling my cock totally out of his hot ass, I slammed home knocking the breath out of him. I'm a big man, I'm talking bulk here not cock size and even though he is a big man himself I tower over him, so his body was buffeted on the table as I picked up the pace, bruising his ass as my cock dominated his butt, claiming it, hitting his prostate until his cock twitched and oozed its appreciation.

"You're mine now, Blake," I whispered, half in hope, half in suggestion. "Your ass belongs to me. I'm the only one who will ever satisfy you."

If he didn't like my dialogue, he never said so. It was probably a one-time thing but I wasn't going to let him go without some attempt to stake a claim in his affections.

"I'd be good for you, Blake. I can give you what you need."

"Oh, yes," he hissed. "I need your mammoth cock buried in my guts."

I pulled out slowly, then back in hard and fast, feeling him clench his muscles at each action. He knew how to please a man just as I hoped I knew how to please a guy on the end of my rod. Not just any guy, but Blake Kendall.

Much as I wanted to, I knew I couldn't keep going forever, and I built up a head of steam as I powered my way to climax. Blake mewled funny little sounds as I pounded his ass, his eyes rolling back in his head, until the friction caused him to squirt a copious load all over his belly and chest. I licked up the puddles I could reach with my tongue as his sphincter pulsed around my cock and I blew my load inside him.

There was a scattering of applause from some of the guests who'd been watching us. That alone made us all too aware of our surroundings. After my cock popped free, I dressed quickly to get back on duty. Handing Blake his clothes, I whispered, "I think there's a few others who have designs on your ass here tonight. If you want to stay, that's..." I was going to say 'fine' but it wasn't. I liked the man. He was mine. If I was getting possessive, it could only mean one thing: I really liked the man.

He looked at me to finish the sentence.

"If you want to stay here, that's your choice."

"Do I have a choice anymore?"

There were so many interpretations to that one question; although I hoped the one he meant was he liked me so much there was only one plausible answer. I plunged in.

"Come on," I said, helping him dress. "I'll take you to the staff rest rooms where you can tidy up and I'll escort you off the premises."

"I'd like that," he said, leaning against me to put on his shoes.

I gave him space but protected his back as we left the party room, closing the door on Nicola's pleading and a group of horny men advancing on her and Grant. I kept a respectable distance as I let Blake into the staff rest area, closing the door firmly behind us. He was in my face the moment the door clicked shut. He pulled me to him, burying his tongue in my oh-so-receptive mouth, giving me a fair indication that a repeat of our earlier exploration of each other's body might be on the cards.

He kneaded my ass cheeks until I whimpered, "I'm a pretty versatile guy if that's a direction you'd like to take."

"Fuck, yeah," he said, his eyes going all dreamy. I loved those eyes and their bottomless capacity for love. I stroked the hair from his eyes.

We heard someone clear his throat and I turned to see Marty, open mouthed, watching us from the small table where he was having his coffee break.

"I'll be right with you Marty. Blake just needs to tidy up a bit before he faces the press on his way out."

"No hurry, mate," he said, patting me on the back as he left the room.

"You'll be okay now," I said.

"Not so sure I'll ever be okay again," he said wistfully.

"Take your time. If the press guys get too pushy when you leave just holler."

"I appreciate it, Vlad. You're a good man. I won't forget you."

My heart sank. It sounded like I was being dismissed. No use beating myself up over it. What did I expect? The man was a big star, what was I? A bouncer at a club. And I thought this could lead somewhere? Who was I kidding?

I joined Marty at the front entrance.

"Aren't you the sly one?" he laughed.

"Not now, Marty."

He must have seen the look on my face because he dropped it. I'd explain another day.

About ten minutes later, Blake appeared and a shriek of recognition came from the crowd waiting to get in. The photographers mobbed him. He was happy to pose, and then held up his hand for quiet.

"As you know, tonight was to be a celebration for my forthcoming wedding to one of the most beautiful women in the world, Nicola Green." There were a few hisses from the crowd. "Instead, it became the wake for our relationship." There was an audible gasp. This was the scoop of the year. "It sometimes happens that people fall out of love and Nicola and I have done just that. No hard feelings. We spent tonight crying our eyes out over what might have been had we both not fallen in love with other people."

That was laying it on a bit thick, but I guess he wanted to save face as much as Nicola did. It would have been better, though, if he'd played the aggrieved boyfriend. Still, it was his career, nothing to do with me.

"Nicola has found herself falling for a young man who...But I'll let her tell you all about him. As for me, well I think I might just have found that special someone, but it's early days yet and we'll have to wait and see how things pan out."

If he wasn't bullshitting to save face then she'd better be very understanding.

The press pushed for more details but Blake refused with a smile that brooked no argument. Then with another wave and corresponding shriek from the crowd, he was gone.

Nicola didn't make an appearance that night, obviously using her father's escape route as usual. She'd read Blake's gentle ending of their relationship in the press and she and her publicist would undoubtedly come up with a response sympathetic enough to her it would knock Blake off the front pages of the tabloid press.

The night dragged unbearably for me after Blake left. I just wanted to get home, shower, and relax. Sunday was my day off and I was looking forward to examining where my life was headed. If nothing else, my brief time with the star had woken me up to the fact I was cruising through life, wasting my time. Suddenly, I was dissatisfied with my cozy little existence.

"Night, Vlad," Marty called as he let himself out the front door. Adrenaline was closed now, the street awash with stragglers going home from party central. I turned off the lights, programmed the security system, and let myself out, pulling down the shutters to lock them.

Dawn shit streaked the early morning sky. It would be a lovely day. I went to hail an empty cab for the short ride home but, before I could attract one, a Harley growled to a stop in front of me. The rider lifted the visor on his helmet.

"Going somewhere?" he enquired.

"Anywhere you're going," I smiled.

He handed me a spare helmet as I hopped on behind him, my cock sliding between the crack in his ass, now clad in tight fitting jeans.

"I was serious about what I said earlier," he commented, obviously hoping I'd picked up on it.

"The bit about maybe finding that special someone."

"Yeah. I guess I should have asked you first."

"I'll forgive you this time," I joked. "Just don't let it happen again."

I grabbed him by the waist as we took off down the road headed who knows where. It was early days yet.

*M*ETA-ANALYSIS *O*F *T*HE *E*FFECTS *O*F *L*OVE *O*N *T*OFU

"*B*UT why would they name a town after the past tense of a verb?" The little voice came from the plane seat next to me. Wally, who was a seat farther over ignored the question and squeezed closer to the window as if he didn't know me or our little baby dinosaur strapped in the seat between us who had asked the, in my estimation, quite reasonable question.

We'd hit Bled in northwestern Slovenia in search of the world's greatest pastries as we are both of an inquisitive culinary disposition, especially of the cream kind, and had heard rumors that kremna rezina, created there in the 1950s, was a source of national pride. Our pilgrimage was to the small café, Slaščičarna Šmon, near the bus station, awash with a sea of yellow custard and flaky pastry.

"But it's just a plain old vanilla slice," Wally complained when he first saw it. He couldn't keep the disappointment out if his voice when it was brought to our table and he proceeded to prod it with his fork like it was some alien custard life form.

"Mmph, wait till you taste it," I said as I hoed into more of it. It may have been plain old vanilla slice back home in Sydney but here it was like biting into a small pocket of vanilla-flavored cloud. It melted in the mouth like custard cotton candy. No wonder it was considered Bled's national treasure.

"Oh

"My

"God!"

Wally said as he scooped it into his mouth. "It really was worth coming all this way for it."

We'd come 'all this way' because Wally had returned home, a few months earlier, from his 58th straight week of overtime and exploded, "I can't take it anymore!!!!!!!!!!!!!!!" The line of exclamation marks does not signify semantic laziness, rather an attempt to express, rather poorly in print, the combination of explosive emphasis on 'more' and the grinding of teeth.

It was approaching the thirtieth anniversary of our decision to live together after a whirlwind romance of three months and his total capitulation to my needs which necessitated his cross border resettlement. In the intervening years we'd systematically pepped up our relationship with drugs, alcohol, adultery, acupuncture, Atkins, group sex, pornography, chiropractic and ESP therapy, in no particular order or combination. Now we were after some 'alone' time. Time away from friends, acquaintances, utility bills, being locked into cable television schedules and the constant anxiety of the new millennium, as well as having to douche every Friday night for those sudden unexpected visitors who would crawl round for a quickie after their girl friends had closed the vaginal gate.

In a sudden pique of consideration for his care of me during my convalescence from being surgically rendered an almost overlooked form of punctuation, a semi-colon, from my tussle with cancer I allowed him to choose the destinations that most appealed to him. He'd worried and cajoled me through chemotherapy and a stomach wound so stubborn it spat parsley and soy sauce if I even so much as laughed.

"I'd like to go home," he said without having to think about it, immediately pricking my romantic notions of trekking the Himalayas in Bhutan or snuggling up to a cute Mongolian in his yurt.

And home did not mean our heavily mortgaged inner city apartment, but rather Malta, a tiny lint speck in the Mediterranean dislodged from the boot of Italy, from whence Wally had migrated with his family fifty years before at the age of five, and to which he had not, as yet, returned. And as an added tease to make the anticipation of 'going home' that much sweeter, we decided to make our approach leisurely – by way of Italy, and Slovenia, the home of vanilla pastries.

So with a list of his most sought after destinations and instructions to track down the elusive kremna rezina here we were...

We scoffed it down making a mental note to buy half a dozen to take back to Ljubljana on the bus, realizing that if Dr. Atkins of the famed low carbohydrate torture had ever tasted one of Bled's finest he may never have devised his torturous regimen. But before the bus we had one final thing to do. We were accompanied on our travels by our lucky mascot, Tofu, a tiny intractable, opinionated baby dinosaur. The more psychologically inclined of our friends sagely, but wrongly, perceived our adoption of said creature as frustrated paternal desire, instead of the fact that I could ventriloquize the most childish and sarcastic aspects of my personality into the little 'stuffed toy', their dismissive description of him.

When Tofu read up on our itinerary, and you will just have to accept him as a living entity or cease reading now, he made one request. Well, he made hundreds being the selfish little shit he is, but this one was, at least, poignant. On an occasion when he had been propped up in front of the television with his own remote control he'd come across a version of *Pinocchio* and from that moment his obsession had been to become human. Wally and I knew it was fantasy (yes, we can discern fantasy from reality even though it may not seem like it) but Tofu had read that the teardrop-shaped island, Blejski Otok, an added touch of perfection on Bled's postcard-perfect alpine lake, was home to an ancient church, the Church of the Assumption, which houses a fifteenth-century magic bell. The legend is that it grants a wish to anyone making it peal from their first tug on the rope. Tofu believed, in the depths of his little plastic heart, that he would ring that bell and become a real little boy or, actually, a real little boy dinosaur.

We couldn't deny him, and anyway, the flight was cheaper into Slovenia than it was into Italy.

His excitement on the hand-propelled gondola ride over to the island was matched only by his eagerness to scale the arduous South Staircase, with scant regard for the historical architectural niceties along the way, and barrel his way to the belfry. Being only six inches tall, Tofu, of course, needed my help. The other tourists in the chapel were most amused that a tiny dinosaur was attempting to ring the bell that they'd already failed miserably to clang.

So with his little hands (do dinosaurs have hands?) gripped in mine and Wally attempting to chameleon himself into the woodwork of the pews in embarrassment, we gave the bell rope one almighty tug and waited for the Almighty to do his thing. The silence was painful. "Pull it again," someone shouted but we both knew if it didn't ring the first time the wish was void. Then, just a whisper of a strike before the bell pealed high up the tower and Tofu's little plastic face lit up with excitement at the metamorphosis to come. But it didn't. And by the time we'd reached the lake shore on the tourist gondola he realized he was still nothing but a plastic replica of a television sitcom character. And one whose series had been cancelled over a decade before.

"Maybe it's because you're not a Catholic," Wally suggested to prevent his becoming too depressed. "Or maybe the Lake Bled god doesn't like dinosaurs. Especially gay dinosaurs"

"Why do you want to be human?" I asked. "You just get to feel lots of pain and misery and disappointment. Just like now."

"You just think I feel these things," he said. "They're just words I've seen on television but I don't feel them. And I want to feel that one that everybody talks about all the time."

"What one's that?" Wally said.

"Love."

Tofu insisted we head to Rome where he fully intended to lodge a complaint with the Pope about the Bled church's false advertising. Fortunately for the Pope, he was out the day we arrived.

Wally, the lapsed Catholic, was less than pleased to be dragged through the Vatican Museum while Tofu got a crick in his neck from admiring the ceiling of the Sistine Chapel where we'd taken him to assuage his unfulfilled close encounter of the papal kind. He was further placated by the Sistine Chapel souvenir coloring book we'd bought for him at the Vatican shop. He just knew he could improve on Michelangelo's color palate. "It needs lots more red. And if you add a few dicks it'll have queens flocking to see it. Don't the pope's men know anything about marketing?" Tofu asked in his wide-eyed no eyelids sort of way. "And what's with all the gold plates around everybody's head in the paintings?"

"It symbolizes that person is a saint," Wally explained as patiently as anyone could to a piece of molded plastic. Wally was embarrassed only by Tofu's public pronouncements but was highly amused by his private opinions.

"What's a saint?"

"A saint is a special person who performs miracles."

"Like turning plastic dinosaurs into living, feeling creatures?'

"Uh huh."

"So what you're telling me is all I need is a gold plate stuck to the back of my head and then I can perform a miracle and make myself feel love?" he said with commendable common sense.

"Um, I think the miracles have to come first," Wally said.

We could see his little hollow head was attempting to think it over as we placed him in the hotel drawer for safekeeping during the night.

"He won't give up," I said. "But I have an idea that might please him."

The next day we headed for Malta, Wally's greatest fear being that I would use the smattering of Maltese curses I had picked up over the years on one of the customs officials, or that Tofu would let fly with his favorite Maltese expletive which roughly translates as "dick breath" if one of the said officials should prod him to see if he contained drugs. "I don't have even a rudimentary anal canal so how could I conceal drugs?" he said when I warned him.

My fear was that Wally would find his homeland a disappointment.

Wally was keeping his emotions in check on the short plane flight which was all to the good as Tofu was, as usual, causing a ruckus. He hated it when a plane was capacity and he was assigned an uncomfortable berth in the magazine rack at the back of the seat in front. He would sit in what he called 'string bag' class and glare for the entire trip. Or until he forgot his funk.

"How can I be a saint? The plate's not gold. It's white and it's made of plastic," he grizzled.

"How ungrateful can you be?" I remonstrated.

"And it smells of pastries. I bet real saints don't smell like a bakery."

"It's the best we could do on the spur of the moment," I said.

"You're so cheap. I bet this is the plate left over from the take-away vanilla slices you bought in Slovenia and you thought I wouldn't notice."

He was right of course.

"And I bet the Pope didn't bless it at all."

I had told him a small lie to keep his hopes alive. I shook my head.

"Well, fuck the Pope," Tofu said.

Wally gave me a withering look.

"I'm going to start my own religion. I hereby declare myself a saint. And to show my purity I have a white plastic halo. And no mention please that it's plastic."

"If you're a saint," Wally said, "You need to be Saint somebody or the other."

"Open the map of Malta," Tofu said and putting one arm over his eyes his little hand poked the map. "There, that's my name. Saint um Bugger er Saint Buggybar."

"It's pronounced Boo-jee-ba," Wally smiled.

"Okay, so I'm Saint Buggiba. That sounds good."

He fell asleep while calculating all the ways he could bilk money from what he hoped would be his future considerable congregation.

We sailed through customs uneventfully, Wally flashing his Maltese passport for the first time in the twenty years he'd had one, and me managing to keep my tongue in check as Tofu, all sweetness and piety, protruded from my backpack, his head and his outstretched arms beseeching all and sundry to worship him or at least come along for a hug.

Wally was emotionally raw so Tofu and I backed off and gave him time to acclimatize himself to the womb of his formative years. We unpacked in silence at our self-contained apartment until Tofu discovered that, from our third-floor balcony, we could see straight into the dormitories and showers of the backpackers' hostel opposite. As it was the height of summer all the windows were wide open revealing male and female backpackers who had the modesty of a *Playgirl* centerfold.

"You chose the accommodation well," Wally smiled.

"It wasn't deliberate. I had no idea."

And his few remaining relatives on the island had no idea he had returned. The family bond remains tight among the Maltese and their expatriate kinfolk. We'd learned from expat friends that once they know you're 'coming home' they turn up at the airport and ferry you from one relative to another and all you see of the country is the inside of people's residences spruced up for the occasion, and the vista that can be readily viewed from a car window. We did, however, have one date lined up. With Wally's aunt, his mother's sister, who still lived in the same house she did when Wally and his family had left for Australia in the 1950s.

The date was for dinner at her house on the very last night of our stay, that way no one could monopolize our time and we were free the preceding week to wander the seafront for our afternoon 'parmigiano' as Tofu called it, sitting at the waterfront cafés of Sliema nibbling on pastizzi or taking a dip in the Mediterranean with locals of all ages who didn't give my portly scarred body a second glance even in disgust, unlike the slim lithe gay youngsters at Bondi. We strolled through the old sandstone capital of Valetta and explored the megalithic temples at Tarxien, and the walled city of Mdina. And best of all we relaxed and snuggled and snogged as Wally's apprehensiveness relaxed into joy.

He had found his birth home, for all its annoyances, a most welcoming place.

We ignored the newspapers, there was no television in our self-contained apartment, and the tension oozed out of our bodies along with the perspiration. We sipped wine on the balcony and watched the young backpackers across the street or listened to the young men on the balcony below ours luxuriating semi-naked with pick-ups of the previous night until their smoking drove us indoors.

And then, the all-too-soon dinner date with the aunt. We traveled by bus to Marsaxlokk, impressed that the driver had turned his cabin area into a mini shrine to some patron saint or the other.

Tofu made a Post-It note reminder to get some 3-D postcards of himself in official robes with his plastic plate on our return to Australia.

"Oooh," Tofu had squealed when he heard of our destination. "I love all those Maltese names with the unpronounceable x's and q's. No one back home will know how to pronounce them so I hereby declare myself to be St. Buggiba of Marsaxlokk." Admittedly it took him three or four attempts to wrap his little plastic tongue around the correct pronunciation.

"You're not taking him," Wally said horrified at the thought.

"You're certainly not going without me," he huffed.

We compromised and Tofu was tucked into my backpack as we made for the bus the only evidence of his existence the muffled cries of "Let me out! Let me out!" which continued until we neared the aunt's maisonette. Wally was nervous and hung back until I marched up to the door and rang the bell. After a second buzz a head popped over the upstairs balcony and then a shriek of recognition although there was a split second quizzical registration of the strange man with eyebrow rings and ear-rings beside the prodigal nephew.

It was a Whirling Dervish of reminiscences and introductions. I sat outside the eye of the nostalgia as Wally was examined like a foreign insect under a microscope and I was examined peripherally in an effort to place my position in the pantheon. The conversation broke from English into Maltese and back again with the regularity of an English train timetable as aunt and uncle and their assorted adult children who had assembled for the occasion showered him with family news and gossip and showed us from their living room window the house down the street where Wally's father had shouted the news of his birth to the relatives and the neighborhood.

There was the inevitable cramming of fifty years into four hours, the niggling distrust of a returning expatriate from the generation who remained behind, especially as Wally's brother, Joe, was also visiting his homeland and with his girlfriend to whom he was unwed. But it had fallen to poor 'fallen' Joe to explain Wally's and my marital (or lack thereof) situation. The response had been shock followed by stoic resignation and the aunt's, "I never would have believed it. He's the last one in the family I would have expected to turn out that way. When he was born he had the most perfect little tool."

So the cacophonous outpouring of affection and pleasure tinged with a soupcon of disapproval continued through the meal until we all retired to the third floor roof space. It was the feast day of the church that the house overlooked and the locals were crowding the streets, even though it was late, in preparation for the fireworks. Children were pushing molded chairs along the sidewalk in a game they had invented to relieve the boredom causing much consternation in Tofu who shuddered at the thought of fragile plastic scraping along concrete. The adults, ignoring them, drank as they played cards in the streets or else sat in the gutters with their neighbors.

On the rooftop, well lubricated by the wine, we watched the late-night fireworks over the church and, for a moment, could appreciate the comfort of faith without capitulating to its abrogation of personal responsibility to the almighty powerful super being. We'd attempted to discuss it in the past with Tofu whose response had been a simple: "Well, if you don't give me what I want I'll destroy you."

The fireworks bruised the sky with their orgasm of colors and momentary solar system of stars till our group began to wander back down to the maisonette's living room for coffee. Wally and I lingered and I propped Tofu on the edge of the roof parapet.

"Oooh," Tofu said in awe and he clapped his little hands at the last spurts of orgasmic celebration that turned the night sky blue and pink and green. "Is this all for me?"

I held Wally's hand and leaned over and kissed him.

Tofu, confused for a moment, his heart racing at the excitement of his first live fireworks display and the sheer exuberance of a new life experience, reached out for our hands and, as the three of us stood and watched the giant church dome in its final paroxysm of illumination, asked dreamily, "Is this what love is? Dazzling colored lights, big explosions, being with people you really like?"

"Close enough," I said.

Lydian

About the Author

Barry Lowe writes about love and sex so he won't forget how to do it. When he's not scribbling his adventures for the Sydney gay weekly SX, or out doing field research, he's writing about love's wonderful variations for a series of smut eBooks, novels and anthologies for Lydian Press.

He lives in Sydney with his partner, Wally.

Check out his website at www.barrylowe.info

More Romance from Barry Lowe in
COCK-EYED OPTIMISTS

Love is just around the corner…

But if you have your head in your Smartphone or your eBook reader, you might just miss it. While you're waiting, what better way to pass the time than a collection of Barry Lowe's romance erotica in which you'll discover the myriad ways m/m romance runs its course. In this anthology you'll meet a young student from the 1960s who discovers during a front seat quickie hook-up that love between two men is not only possible, it's plausible; a man on the anniversary of his lover's death who may just have found a replacement with his deceased lover's blessing; a country boy who returns to town after four years to lay claim to the man he loves – in a frock; a straight surfer dude who discovers the joys of the 'other side' during a thunderstorm at a nude beach; a guy who can't decide between his three lovers so he invites them all to dinner; a young gay dad who discovers a secret sexual underbelly at the local park; a tour guide who may just have found the love of his life in a rainforest; and a young man who returns to Greece on a promise.

Cock-Eyed Optimists includes: *A Red Rose Before Crying, Too Frocked to Care, The Three Spooges, Love and the Odor of Red Leatherette, The New Dad's Club, Hard on His Heels, It's All Greek to Me,* and *Salted Mixed Sluts* – all previously published as individual eBooks by loveyoudivine Alterotica.

BEAR SKIN

Body hair is making a comeback!

Move over hairless twinks. Stand aside waxed wankers and depilatorized dudes – your bodies look like plucked chickens. Once again, the hirsute look is making inroads into the gay community. Long live beards and moustaches. Here's to the return of pubic hair and furry ass cracks. Let's hear it for thatched tummies, chest pelts, and back hair.

In this bearotica anthology, bears, cubs, otters, and their admirers, rub hairy body parts in a myriad of fashions as only Barry Lowe can write them. There's humor in a young twink who wants to top his best mate's Daddy Bear; sizzling cuckoldry when a bear watches his mate triple played on their living-room floor; violence and retribution in a relationship gone stale when a battered partner finds his inner grizzly; love and hope when an older bear finds his cub; and the best kind of revenge when a young twink who is constantly belittled as an ugly hairy duckling discovers he's really a swan.

Bear Skin was originally published by loveyoudivine Alterotica and includes – *Carbon Dating the Bear; Bumming a Fag; Four on the Bear Floor; Beauty, Mate; There's a Bear in There; Busting a Gut; Steam Punk; Piss Elegant;* and *The Bear's Guide to Depilatory Wax.* – all previously published as individual eBooks by loveyoudivine Alterotica.

ANTHOLOGIES By Barry Lowe

BUSTING BILLY'S BUTT - eBook & Print

Four On The Floor
Jolly Rogering
The Devil His Due
Never Take Candy from Strangers
Done Like A Dinner
In The Family Way
Right Up His Alley
Group Therapy

THE MAJOR AND THE MINERS - eBook & Print

A Serpent in Paradise
Desperate Remedies
Joshua's Story
Emerald City
Danny's Revenge
Future Tense

THE MORE THE MERRIER - eBook and Print

Marine Biology
Flesh for Fantasy
Buck's Night
Four On The Floor
Sluts & Satyrs
Framing the Picture of Dorian Gray
Fuck Buddy
Seven Card Studs
Dude, Where's The Bar?
New Year's Steve

LIKE FATHER LIKE SON - eBook and Print

Man of the Hour
Like Father Like Son
Sonny & Shared
Sonny Side Up
Eclipse Of The Son
Son & Games
Where The Sun Don't Shine
The Sun Shines Out Of His Ass
Have Son Will Travel

YOUR BOYFRIEND IS HOT - eBook and Print

From Here to Fraternity
Stripping His Assets
Indecent Exposure
Middle Man for Madame Blavatsky
A Cook's Tour
Topping the Pizza Delivery Boy

THE BOY IS A BOTTOM - eBook and Print

Marine Biology
Marine Animals
Attack of the Ass Bandits
The Arab Downstairs
Clockwork Derriere
Creaming the Party Dip
Top of the World
Route 666: Signal Driver
The Butler Did Him
Fifty Shades of Fey
Spinning the Bottom

BEAR SKIN - eBook & Print

Carbon Dating the Bear
Bumming a Fag
Four on the Bear Floor
Beauty, Mate
There's a Bear in There
Busting a Gut
Steam Punk
Piss Elegant
The Bear's Guide to Depilatory Wax

ROUGH & READY - eBook and Print

Stocks & Shared
Scarface
Ceps: Mad about Muscle
The Plumbers' Mate*
Climbing Up the Wall
Little Red Rides da Hood
The Dex Factor
Jailhouse Cock
The Skinhead Upstairs

COCK-EYED OPTIMISTS - eBook & Print

A Red Rose Before Crying
Too Frocked to Care
The Three Spooges
Love and the Odor of Red Leatherette
It's All Greek to Me
Hard On His Heels
Salted Mixed Sluts
The New Dad's Club

OMG! NOT ANOTHER GAY EROTICA ANTHOLOGY?

OMG! My Dad's a Stripper!
OMG! The College Jock's a Nudist!
OMG! Put Some Clothes On!
OMG! My Uncle's a Fairy!
OMG! Satan Wants a Blow Job!
OMG! My Dad's Got Tits!
OMG! Santa's Got a Six-pack!

BABY, I'M NOT A MONSTER - eBook and Print

The Vampire's Guide to Dental Hygiene
Stupid Cupid
Gadigal
Pride & Joy
Seeing Things
My Dad's a Vampire
Guys & Trolls

THE GRAVY TRAIN - eBook & Print

In the Soup
Salad Days
Whores d'Oeuvres
Beefed Up and Porked
Torte A Lesson
Café or Lay

For all Barry's titles please visit his page at:

lydianpress.com

Lydian Press is dedicated to bringing you the finest GLBTQ erotic literature on the web.

Visit us on the web at:

http://lydianpress.com